P9-CDB-099

Kissed by an angel . . .

"I can't stop thinking about you. I have no idea who you really are—an accomplished liar, or a desperate woman in terrible trouble," Reid said.

His finger moved from her cheek, trailing across her lips. Then he cupped her chin, tilting her face up to his. Her blood ran hot. A wave of unexpected and reckless desire shot through her body. She caught her bottom lip between her teeth, knowing that if he didn't move, then she should, because nothing could happen between them. But when his gaze moved to her mouth, her lips tingled in anticipation. He lowered his head so slowly she had plenty of time to move, yet she couldn't take a step.

She wanted to feel his mouth on hers. She wanted him to wrap his strong arms around her and pull her into his hard body. She wanted to lose herself in him for just a minute . . . a minute when she didn't have to be strong and protective and fierce. . . . It was foolish. Reckless. Dangerous. Impossible . . .

Praise for award-winning author
Barbara Freethy

"This book has it all: heart, community, and characters who will remain with you long after the book has ended . . . a wonderful story with a bit of angelic intervention."

—*New York Times* bestselling author Debbie Macomber

"Freethy is an expert at creating believable characters."

—*Library Journal*

"Poignant, romantic and suspenseful . . . gifted author Barbara Freethy creates an irresistible tale."

—*New York Times* bestselling author Susan Wiggs

"Fans of Nora Roberts will find a similar tone here, framed in Freethy's own spare, elegant style."

—*Contra Costa Times*

"Barbara Freethy delivers strong and compelling prose. . . ."

—*Publishers Weekly*

"Freethy skillfully keeps readers on the hook. . . ."

—*Booklist*

"Barbara Freethy writes with bright assurance, exploring the bonds of sisterhood."

—*New York Times* bestselling author Luanne Rice

"A master storyteller."

—Romance Reviews Today

"Freethy deftly weaves the evocative tapestry of family life, love, and pain with a delightful splash of whimsy."

—*BookPage*

"Freethy is a strong storyteller with an unerring ear for dialogue."

—The Romance Reader

"Warm and wonderful."

—*New York Times* bestselling author
Susan Elizabeth Phillips

"Kudos to Barbara Freethy for a first-class reading experience."

—*Affaire de Coeur*

BARBARA FREETHY

Suddenly One Summer

POCKET **STAR** BOOKS
New York London Toronto Sydney

The sale of this book without its cover is unauthorized. If you purchased this book without a cover, you should be aware that it was reported to the publisher as "unsold and destroyed." Neither the author nor the publisher has received payment for the sale of this "stripped book."

Pocket Star Books
A Division of Simon & Schuster, Inc.
1230 Avenue of the Americas
New York, NY 10020

This book is a work of fiction. Names, characters, places, and incidents either are products of the author's imagination or are used fictitiously. Any resemblance to actual events or locales or persons, living or dead, is entirely coincidental.

Copyright © 2009 by Barbara Freethy

All rights reserved, including the right to reproduce this book or portions thereof in any form whatsoever. For information address Pocket Books Subsidiary Rights Department, 1230 Avenue of the Americas, New York, NY 10020

First Pocket Star Books paperback edition July 2009

POCKET STAR BOOKS and colophon are registered trademarks of Simon & Schuster, Inc.

For information about special discounts for bulk purchases, please contact Simon & Schuster Special Sales at 1-866-506-1949 or business@simonandschuster.com

The Simon & Schuster Speakers Bureau can bring authors to your live event. For more information or to book an event contact the Simon & Schuster Speakers Bureau at 1-866-248-3049 or visit our website at www.simonspeakers.com.

Designed by Jill Putorti

Manufactured in the United States of America

10 9 8 7 6 5 4 3 2 1

ISBN 978-1-4391-0156-8
ISBN 978-1-4391-2696-7 (ebook)

To Terry, Kristen, and Logan—you're the best!

Acknowledgments

Special thanks to my writing friends who provide moral support, brainstorming, and chocolate when needed—Jami Alden, Bella Andre, Carol Culver, Diana Dempsey, Tracy Grant, Lynn Hanna, Anne Hearn, Candice Hern, Monica McCarty, Barbara McMahon, Kate Moore, Christie Ridgway, Penelope Williamson, and Veronica Wolff. Thanks also to my terrific agent, Karen Solem, and my wonderful editor, Micki Nuding, who helped bring Angel's Bay to life.

For more information on my books, please visit my website at http://www.barbarafreethy.com.

One

Jenna Davies shivered as she headed out of the market and down the dark, shadowy street that faced the harbor. Thick fog rolled in off the Pacific Ocean, blowing a cool, wet mist against her face. If she hadn't needed milk for Lexie's breakfast, she wouldn't have dragged Lexie out of their cozy, warm house into the cold night air. But she certainly couldn't leave her seven-year-old home alone.

Although she liked Angel's Bay for its remote location on the rugged central California coast, there were moments when the isolation made her nervous. In the distance she could hear music coming from Murray's Bar, the popular pub where the locals and tourists hung out, but this part of town was deserted. While the marina bustled during the daytime, now the boats bobbing on the water took on ghostly shapes that made her feel uneasy.

Jenna told herself not to let her imagination get the best of her, but the eerie glow of the streetlights didn't help—nor did the feeling that someone could be following her and she wouldn't even know it. Though she'd covered her tracks, she still didn't feel safe deep down in her bones. Sometimes she wondered if she'd ever feel that way again.

But Angel's Bay was home now, and after two months she and Lexie were beginning to fit in. The private piano lessons she taught made her enough money to live on. Lexie had just finished first grade and would begin summer school next week. Her nightmares continued, but she wasn't so panicked anymore.

There was no reason to be nervous. Still, Jenna tightened her hand around Lexie's as they hurried toward her car.

Lexie stopped abruptly, pointing at the pier. "Look, there's an angel."

Jenna sighed. Lexie had been obsessed with angels ever since they'd moved to town and heard the legend of the famous shipwreck—the people who hadn't made it to shore, and the angels that protected the bay. Lexie's imagination had been fueled even more in recent days when an Internet video had appeared showing apparitions dancing across the water, and mysterious symbols appearing on the cliff face. The video was drawing a flock of visitors to the town just in time for the summer festival that would kick off tomorrow night.

Jenna was about to tell Lexie she was imagining things, when her gaze caught on the shadowy figure at the end of the pier. It appeared to be a woman in a flowing dress, her long blond hair billowing out behind her as she swung one leg over the railing, straddling it as she stared down at the water below.

Jenna's heart began to pound. The hair reminded her of Kelly—but that wasn't Kelly on the pier, it was someone else. Someone who was in a very dangerous position.

The woman moved her other leg over the rail and stood on the narrow board that was the only thing between her and the cold water below. Holding on to the rail behind her, the woman lifted her face to the sky as if offering up a silent prayer.

"Do you think she's going to fly?" Lexie asked. "Is she going to heaven now?"

"That's not an angel." Jenna quickly opened the car door and put her shopping bag on the backseat. Damn! The last thing she needed was more trouble, but there was no one else around, and as she glanced toward the pier once again, the woman seemed to be swaying precariously. "Let's go say hello. Make sure she's all right." Jenna grabbed Lexie's hand again and they walked swiftly toward the pier.

The wind made Jenna's eyes water, and she had to fight the almost irresistible desire to turn around, go back to the car, and drive away. This wasn't her problem; it could be dangerous to get involved. But still, she kept moving forward.

"Hello," she called as they neared the end of the pier. "What are you doing? Do you need help?"

The woman didn't respond. She lifted her face to the sky once again. She let go of the rail—first with one hand, then the other—stretching her arms out in front of her. A moment later she let out a shrill, piercing scream and plummeted off the pier.

Adrenaline surged through Jenna, and she yanked off her coat and shoes. "Stay here, Lexie. Don't move a muscle. Do you understand me? Do *not* go near the rail."

"What—what are you doing? Where—where are you going?" Lexie stuttered, fear in her eyes. "Don't leave me." She grabbed onto Jenna's arm, her tiny fingers tightening in terror.

Jenna squatted down so they were eye to eye. "I'll be right back, Lexie. I have to save her, honey. There's no one else." God, she wished there was someone else, but not even the girl's scream had brought anyone out of the nearby buildings or boats. She gently disengaged Lexie's fingers from her sleeve, took out her cell phone and punched 9-1-1, then handed the phone to Lexie. "When they answer, tell them to come to the pier, that a woman is in the water. Do you understand?"

Lexie nodded.

"And you stay right here," Jenna repeated. "Don't take one step from this spot."

Her heart pounding, she quickly moved to the rail and climbed over. Fear ripped through her as she looked down. It was a good fifteen to twenty feet to the water below, and she wasn't a strong swimmer.

Jenna heard Lexie yelling into the phone, but help wouldn't arrive soon enough: the girl was flailing her arms, sinking beneath the dark waves.

Holding her breath, Jenna closed her eyes and jumped.

When she hit the water, the icy cold stopped her heart. Weighted down by her clothes, she seemed to take forever to get to the surface. Taking welcome gulps of air, she treaded water, searching for the woman. It was dark and the current was moving fast, pushing Jenna under the dark pier where there was no sign of the woman. Was she too late?

Then she saw a swirl of bubbles and a hand, the top of a head bobbing under the small waves. Swimming quickly, Jenna dove under the water, grabbing the woman by the hair, then by the arm. The woman struggled but Jenna held on tight, kicking and pulling until she got them both to the surface. The woman coughed and blinked, her eyes dazed.

"It's okay. You're okay," Jenna said, but the woman's eyes closed and she began to slip out of Jenna's grasp.

With her arm around the woman's neck, Jenna swam toward the ladder at the end of the pier. The current was working against her, and she was already getting so tired, so cold. What if she wasn't strong enough to get them both to safety? An old, familiar, and painful refrain ran through her head: *"You're not good enough. You need to do better, work harder, or you'll always be a failure, a disappointment."*

She thrust his voice out of her head. She *wasn't* going to fail. She couldn't.

The sound of a siren gave her new strength, and she swam harder. She could do this. By the time she reached the ladder, she could hear pounding footsteps on the pier. She had her hand on the first rung when a fireman appeared. He climbed down to meet her, pulling the unconscious woman from her grasp. Once he was up, another fireman came down to help Jenna.

She was grateful for his strong hand, because she was suddenly exhausted. Her arms burned from the exertion and her legs felt weak and wobbly. When she got back on the pier, she fell to her knees as Lexie hurtled herself into her arms and began to sob.

"It's all right, honey. I'm fine," Jenna said comfortingly, rubbing Lexie's back. "You did really well. I'm so proud of you." Lexie continued to cry, her small arms tight around Jenna's neck. "It's okay, baby. It's okay," Jenna soothed.

Finally Lexie lifted her head, tears running down her cheeks. Jenna was more than a little sorry that she'd scared Lexie so badly. Fear was the last thing Lexie needed in her life.

"I didn't think you would come back," Lexie sobbed.

"I'm not going to leave you, Lexie. Not *ever.*"

The fear slowly faded from Lexie's eyes as she searched Jenna's face for the truth. Finally satisfied, she nodded. "Okay." She wiped her face with the sleeve of her sweater. "How come the angel didn't fly?"

"She's not an angel, honey." As Jenna looked over at the young woman on the pier who was now coughing up seawater, she let out a relieved breath that she was alive. The girl was much younger than she'd realized, probably sixteen or seventeen. Her long blond hair hung in wet strands against her pale cheeks. Her eyes were now wide open and confused. Did she realize how close she'd come to dying? Why on earth would she have wanted to kill herself?

Jenna looked up as a police officer approached—Joe Silveira, the chief of police. She'd seen him around town. He was in his mid to late thirties and had most recently been with the Los Angeles Police Department. He had a reputation for being highly intelligent and keenly perceptive, two reasons she'd avoided talking to him. Blending in, not standing out, had been her goal—until now. Her nerves tightened.

"Why don't you wrap this around you?" the chief suggested, holding out a blanket. "You must be freezing."

"Thank you." Jenna stood and wrapped the blanket around her shoulders as a chill rocketed through her body, making her teeth chatter. She needed to get home, get warm, and get the hell away from the cops.

"I'm Chief Silveira. I don't think we've officially met, although I've seen you at the café a few times."

"Jenna Davies. This is my daughter, Lexie."

The chief smiled at Lexie and then looked back at Jenna. "Why don't I take you to the clinic, get you checked out?"

At the medical center there would be forms to fill out, questions to answer. "No, I'm fine," she said quickly. "A little cold, that's all. I just need a hot bath."

"Are you sure you don't want to see a doctor?"

"Positive."

"All right. I don't want to keep you out here in the night air, but can you tell me what happened?"

"Lexie and I were coming out of the market, and we saw the girl climb over the railing. When she jumped into the water, I jumped in after her."

"That was very courageous," the chief commented. "I'm impressed."

She didn't want him to be impressed. She didn't want him to think about her at all. But it was too late for that. "I did what anyone would have done," she said with a shrug.

"I sincerely doubt that. Do you know who the girl is?"

"I've never seen her before."

"Neither have I," the chief said heavily, casting a quick glance back at the young woman who was being loaded onto a gurney. "And I know just about all the teenagers in town. So you're saying she jumped? She didn't fall? It wasn't an accident?"

Jenna shook her head. "She definitely climbed over the railing and let go. I hope she'll be all right."

"I imagine you saved her life." He paused, his gaze focusing once again on her. "She didn't say anything to you when you were in the water?"

Jenna shook her head. "Nothing. Can I go now?" She handed the blanket back to the chief and grabbed her coat and shoes from the dock.

"Sure. I might have more questions for you in the morning, if you don't mind."

"I've told you all I know. It happened very fast."

Chief Silveira nodded. "Take care of yourself, then."

"I will." Jenna quickly made her way through the gathering crowd. She heard a few people call her name, but she kept on moving. She had just gotten Lexie into the car when a camera flash went off in her face. Blinded, she put up a hand, but not before the man snapped another picture.

She threw her coat and shoes into the car, then turned on him, anger ripping through her. "What the hell are you doing? Why are you taking my picture?" For a moment, she had the terrible fear that she'd been tracked down.

"You just saved a girl's life," the man said, lowering his camera. "You're a hero."

She frowned. In the shadows, all she could tell was that he was a tall man with broad shoulders and wavy brown hair, wearing jeans and a black jacket over a dark T-shirt. "Who are you? You're not from the *Angel's Bay Daily News*." The local photographer was a sixty-year-old woman named Gladys.

"Reid Tanner. And, no, I'm not from the *Angel's Bay Daily News,* although I have come looking for angels," he drawled.

She should have guessed he was here because of the popular Internet video. "You won't find any angels around here."

"Too bad. So, what's your name?"

"That's not important." Before he could move, she grabbed his camera and dove into her car, slamming and locking the door behind her.

"Hey, I need that," he said, knocking on the window.

Jenna ignored him, fiddling with the buttons on the obviously expensive digital camera.

"What are you doing? Why did you take that man's camera?" Lexie asked. "He's get—getting mad," she added with a worried stutter.

"It's okay, honey. It's rude to take pictures of people when they're—when they're wet." She erased the last two shots, then rolled the window down a few inches and handed the camera back.

"You're crazy," he said with a disbelieving shake of his head. "I can take another picture of you."

"Not tonight, you can't." She started the engine and pulled away. In her rearview mirror she saw him watching her, and she had the feeling she'd just made a terrible mistake, thrown down a challenge. But what choice had she had? She couldn't afford to have her photo in any newspaper. She hoped he'd go back to wherever he came from and forget he ever saw her.

If not, they might have to run again.

Reid stared at the disappearing taillights, feeling as if he were awakening from a long, deep sleep. The last eleven months had passed in a mind-numbing blur of one endless day after another, weeks in which he spent most of his time trying not to think or remember. He'd taken this freelance assignment for *Spotlight Magazine* to make some quick cash while he decided whether he wanted to return to the career that had once been his obsession.

When he'd graduated from Northwestern and gotten a job at *The New York Times,* he'd never imagined that twelve years later he'd be covering anything less important than a story of political or global significance—certainly not sensationalist fodder like angels. At one time he'd been a passionate pursuer of truth and justice, but his desire had made him reckless. He'd been willing to do anything for a story, and a good friend had paid a terrible price for his ambition.

In the deep of the night when he couldn't escape from his thoughts, he could still see her casket being lowered into the ground. He could hear the sobs coming from the crowd and see the accusations in so many eyes. No one came out and said, *"This is your fault,"* but they didn't have to. He knew it down deep in his soul, and doubted he would ever escape the unrelenting pain of his memories. He'd spent most of the past year trying to drink his way into oblivion, but the problem with getting drunk was that at some point he always sobered up.

Turning away from the action on the pier, Reid headed down the street toward Murray's. He'd been on his way to the pub when he'd heard the sirens and decided to follow. Old habits died hard, and he'd been an ambulance chaser since he was a kid. In the neighborhood where he'd grown up, police sirens had been standard fare. He could still remember the flashing strobe lights playing off his bedroom ceiling in the middle of the night, the times when he'd crept to the window to watch the cops arrest someone in the alley behind his apartment building.

Blowing out a sigh, he silently repeated his favorite mantra. *Don't look back, don't look forward, and don't give a damn.*

So what if he'd had an unexpectedly intriguing conversation with a stranger? He wasn't here to investigate a suicide attempt or get distracted by a courageous heroine. His focus was the Internet video that had sparked nationwide interest and the hope that there was finally proof that angels existed—a hope he would shortly put an end to. Angels were no more real than any other fairy tale character. They certainly weren't walking the streets of Angel's Bay.

Or were they? The image of the ocean-soaked brunette with the wary, angry eyes flashed through his head. She'd jumped into the dark sea to save a stranger's life. What kind of a woman did that?

Hell, maybe she *was* an angel.

An angel with something to hide.

An irrepressible tingle of curiosity ran down his spine. He didn't want to give in to it. He was over caring about truth, justice, and shining a light on the evil in the world. He was not going to chase her down. He wasn't.

At least not tonight . . .

Two

Redwood Medical Center sat on a bluff surrounded by enormous redwood trees on the outskirts of Angel's Bay. The center handled basic medical problems, sending the more seriously injured or ill thirty miles down the road to St. Mary's Hospital. As an obstetrician at the medical center, Charlotte Adams was used to dealing with happy pregnant women. The young woman who'd tried to kill herself the night before obviously didn't fit into that category.

Charlotte moved into the room where the girl lay sleeping. The young woman had been examined by the doctor on call after being brought in by the paramedics. After an impassioned plea in the ER to make sure her baby was okay, she'd fallen into an exhausted sleep and had remained that way ever since. It was now nine o'clock in the morning. They'd tested for drugs, but found nothing in her system. There didn't appear to be any physical reason for her long sleep, except perhaps exhaustion and mental stress. Picking up the girl's chart, Charlotte checked the vitals the nurse had taken a few moments ago. Everything was normal.

The young woman's hair was long, almost down to her waist, and very blond. Her skin was pale, and she was bone thin with the exception of a small, round tummy. Charlotte picked up the girl's arm and checked her pulse. The beat quickened and she saw a flutter of an eyelid. Was the girl just pretending to be asleep? She had to be scared, disoriented, confused, and probably feeling very alone.

She'd had no identification on her when they'd brought her in, and so far no one had come to inquire about her. While Angel's Bay was a relatively small community, there were many people who lived up in the mountains or down the long rural roads outside of town. Perhaps her family didn't realize she was gone yet.

Or maybe they'd sent her away. Maybe that was why she'd tried to kill herself.

Charlotte drew in a deep breath at the bitter pain that swept through her. Ever since she'd set eyes on this girl, she'd been struggling to keep some bad memories at bay. Images from her past flashed through her mind—her own positive pregnancy test taken in the bathroom at her best friend's house, the horror and disappointment on her mother's face when she'd finally had to confess, and later the terrifying trip to the hospital. She'd been too young and too weak to deal with any of it. She wondered if this girl felt the same way.

"It's all right," Charlotte said gently. "You can wake up now. You're safe here."

For a moment there was no reaction, then the girl's eyes slowly opened. Charlotte looked into those gold-flecked brown eyes and saw childlike innocence and very adult fear.

"I'm Dr. Charlotte Adams. You're in the Redwood Medical Center. Do you remember what happened?"

The girl hesitated, then said in a dry, scratchy whisper, "Why didn't she let me die?"

"What's your name?" Charlotte asked, diverting the conversation away from the suicide attempt.

The girl stared back at her, and she saw indecision, not confusion.

"You can tell me," Charlotte persisted.

The girl slowly shook her head.

"Someone must be worried about you," Charlotte tried again.

"No," the girl said flatly.

"What about your parents?"

"I want to leave. Where are my clothes?" The girl's gaze swept the room.

Charlotte could have told her there was no way she was leaving, since legally they had to hold anyone for seventy-two hours after a suicide attempt or until a psychiatrist determined the patient could be discharged. Instead, she tried a gentler tack. "You need to rest and eat, and I want to run some tests on your baby, make sure everything is all right.

"You look like you're about sixteen weeks along,"

Charlotte continued. "Past the morning sickness stage, hopefully. I'm an obstetrician. I deliver babies all the time and I take care of the mothers, too." She paused. "I'd really love to know what I could call you."

The girl picked at the edge of the blanket, then finally lifted her gaze. "I guess you can call me Annie."

Charlotte smiled. "Okay, Annie. Have you seen a doctor since you became pregnant?"

"No."

"I'd like to do an ultrasound. It takes a picture of your baby and helps us pinpoint the dates."

"Does it hurt?"

"Not a bit."

"I suppose it will be okay." Annie licked her lips. "I'm kind of hungry."

"Good, I'll send someone in with your breakfast. I'll do anything I can to try to help you, Annie. Can you tell me how old you are?"

"Eighteen."

She looked younger, but she might be telling the truth. She hadn't hesitated in her reply.

"Are the police coming back?" Annie asked.

"Yes. They'll be worried about you, wanting to make sure you're okay."

"You'll tell them I'm fine, and then they'll leave, right?" A slight Southern twang to Annie's voice indicated a past outside of California.

"*Are* you fine?" Charlotte asked.

Annie hesitated, then said, "I had to do it. I had

to see if the angels would save me, if I was worthy, and they did. So everything is okay now."

It wasn't an angel who'd saved Annie. If someone hadn't seen her jump off the pier and gone in after her, she'd be dead now. But that was a discussion better left to another time. "I'm sure there are people who are worried about you, Annie. Can I call someone for you?"

"No. Please don't tell anyone I'm here." Worry filled Annie's eyes. "Promise me."

"Just rest for now," Charlotte soothed. "Someone will be in shortly with your breakfast."

Charlotte closed the door behind her and walked down the hall toward the nurse's station. Her pulse sped up as she saw Angel Bay's chief of police waiting there. Joe Silveira was a darkly handsome man with olive skin, deep brown eyes, and jet black hair. He'd no doubt set a few hearts racing in his time, but he was married—at least that's what the local gossips said. Where his wife was, nobody seemed to know.

"Chief," she said lightly, trying to ignore her foolish reaction. It wasn't like her to feel attraction for a married man. Actually, she hadn't felt attraction for anyone in a long time, and this was definitely not the time to have her libido jump back into action.

"Dr. Adams," he said with a smile that warmed up his face. "I haven't seen you in a while."

"Not since you delivered that baby down on Oak Road."

"Couldn't have done it without you talking me

through it, but I'm hoping never to repeat the experience. I'll leave that to you." He paused, tipping his head toward the room she'd just left. "How's our girl?"

"She's awake. She told me I could call her Annie, but I'm not sure that's really her name."

"Actually, it is. We found her backpack next to a motorbike by the pier. Her name is Annie Dupont and she's eighteen years old, according to the school records, although she hasn't been at school in a couple of years. Her family lives up in the mountains and apparently was homeschooling her."

"Have you contacted her parents?"

"Not yet. I sent an officer up the mountain, but he found an abandoned shack at the address we had. Do you think Annie will give me her current address?"

"Not a chance," Charlotte said frankly. "She wanted me to promise not to tell anyone she's here. She's obviously scared. If you press her now, I'm afraid she'll try to run, and I really don't want to have to restrain her. She's a young girl, emotionally fragile, and pregnant. I'd like an opportunity to make her feel safe here and see if I can get her to open up. Our psychiatrist, Dr. Raymond, needs to see her, but he won't be back until this afternoon. Can you put off talking to her at least until later today?"

"She is eighteen; I suppose I can wait. Did she by any chance say why she jumped?"

"She wanted to see if the angels would save her."

"That damn video," Joe said with a disgusted

shake of his head. "It's bringing out the crazy in everyone."

"I take it you don't think the angels are carving a message on the cliff wall."

"I think someone is up to something and using the angel legends for either a cover or a distraction."

"You know, Joe—I mean, Chief—"

"You can call me Joe."

She cleared her throat, feeling uncomfortable under his warm gaze. The man really needed to rein in that smile of his. She forced herself to focus on the conversation.

"I grew up here, Chief, and the angel legends aren't as easy to refute as you might think. Things have happened here that are completely unexplainable—good things and bad." It was that darkness that had made her want to stay away, but duty had called.

His gaze settled on her face. "You're sounding awfully mysterious. I thought you were a woman of science and logic."

Charlotte sighed. "I used to be. Then I came home."

Jenna winced as Stella Rubinstein, a fifty-two-year-old woman in the midst of a midlife crisis and a divorce, murdered Tchaikovsky's *Love Theme from Romeo and Juliet.*

As Stella finished playing, she gave Jenna a delighted smile. "I'm getting better, don't you think?

Sydney will not believe it when I play this at Carole's wedding."

Sydney wasn't going to believe it, all right. Jenna cleared her throat, choosing her words carefully. "You might want to unveil your talent in a more private setting. You should enjoy your daughter's wedding, and if you're worried about playing, you won't be relaxed."

"Are you kidding? I am going to be the talk of the town. Sydney said I was stuck in a rut, that I couldn't learn anything new, couldn't be exciting anymore. He said I couldn't compete with a younger, more talented woman. As if that waitress at Murray's has more going for her than big boobs. Syd was wrong to leave me, and I'm going to prove it to him," Stella declared. "I'll make him see me as more than the woman who washed his socks and cooked his dinner for twenty-three years. The woman he walked out on because she was boring. Well, I'm not boring anymore."

"You certainly aren't," Jenna agreed. In fact, warmhearted, loud-talking Stella was one of the more colorful personalities in Angel's Bay. Jenna wasn't sure why Stella had picked the piano to make her stand, but she knew that music had a way of healing the soul. That's what it seemed to be doing for Stella. When she'd come for her first lesson six weeks earlier, Stella had been lacking in confidence and had seemed almost lifeless. Now she'd colored her hair, lost a few pounds, and exchanged her usual sweats for tighter jeans and a sweater. Her blond hair had been recently highlighted and cut, giving her a fresh, younger look.

"I just love how I feel when I play," Stella continued. "As if I'm making something important, as if I'm not me anymore. It's silly, I know. It's not like I'm good or anything."

"It's not silly. Music speaks to the heart. It transforms you." Jenna had always turned to the piano when she was unhappy or lonely, losing herself in the technical challenge of Prokofiev's *Piano Concerto No. 3* or Beethoven's *Pathétique*. But despite Stella's newfound belief in herself, Jenna hated to see her play before she was ready—although there was a good chance Stella might never be ready. While she found joy in the piano, she had little sense of timing, and her fingers often collided on the keys. But she did play with enthusiasm, and there was something to be said for that.

"Why don't you come twice next week?" Jenna suggested. "Just to polish things up. You want to make your daughter proud, too."

"Carole is the one who bought me these piano lessons. She said, 'Mom, stop whining about having nothing to do and *do* something. You're not that old. You could have another life. You could meet another man.' " Stella laughed. "As if I want another man to pick up after. But I wouldn't mind having another life. I know I'm not as good as I think I am, Jenna, but I'm having fun. I haven't felt this good in a long time." Stella's eyes grew misty. "It's going to be hard, seeing my little girl get married. I hope she picked a better man than I did." Stella paused. "Are your parents still together?"

Jenna shook her head, knowing she was about to tell another lie. There seemed to be no end to them these days. "They've both passed on."

"Oh, I'm sorry."

"It was a long time ago." She hoped that would be the end to the questions.

"I'm sure it still hurts. My mama has been gone fifteen years now, and I still wish I could talk to her. Every Thanksgiving when I make her stuffing recipe, I see her face and hear her scolding me about using too much butter." Stella blinked back a tear. "Good grief. I'm welling up already."

"I miss my mother, too," Jenna confessed. "She died on Christmas Eve. She was on her way to play the piano for our church. She had to get there early, so we didn't go together." Jenna paused, her mind flashing back to that terrible night. At first she'd thought the red and blue lights were Christmas lights, but soon it became clear that they belonged to a police car and an ambulance. Her father had screamed—a horrible sound that she could still hear in her dreams. Jenna cleared her throat, realizing that Stella was watching her with compassion in her eyes. "Anyway . . ."

"I know. I should go. Thank you, Jenna."

"You're welcome." Jenna stood up and found herself enveloped in Stella's warm arms. Instinctively, she stiffened. After her mother died, hugs and kisses had vanished from her life, and she'd never been a touchy-feely kind of woman. She'd never had that relationship with friends, and boyfriends had been few and far between. In the last few months she hadn't let anyone but Lexie get close enough to touch her. The contact felt surprisingly good.

"You're a skinny thing. You should eat more. I know it's none of my business, but I can't help it." Stella grinned as she let Jenna go. "Bye now." She grabbed her purse off the table, gave a wave, and headed out the door, humming off key.

As the door closed behind her, Jenna checked her watch. She had a few minutes before her next lesson, so she sat down at the old upright piano that had come with the furnished cottage. When she'd seen the house and the piano, she'd felt as if she and Lexie had landed in exactly the right spot. With music, she could get through anything. The piano was at least seventy years old and a far cry from the grand piano she used to play, but it was good enough. Better than good enough, because the old piano made her remember what it was like to play without any pretensions, ambitions, or pressure. Music had been both her best friend and her worst enemy, and right now she needed it to be her friend.

As she stared down at the keys, a wave of reckless temptation swept through her. She knew she should resist. She couldn't let herself get seduced. If she started playing anything more than simple notes, plain melodies, she wouldn't want to stop, and she *had* to stop. Her life was different now. She could never have what she'd had.

But the lure of the keys drew her forward. Maybe just a few chords, just enough to satisfy her ears, which were still ringing from Stella's performance. She knew she was rationalizing, but couldn't stop herself from placing her fingers over the keys, from feeling the sense of anticipation that she always felt right before she hit the first note.

As soon as her fingers touched the smooth ivories she was lost, back in another world, another place. At first she was content to play the tunes that she couldn't remember not knowing. Her parents had taught her to play before she could read. As the music ran through her, the melodies changed, the emotions of the past flowed through her, memories of a time when music had driven her life . . .

The crowd hushed as she walked across the stage in the Isaac Stern Auditorium at Carnegie Hall. It had taken forever to get here—all those hours of practicing, of worrying she wasn't good enough. But here she was. As she began to play, the fear ran away. She wasn't herself anymore. She was a conduit to the music that came not only from her piano, but also from the venerated musicians who had played in the old hall. She was one of them now, connected to the past, the music running through her veins. When she finished her solo, there was dead silence. Then the applause echoed through the auditorium. She had almost forgotten she was playing for anyone but herself.

Standing up, she took her bows, her gaze catching on the man in the front row. He wasn't smiling. Nor was he clapping.

Maybe she hadn't been good enough. But dammit, she was the one on the stage, not him. She glanced away. She would pay for that small act of rebellion later. . . But tonight she would just enjoy the moment. It was her moment—and it belonged only to her.

Reid Tanner pulled up in front of a one-story cottage at the end of Elmwood Lane. Jenna Davies's house backed up to a grove of redwood trees and stood apart from its neighbors, an empty lot between it and the next house. On the other side of the home were more trees that wound along a steep cliff that dropped to the ocean.

Her street was a few blocks inland from the harbor and in a quieter part of town, but still only about a ten-minute walk from the action. It was a modest house, the lawn neatly trimmed, a few bushes by the porch, but nothing bright, colorful, or inviting. The windows were covered with curtains or blinds, none of which was open to let in the midday sun.

It was a lonely house, a place that felt separate and a bit outside, perhaps exactly like its owner. Or tenant, Reid amended. He knew from the town gossips that Jenna Davies had moved into the house two months ago and while she was friendly, she was also reserved. No one knew anything personal about her or her daughter, Lexie. He planned on changing that.

Reid was about to knock on the front door when the sound of music made him pause. Whoever was playing the piano had incredible talent. But there was a painful, angry violence to the melody, a rumble of thunder, a gathering storm. His pulse began to pound in anticipation, of what, he didn't know. The music seemed to fill the air that he breathed, flowing through his veins, sharpening every nerve in his body. He fought its pull, sensing that it was taking him somewhere he didn't want to go, making him think, making him feel . . . Dammit, he didn't *want* to feel. He needed to walk away, but he couldn't seem to move.

The melody ended in a crashing crescendo of notes. He drew in a deep breath, unsettled by the fury he'd heard, the feeling of desperate despair, the sense of terror. He waited a moment to see if the music would start up again, but all was quiet now. The calm before another storm, or was the storm over?

Who could tell? He'd spent many a day wondering if the nightmare he was living would ever go away or if it would always lie in wait, striking when he least expected it, reminding him that he'd never be free.

Was that how the person inside felt? The one playing the piano with an intensity he'd never heard before? As he considered the thought, he debated the wisdom of his course. He really should be interviewing people in town about the angels. Unfortunately, he was far more interested in the woman who'd blown him off last night than he was in angels, and if she was the one who'd just played the piano, then he had even more questions.

Reid rang the bell then lifted his camera, feeling a rush of adrenaline.

God, she was going to be pissed. He felt more alive than he had in a long time.

She opened the door.

"Smile," he said, snapping her photo. He caught the drop of her jaw, the flash of anger in her dark blue eyes, the tightening of her lips, and the dismay that crossed her face. He took another shot and then stuck his foot out as she tried to slam the door in his face. "I told you I could take another picture."

"And I told you that I'm not your story. Why aren't you down at the cliff with the other reporters?"

"I don't like to follow the pack, Jenna."

She frowned at his deliberate use of her name, her expression an intriguing mix of anger and wariness. He had a feeling Jenna Davies was a complicated woman, another reason he should probably not be standing on her porch.

"How did you find me?" she asked.

"It wasn't difficult. Everyone at Dina's café was talking about your heroic rescue last night. Most people can't imagine doing what you did. I'm surprised the local paper hasn't been after you for an interview." A look of discomfort entered her eyes. "They have, but you turned them down, didn't you?"

"I'm not interested in press coverage. I only did what anyone else would have done. The local paper respects my right to privacy."

"Then they must be a bunch of pansy-assed reporters."

"What do you want?" she asked impatiently.

"I want to know why you did it. Most people wouldn't get off the couch to save their own mother, but you jumped into an ice-cold bay to rescue a stranger. That's why I'm interested in you."

His gaze ran down her body. She'd been soaked the night before, and in the shadows he hadn't been able to see her clearly. She was pretty in an understated way. Her thick brown hair was swept up in a ponytail, and except for two bright spots of pink in her cheeks, he doubted she was wearing a speck of makeup. Nor did she have on any jewelry, not even a wedding ring, which he found much too interesting. Her jeans were cheap and baggy. Her long-sleeved T-shirt looked like it had seen better days, and was at least a size too big. She appeared to be a woman who lived a modest life, yet it seemed contrived, as if she were deliberately trying to downplay her features. He had the distinct feeling that she'd made herself up to appear very forgettable, which only intrigued him more.

"What will it take for you to delete those pictures?" she asked, crossing her arms in front of her chest.

The motion drew the material close around her breasts, and he noticed that she had some very nice curves. His body tightened in appreciation. He cleared his throat as he met her eyes. "How about an explanation for why you're so camera-shy?"

"I want to live a quiet life, that's all. Who do you work for, anyway?"

"*Spotlight Magazine.*"

"I've never heard of it."

"Well, six million people have," he drawled. "We cover whatever stories people are interested in."

"No one is interested in me."

"I am."

"I can't imagine why."

"Why are you teaching piano to beginners when you play like a concert pianist?" he challenged.

Her eyes widened in alarm. "You heard me?"

"Yes, and you're very good. But you know that, don't you?"

"Not good enough," she said with a shake of her head.

"You must have extremely high standards. I'm curious as to why you chose to play such a dark piece. It sounded as if you were incredibly angry or in terrible pain, or maybe both."

She looked away, glancing down at her watch. "I really don't have time for this. I have a student coming in a few minutes. Look, Mr. . . ."

"Tanner. Reid Tanner. Here's the thing, Jenna. I have some time to kill until the angels make their next miracle appearance. Now, I can ask you my questions or I can ask around town. I'm sure people will be more than willing to talk about you. They already are because of what you did last night. But it's your call. If you want me to go away, you have to give me something."

She hesitated for a long moment, an internal battle going on in her beautiful blue eyes. He sensed that she wanted to slam the door in his face, but since that hadn't worked the first time, she needed another game plan.

He didn't usually have much trouble getting women to talk to him, but this one was as prickly as a cactus.

"Fine," she said. "Here's the deal. You took two pictures. You get two questions. Then you delete my photos."

"Will you tell me the truth? And that's not my first question," he added quickly.

"We'll see."

"All right." He thought for a moment, choosing his words carefully. "Where's Lexie's father?"

"He's dead," she said shortly. "Next."

"Who are you afraid of?"

She didn't answer right away, her lips tightening. Then she looked him straight in the eye and said, "Right now—you."

Three

"Me?" Reid echoed. "Why would you be afraid of me?"

"You're out of questions," she said, a determined glint in her eye. "Now give me the camera."

"I'll do it." He stepped back in case Jenna decided to grab his camera again, then pressed a couple of buttons. "Satisfied?"

"Don't come back here," she warned.

"You don't have to be afraid of me. I'm not a bad guy."

"That's what all the bad guys say," she replied, a disillusioned note in her voice. "Good-bye, Mr. Tanner."

A second later, Reid found himself staring at her front door. He really hated the fact that she'd gotten the last word again. And he'd gotten nothing. He didn't have her photo, and her answers had only left him with more questions.

He turned and walked down the steps to his car. Every instinct he had told him to go after her story.

He knew she had one. That's why she was afraid of him. She had a secret to protect. He'd never been able to resist a good mystery—but she was trouble, and he didn't need any more of that.

He started the car and pulled away from the curb. When he made a U-turn in the cul-de-sac, he saw the flutter of a curtain at her window.

She was watching him.

Just keep driving, he told himself. But he found himself looking in the rearview mirror, knowing he'd be back.

Jenna knew she would have to do something about Reid Tanner. He was gone for now, but he'd be back. Like a shark, he smelled blood in the water—but she wasn't going to tell him her secrets, no matter how often he flashed that charming cynical grin at her or gazed at her with those very interested dark brown eyes. She couldn't trust anyone—especially not a journalist.

When the doorbell rang again, she looked through the peephole this time, then opened the door to her next student.

Marly was a twenty-two-year-old grad student getting her teaching degree, who wanted to learn some basic piano to use in her elementary school classes. The plump blonde gave her a cheery smile. "Hello."

"Hi. How did the practicing go this week?"

"Not very well. I had so much other work to do, but I really hope to make more time this week."

Jenna's cell phone rang. She started in surprise. Only one person had the number of her prepaid phone. Her heart began to pound.

"Why don't you get warmed up, Marly? I'll be back in a minute." She headed into her bedroom, closed the door, then redialed the number. It was answered almost immediately by a soft female voice that was quickly becoming very familiar. "Has something happened?" Jenna asked.

The woman Jenna knew only as Paula said, "Brad put the house up for sale."

"He's moving?" Jenna asked in shock. "What about his job?"

"He might be staying in the area, just not in the house."

Jenna felt sick. Brad had some plan, and she had no idea what it was.

"Is everything okay there?" Paula asked. "How is Lexie doing?"

"Better. She only wakes up a couple of times at night now. She's making friends. Stuttering less. I really hate to move her. I think she's finally starting to feel safe."

"You'll do what you have to do."

"Yes, I will."

"She's lucky to have you."

"Lucky? There's no way in hell I'd ever call Lexie lucky," Jenna whispered as she ended the call.

* * *

The Angel's Bay Marina bustled with afternoon activity. The smell of frying fish permeated the air as Reid passed by Carl's Crab Shack, where a line of people stood at the take-out window for fish sticks and fries. He sidestepped a group of tourists who had just returned from a whale watching trip on the *Angel Shark,* one of Angel Bay's larger charter boats, run by the Murray family. The most prominent family in town, they were definitely on his list of people to interview, but right now he was in search of seventy-nine-year-old Henry Milton, who was rumored to spend most of his days and nights on his boat, the *Mary Lynn.*

The twenty-two-foot fishing boat, which Reid spied on the other side of the *Angel Shark,* looked like she'd seen a few storms—much like the man who was puttering around on deck. Henry Milton's face was as weathered as his boat, a crisscross of tiny lines on skin that was dark reddish brown. His white hair stood up in tufts on top of his head, and his lean frame could have used a few pounds. As Reid approached, Henry gave him a friendly smile.

"Mr. Milton, may I come aboard?" Reid asked.

"That depends. If you want to talk to my grandson, Timothy isn't here."

"I understand that. He seems to be difficult to find these days." Every effort Reid had made to talk to Timothy and his pal James, the makers of the angel Internet video, had been blocked. The two young men had apparently gone on a deep-sea fishing trip and wouldn't be back until the next day. They were probably feeling the heat of national scrutiny, but they wouldn't be able to stay away forever. "Actually, I want to speak to you," Reid continued. "I'd like to get your take on the angels and the alleged pictures on the cliff wall."

"My take, huh? Hold on." Henry disappeared down the stairs, then returned with two bottles of beer. He tossed one to Reid. "You look thirsty."

"Thanks." Reid sat down on the bench across from the old man, unscrewed the bottle cap and took a long swig. It tasted too good. It tasted like forgetfulness. But he couldn't afford to take that slide right now. He set the beer down next to him. "So, any thoughts on the angels?"

"There are a lot of legends in this town. Hard to know where to start."

"You've lived here your entire life; is that correct?"

"Same as my parents and my grandparents and their grandparents before them. My great-great-great granddaddy was one of the twenty-four survivors who made it to shore after the wreck of the *Gabriella* in the mid 1800s. He was originally from New York, made the long trek around the Cape and up the coast to San Francisco in search of gold. He didn't find much gold, but he did fall in love and get married. He was taking his new wife back to the East Coast when the ship went down. She didn't make it. He ended up marrying one of the other survivors and having a family, staying right here." Henry scratched his chin. "A lot of people died that night. More than thirty bodies were found in the bay, just a few yards away from land. Another forty or so must have floated back out to sea, because they were never found."

"So your ancestor was one of the fortunate ones," Reid said.

"Yep."

"Is this video, the angels, and the pictures on the cliff just a way to bring in more tourists for the summer festival that starts tomorrow? Add color to the town?"

Henry gave him a sharp look. "Timothy said he saw angels. They were as clear to him as his own hand. He could see their faces, not just shapes. One was a female with long blond hair. She's not so clear on that video he made, I guess, but he said he'd recognize 'em again if he saw 'em."

"Really?" Reid tried to keep the cynical note out of his voice. He had Henry talking and he didn't want to do anything to make him stop. "Is your grandson very religious?"

Henry shot him a quick look. "No, not at all. He lost his faith in a lot of things when his parents split up. You're not a believer, are you, Mr. . . ."

"Tanner. And no, I'm not." Reid paused. "I heard that the *Gabriella* was filled with massive treasures from the Gold Rush, yet no divers have ever found the wreck or any evidence of gold."

Henry nodded, an admiring expression filling his eyes. "You've done your homework. But just because you can't see something doesn't mean it's not there. I've been fishing and diving off this coast my entire life. There are underground canyons, mountains, unbelievable spectacles beneath the water that can only be seen when the tides are just right. There is no doubt in my mind that somewhere not far from here sits the remains of the *Gabriella* and all she contained." Henry paused. "Some people think the angels are trying to make a map on the cliff face to point to where the *Gabriella* lies. They want something to be found—something that's been lost too long."

"Treasure," Reid murmured, a tingle running down his spine. The thought of undiscovered gold was undeniably exciting.

"That's right." Henry gave Reid a grin. "Got your attention now, huh? The angels you could ignore, but not buried treasure. Temptation, greed, desire changes a person. Desperation, too." Henry paused and lifted the beer bottle to his lips, taking a long, thoughtful swallow. "This place has always been about the battle between good and evil, the two sides of every human being's soul. In my family there are journals passed down from generation to generation, each retelling the story of that night: the terrible storm, the ship splintering apart on the rocks, the rush for lifeboats—the knowledge that there weren't enough, that not everyone would survive, that some would not act heroically."

Reid stared at the old man, caught up in the story. "Was your ancestor one of the heroes?"

"In his writing it seems so, but who knows?

Sometimes a man doesn't want to look too closely at his soul. You know what I mean, Mr. Tanner?"

Reid had spent the better part of a year not looking at his soul. He had the distinct feeling that old Henry could see that. The thought unnerved him. He'd always considered himself a good poker player, not a man to give anything away.

Henry continued, "The lines between good and evil can be razor thin. Sometimes they're blurry, and sometimes they're impossible to see until you step over them. You think you're doing what's right, and suddenly you realize just how wrong you are." He sat back in his seat and took another sip of his beer.

Surprisingly rattled by the conversation, Reid swung his gaze toward the town, needing a minute to compose his thoughts. Small shops lined Ocean Avenue, the waterfront looking like a picture postcard with antique shops, sidewalk cafés, art galleries, clothing boutiques, a quilt store, and shops selling Angel's Bay memorabilia.

The homes in the older part of town were on the smaller side, but on some of the adjacent bluffs and hillsides, large seaside homes were being developed. It wouldn't be long before Angel's Bay had more business and more people than it could handle. Actually, maybe that time had already come. The manager of the Seagull Inn, where he was staying, had told him that all the rooms in town were booked. They'd never had so many tourists. Perhaps that's exactly what the makers of the video had intended to accomplish.

"You should talk to Fiona Murray," Henry said, interrupting Reid's thoughts. "If you're interested in the history of the town, that is. She runs the Angel's Heart Quilt Shop, where all the ladies go. It's that big red barn over there." He pointed toward the far end of the street. "Fiona knows a lot about the *Gabriella* and the people who survived—what happened to them, where they are now. History says that some of the survivors tried to leave town, but they never made it. It's as if those who died in the wreck had a grip on them and wouldn't let go." Henry stroked his lightly bearded chin with one hand. "Story goes that something bad happened on the ship before she went down."

"Like what?" Reid asked, his attention captured once again.

"Murder," Henry said bluntly. "Some think that's why the angels are getting stirred up. They're tired of waiting for the truth to be revealed. They want someone to pay attention." He paused, his gaze drilling into Reid's. "Maybe that someone is you."

Murder, lost treasure, a mysterious woman . . . Every time he turned around, there seemed to be a new story in Angel's Bay. Reid felt an inexplicable run of goose bumps down his arm, as if the weather was about to turn, or something was about to happen, which was crazy. He was just getting caught up in the old man's imagination.

"Sounds like quite a story," Reid said lightly. "Someone else will have to tell it."

Henry gave him a speculative look. "Why don't we go for a ride out to the cliffs? The markings on the cliff are best seen from the ocean."

Reid looked at the distant bluffs that dotted the rugged coastline. Beyond the calm waters of the bay, the water appeared more turbulent and treacherous. "How far is it?"

"Just past the breakwater. Takes about twenty minutes to get out there. You got something more important to do? I wouldn't have taken you for a man content to write a story from the sidelines." Henry threw down the challenge with a smile.

Reid picked it up with an answering grin. "You got that right. Let's go."

"Great." Henry jumped to his feet and prepared the boat to sail. He untied the ropes, started the engine, and they were off. As they pulled away from the dock, Reid moved to stand next to Henry at the wheel. There was a glint of excitement in Henry's eyes.

"You love the sea, don't you?" Reid asked.

"I've been on it my whole life. It's in my blood. Wouldn't know what to do with myself if I couldn't see the ocean, taste the salt in the air, feel the wind in my face. There's nothing better." Henry gave him a regretful smile. "My sons don't feel the same way, though. One of 'em lives in Detroit, the other in Nebraska. Landlocked, the both of them, and they're happy."

"I guess one of them is Timothy's father."

"My oldest, Paul. He and Erica divorced about six years ago. Erica was here for a while, but she remarried last year and moved to Los Angeles. Timothy decided to stay and moved in with his buddy. I see him as much as I can, but he's a young man. He doesn't care to spend much time with his old grandpa. What a beautiful day. God, I love this," Henry added with a slight slur.

Reid's gaze narrowed. "How many beers have you had?"

"Now there's a question you should have asked before we left," Henry said with a laugh. He gunned the motor, and Reid grabbed onto the rail to steady himself. "Trust me, I know what I'm doing."

The old man's statement sent a wave of pain through Reid. The last time he'd heard those words, someone had died.

"You okay?" Henry asked, shooting him a quick look. "You look a little green. How many beers have *you* had?"

"Just the one you gave me. Not nearly enough."

Henry gave a nod. "I could see the light in your eyes when I handed you the drink. You've been losing yourself in it, haven't you? Don't you know that when the bottle is empty, so are you?"

"That has occurred to me, yes."

"Afraid you'll forget, or afraid you'll remember?"

Reid tipped his head in acknowledgment. "Maybe a little of both. I didn't think I was that easy to read."

"I've been on this earth a long time, son."

Reid looked away, feeling another odd rush of emotion at the simple word. He'd never had a father, never heard a man call him son, and had thought that he'd gotten used to that fact. Strangely enough, he felt comforted by the word. In fact, with the wind in his face and the sun burning down on his head, he was feeling better than he had in a long time. Summer had arrived, and it had always been his favorite time of the year: long days, warm nights, and nothing but blue skies. It was a season of possibilities. He was surprised by the hopeful thought, not sure where it had come from. The ocean, probably. Henry was right. There was something about being out on the sea that made a man feel powerful and free.

As he glanced back at Henry, he saw a look of pure joy on the old man's face. "I can see why you love this."

"Out here, I rule the world," Henry said with a broad sweep of his hand. "You know what that feels like, I bet."

"I used to," Reid admitted.

"On the sea, I control my destiny—at least until Mother Nature decides to play, but I can handle her. Back on land, there are too many people telling me what to do."

"Probably people who care about you."

"Who think I'm too old to cross the street," Henry grumbled.

Reid grinned and pointed toward a burned out two-story house on one of the bluffs. "What's that over there?"

"That's the Ramsay place. It's cursed. People keep trying to rebuild it, but something always happens."

"I suppose it's haunted, too. Or maybe that's where the angels hang out when they're not drawing pictures on the cliffs."

"Could be," Henry said, ignoring his sarcasm. "All I know is that no one has been able to live in that house for more than a few days in the last thirteen years, ever since they found fifteen-year-old Abigail Jamison's body in the basement. She'd been murdered. The house was empty at the time, between rentals. One of the local boys, Shane Murray, was a suspect for a while, but they didn't have enough evidence to hold him and the crime has never been solved. Since then the house has gone through a couple of owners, but something always goes wrong. The people who have stayed there say they hear screams coming from the basement—Abigail's screams, no doubt."

"You should be writing books, Henry," Reid said with a grin. "You're a born storyteller."

"Just telling it like it is."

"When was the fire?"

"About six months ago. A new owner decided to remodel the house and then it went up in smoke. Arson—but no one was ever caught. I hear the property is on the market again, but I doubt anyone will touch it. At least not a local."

As they made their way up the coastline, the waves rocked the boat up and down. "Is it always like this?" Reid asked, holding onto the rail, his stomach beginning to rumble.

Henry's weathered smile widened. "This is nothing. The ocean is just playing with us, giving us a ride."

"Have you ever been caught in a bad storm?"

"Three of them—the last one about ten years ago. The waves were pounding the boat hard, and it was taking on water fast. I thought I was going down for sure. I figured I'd had a good run, and it was my own damn fault for sailing into bad weather. Then I started hearing voices in my head, people in my life who had died—my grandmother, my mother, my sister. I followed the angels, and they led me home."

"Did you actually see these angels?" Reid asked, unable to keep the skeptical note out of his voice.

"Nope. But I felt their presence."

"I think most people look for angels and spiritual guidance when they think they're about to die."

"I expect that's true. But I didn't die, did I?" Henry cut the engine and pointed toward the cliff. "That's the one."

A large number of people were gathered on the bluff, angel seekers out in full force.

"How close can we get?" Reid asked.

"Not too close, but you can use these." Henry pulled out a pair of binoculars. "You'll have a better view than those up on the bluff. A few folks have gotten so crazy as to try to climb down the cliff. One fell onto those rocks day before yesterday and broke both legs. They had to airlift him out of there. That's why they've got that fence set up now."

Reid looked through the binoculars at the onlookers behind the temporary wire fence on the edge of the cliff. Most looked like normal tourists checking out the scene, but there were a couple of people on their knees, their heads bowed in prayer. He zoomed in on the cliff face. The video had focused more on the angel shapes than the cliff, although subsequent film had showed what appeared to be random markings. As he looked through the binoculars, Reid was surprised to see that the markings appeared to form the outline of a face. There was an oval shape to the head, two wide eyes, an upturned nose, a beautiful mouth, and what appeared to be hair streaming off to one side—reddish gold streaks that stood out in contrast to the otherwise pale rock face.

His heart began to beat faster as the image took shape, searing into his brain.

"What do you see?" Henry asked.

"I'm not sure." He couldn't give voice to the thought running through his head. It was crazy.

"Give it a shot," Henry prodded. "It can't be that difficult to say."

"Maybe a woman's face, maybe not."

"Interesting," Henry commented.

Reid lowered the binoculars, sensing he was about to hear another story from Henry. "Why do you say that?"

"When I look at the cliff, I see a rosebush."

"You do?" Reid took another glance through the lenses. "I don't see that."

"No, you wouldn't. Everyone sees something different. The image has been described as everything from a map to a face to a treasure chest, a house, even a wolf. I think whatever you see is what you need to see. That's why no one can agree."

"Save the bullshit for the tourists." Reid handed the binoculars back to Henry, then lifted his camera and snapped some shots to study later.

The old man laughed. "Who's to say what's real and what's not?"

"Or what's the work of angels, and what's the work of waves pounding against rocks."

"Those markings weren't there a month ago. Every day there are new lines, although the last few days have been slow. Maybe because so many people are camping out on the bluff, scaring the angels away."

"Or scaring away whoever was carving a picture on the cliff."

"It would be almost impossible for a human to reach that part of the cliff. I told you what happened to the last guy who tried."

"There has to be a way." The alternative was even worse to consider.

As Henry turned the boat back toward the harbor, he gave Reid a curious look. "So who was she?"

"What do you mean?"

"The woman's face you saw on the cliff. Did you know her?"

Had he recognized her? Had his brain put Allison's face on that cliff because he couldn't get her image out of his mind?

Turning the question back on Henry, Reid asked, "So if you think we see what we want to see, what's up with your rosebush?"

Henry turned his gaze toward the sea. "My Mary used to tend the roses behind our house. She had a whole garden of them. I was all about the water, she was all about the earth. She loved to plant seeds, tend to them and watch them grow. I'd go to sleep at night smelling the roses on her hands, in her hair, and since she died I can't get the smell out of my head." He gave a sad shake of his head. "We were married thirty-nine years. We were going to take a cruise to Alaska for our fortieth anniversary. I couldn't get her out on this boat to save my life, but she always wanted to go on one of those fancy cruise ships with the big buffets. We kept putting it off—then it was too late. She's been gone almost four years now. Never thought I'd be able to keep going after she passed, but one day somehow turned into the next. Time passes, you know?" Henry looked over at Reid. "You'll know, son."

"What are you—some kind of psychic?" It was uncanny how Henry seemed able to read him better than people he'd known for a lifetime.

Reid moved away from the rail to gaze out over the water as Henry steered the boat back toward the bay. As the cliff grew smaller in the distance, a shadow passed between him and the sun—a shadow that appeared decidedly female. Probably a wisp of a cloud, yet there were no other clouds in the sky. The most ridiculous thought came into his head, and Reid shoved it away. He'd been in town less than forty-eight hours, but he was already getting caught up in its spell. He had *not* just seen an angel. Because if he were going to see a spirit, it wouldn't be an angel; it would be one of the darker ones.

Four

Jenna felt goose bumps run down her arms as the afternoon breeze lifted her hair off her neck. She'd been feeling unsettled all day, rattled not only by the news that Brad had put the house up for sale, but also by Reid Tanner's intrusive appearance in her life.

As she and Lexie walked down Ocean Avenue, she couldn't shake the feeling that someone was watching them. The sleepy town she'd first moved into was now a frenzy of activity with preparations for the weekend festival, a combined celebration of the founding of the town and the official beginning of summer. The festival was set to kick off in two hours with a wine, cheese, and art fair along the waterfront.

Numerous other events were scheduled for the weekend, including a carnival of games and rides in the grassy area at the far end of town. Jenna was already dreading the crowds of strangers and the ensuing chaos. If it were up to her, she'd hide out in the house all weekend and not come out until Monday. Unfortunately, there was no way she could keep Lexie away from the action. She didn't want Lexie to live her life in terror, although some days she wondered if a normal existence would ever be truly possible.

"Kimmy wants us to eat with them tonight," Lexie said excitedly, skipping along next to Jenna. Lexie was always a bundle of energy. She never walked if she could skip or run; never sat without swinging her legs or tapping her feet. Her active movements actually made Jenna feel better. During the first few days of their panicked flight across the country, Lexie had been far too quiet and withdrawn. It was good to see her coming out of that numb state, though with her renewed spirit, her stubborn streak had also returned. "They'll save us seats, okay?" Lexie added, shooting Jenna a purposeful look as if she were expecting Jenna to say no, which is exactly what Jenna wanted to do.

Kimmy was Lexie's new best friend and while Jenna had met Kimmy's mother, Robin Cooper, they'd exchanged little more than casual conversation outside the school. She knew that sitting down to dinner with Kimmy's family would mean questions. She only hoped both she and Lexie could keep the answers straight. "All right, but you need to remember our rules, okay?"

"I remember," Lexie grumbled. "But—"

"But what?" Jenna asked. "There are no exceptions, Lex."

"Don't you think Daddy misses me? Don't you think he's lonely without me?"

Jenna stopped abruptly at Lexie's words. She pulled Lexie to one side and squatted down to look her straight in the eye. "Your daddy is sick, honey. He needs to be by himself right now, so he can get better. That's why we can't call him or tell him where we are. It's important that you remember that—that you continue to play our game."

Lexie's lips turned down in a sulky frown. "But—"

"There aren't any but's," Jenna said, cutting her off. "No exceptions."

"What if he needs *me* to get better?"

"I know you want to help him, but your father has to do this on his own."

"What if the bad guy hurts Daddy?"

Jenna drew in a deep breath. She didn't know what Lexie remembered about the days before their flight, or if what she remembered had anything to do with what really happened. Lexie seemed to mix bits and pieces of fantasy in with reality. Jenna supposed that was normal, but she really had no idea. She knew Lexie needed counseling, but that was a risk she couldn't take right now.

"Your father will be fine," she said, "but you have to promise me that you'll stick to our story. It's really important."

Lexie slowly nodded, the rebellious light fading from her eyes. "But do you think Daddy misses me?"

"I know he does," Jenna said, hoping that was the right thing to say.

Lexie smiled again. "I think he does, too. Look, there's Kimmy!" Lexie pointed down the street to where Kimmy and her mother were entering the Angel's Heart Quilt Shop, then tugged on Jenna's hand. "Come on. I don't want to be late on the first day of class."

The night before, Jenna had succumbed to Lexie's incessant pleading and agreed to take her to the children's beginning quilt class. It had become evident since they'd moved to Angel's Bay that while fishing and tourism were important to the town's economy, quilting was its soul.

Since learning to quilt was the first thing Lexie had shown any real interest in since moving to Angel's Bay, besides the angels, Jenna hated to say no. Lexie needed a creative outlet for the turmoil she'd gone through, and perhaps this was it.

The quilt shop was located in a big converted barn on Ocean Avenue. Every Monday night, dozens of women gathered on the second floor of the shop for community quilting night. In addition to making quilts for new brides and new babies, the Angel's Bay quilts were also sold worldwide, and business was thriving. Jenna had been invited to take one of the adult classes but had managed to beg off. She'd managed to avoid even stepping into the quilt shop until now, knowing that getting any more integrated into the community would mean answering more questions, and it was difficult to keep the facts and the fiction straight in her mind.

"Do you think I can make a quilt for my bed today?" Lexie asked as they approached the store.

"I think it will take a few classes before you can make a quilt." Jenna cast a quick look over her shoulder, unable to shake her uneasy feeling.

"You're hurting my hand," Lexie complained.

She eased her grip. "Sorry, honey." She glanced down at Lexie and saw the worry flash in her eyes. "It's okay. Everything is okay." She said the words firmly as much to reassure herself as Lexie. She let go of Lexie's hand and opened the door to the shop.

The first floor was filled with colorful bolts of fabric, pattern books, an array of sewing machines, and assorted threads, measuring tapes, appliqué materials, and embroidery hoops. The walls were covered with beautiful quilts, including one that was preserved in a glass case on the sidewall.

As Jenna had expected, the shop was crowded with women and children, some shopping, some chatting by the coffeepot, and others sitting on comfy couches working on needlepoint squares. A crowd was gathered upstairs in the loft, where much of the community quilting was done and where the adult classes were held. At the back of the shop were two long tables where children were picking out fabrics they would use for their first quilt project.

Lexie saw Kimmy and immediately headed in that direction. Jenna followed more slowly, realizing with every step that she was fast becoming the center of attention. She smiled nervously at some familiar faces. She'd met a few of the moms while taking Lexie back and forth to school, the library, and the playground, but she'd never had more than a brief conversation with any of them. She suspected that most of the moms either thought she was a snob or very shy. In truth, she hadn't kept her distance just because she was afraid of their questions, but because she really didn't know what to say to them. This world that she and Lexie had landed in was completely different from the world they'd left.

"Here's the heroine now," said Kara Lynch, a pretty dark redhead in her early thirties with friendly brown eyes, a blooming smile, and a ready laugh. Kara's grandmother, Fiona Murray, owned the quilt shop. Kara also worked in the local real estate office and had rented Jenna her house, making her one of the few women in town that Jenna had gotten to know a little bit. Kara was married to Colin Lynch, an officer in the police department, and they were expecting their first child in the fall.

Next to Kara was Theresa Monroe, who was married to Angel Bay's mayor, Robert Monroe. Theresa was a sleek blonde whose hair was cut very short and on the diagonal. She wore a beautifully tailored black dress and looked as out of place as Jenna felt.

"Hello," Jenna said, greeting them both.

"Do you know Theresa?" Kara asked.

"I don't think we've officially met," Jenna replied. "I'm Jenna Davies."

"Theresa Monroe. It's lovely to meet you." Theresa offered Jenna a brief handshake, her eyes cool.

"My husband told me about your incredible rescue last night. We're all very impressed by your courage."

"It was nothing," Jenna said, feeling uncomfortable under their curious scrutiny.

"I can't believe you jumped into the water like that," Kara said. "Weren't you scared?"

"It was a spur-of-the-moment decision. I didn't have time to think. Have you heard how the girl is?" Jenna had been wondering about the young woman all day.

"Colin says she's going to be fine," Kara replied. "She's pregnant, you know."

"I—I didn't," Jenna said, surprised. "She seemed so young."

"Old enough, I guess. But the big question on everyone's mind is—who's the father?" Kara's gaze swung from Jenna to Theresa.

"Probably some teenage boy," Theresa muttered.

"You never know," Kara said. "It could be anyone in town, even one of the married men."

"Well, I really don't have time to gossip about it," Theresa said. "If you'll excuse me, I have to go. I just dropped in to pick up some thread for my mother. It was a pleasure, Jenna. I hope to see you again soon."

"Well, that was interesting," Kara said as Theresa left the store.

"What?"

"Theresa said she came here for thread, but she didn't buy any. I suspect she came for information." Kara cast a quick look over one shoulder, as if she didn't want to be caught gossiping, although from what Jenna could see all the women in the shop were whispering to each other. "The girl you rescued works for Myra's Cleaning Service," Kara continued. "They clean most of the big houses in town, including the mayor's. Word is there are some wives who are mighty concerned that the cleaning service was doing a little more than cleaning at their homes, if you know what I mean."

"Oh." Jenna didn't quite know how to respond. She'd never had a lot of girlfriends growing up, and while she appreciated being the recipient rather than the target of gossip, she was also caught a little off guard.

"Theresa's husband, the mayor, is a big flirt. Good looking man, too. Not that I'm saying anything, but Theresa sure left in a hurry when the conversation turned to that girl."

"The mayor is in his forties. The girl is a teenager," Jenna protested.

"And your point is?" Kara asked, raising an eyebrow.

Jenna sighed. "Right."

"Thank goodness Colin and I can't afford a cleaning service," Kara added with a little laugh. She put a hand on her bulging belly. "The baby is kicking up a storm today."

"When are you due?"

"September. I'm hoping for a girl." Kara gave a guilty smile. "I shouldn't say that, because I really just want a healthy baby, but I've always been a girly girl. I don't think I'd know what to do with a boy."

"Are you going to find out the sex ahead of time?"

"Colin doesn't want to. He wants it to be a surprise at the end. I said it could be a surprise now, but he's a stubborn Irishman. There's no changing his mind once he's made it up. He's a good guy, and he'll make a great father. It took us four and a half years to get pregnant. I didn't think it would ever happen. This baby is such a blessing. Sorry for running on and on—I'm just so happy, I feel like I'm bursting with it sometimes."

Jenna smiled. It was impossible not to. There was so much joy in Kara's eyes, it was contagious.

"So can I help with you anything?" Kara asked. "Do you want to sign up for a class, pick out some fabrics, check out our latest sewing machines? I have to ask, because I'm working right now for my grandmother. She had to step out for a few minutes, and she hates it when customers don't get personal service."

"I'm just dropping off Lexie for her class. I don't need anything."

"You should take one of the adult classes. Since you play the piano I'm sure you're good with your hands, and you might enjoy quilting. It's creative, therapeutic, fun, and practical. The nights can get cold around here, especially in the winter. Quilts come in very handy."

"I don't even know how to sew a seam." Nor could she possibly take on one more challenge in her life.

"It's easy to learn. Believe me, if you stay in Angel's Bay, you'll soon find yourself picking out fabrics and patterns. Quilting is a big part of life around here. It's who we are and who we'll always be. That's what my grandmother says, anyway. She believes that the traditions passed from one generation to the next keep us connected to each other in a world that's getting bigger and faster and more chaotic. I think she's right."

"I do, too." Jenna knew all too well how fragile connections could be, how easily one could be cut off from the rest of the world. "Did your grandmother teach you to quilt?"

"Before I was in kindergarten. My earliest memories are of picking out fabrics with her, listening to her tell me the story of the town, the Murray family, all the generations of women who quilted before me. My mother really doesn't care for quilting, but she was forced into it when she married a Murray. It's a family tradition that started when the town was born. Have you heard the story?"

"Some of it, but I don't want to keep you from your other customers."

Kara gave a casual wave. "Everyone seems happy enough. You've heard about the shipwreck, right? Well, after the survivors made it to shore, one of the first things the women did was make a quilt to honor those who had died. Each square was made by one of the survivors and tells their story. For the men who didn't have wives or mothers, one of the women interviewed them and made their square based on the information they gave." Kara tipped her head toward the wall. "That's the original quilt there."

Jenna followed Kara's gaze to the large glass case on the nearby wall. She moved across the aisle to take a better look. She'd never grown up with quilts—her parents' house had been one of elegance and sophistication. The furniture and décor had been a mix of black and white, with very little color anywhere. And what color there was had disappeared after her mother died, when her father wiped away all traces of the past.

She'd always thought of quilts as homespun art: simple blocks, triangles, squares, patterns. But the Angel's Bay quilt was a complicated pattern of symbols as well as a mix of fabrics and textures.

"It's a story quilt," Kara explained. "Most of the squares are made from the clothes of the loved ones who survived the wreck, or the clothes of some of those who died and washed ashore. For instance, that white square in the center was made from a baby's bonnet."

"A baby?" Jenna echoed. "I thought there were only men and sailors on the ship, fortune hunters from San Francisco."

"No, there were families, too, women and children. A baby was supposedly found on the shore the morning after the wreck, wearing a white dress and bonnet. She was only a few weeks old. She'd probably been born just before the ship set sail out of San Francisco. The town kept waiting for someone to claim her, but it quickly became apparent that she was the sole survivor of her family, so she became everyone's child. Rosalyn Murray took her in and raised her with her own kids. They gave her the name Gabriella after the ship."

"And Rosalyn Murray is one of your ancestors?"

Kara nodded. "That's right. My grandmother, Fiona, is descended from Sean Murray, one of Rosalyn's sons. He was a year or two older than Gabriella, many, many generations back, of course. Rosalyn Murray is the one who organized the making of the first quilt. It was a way for the town to heal, to honor the living and the dead. She put the baby bonnet in the center of the quilt, because the baby was the symbol of a new beginning, and the bonnet was a tribute to her lost parents."

"The thread design in the square looks like a wing of some sort."

"An angel's wing," Kara said with a smile.

Jenna should have guessed that. There were various forms of angels all over the quilt, but as she studied the wing design, something niggled at the back of her mind. She'd seen that marking before.

Her gaze flew to Lexie. The little girl was wearing ankle socks and tennis shoes, but Jenna knew that on the side of her left foot was a birthmark in the exact same shape. Jenna's heart began to beat a little faster. It was a coincidence. It had to be. Or was it? All of a sudden, the steps that had led them to this place, this moment, seemed to make sense in a way they never had before.

"Are you okay, Jenna?" Kara asked.

"What?" Jenna said, her mind racing.

"You look like you just saw a ghost."

"No, I'm fine. I was just thinking about something else." She was thinking about the manila envelope that she'd opened two months earlier, finding in it the directions to Angel's Bay and the name of the person who would help them get here. She'd never questioned any of it. Her only focus had been to get Lexie to safety, and she'd relied on strangers to make that happen.

"They say that the baby, Gabriella, had a birthmark in the shape of an angel's wing—she was saved by the angels, and that was the angel's kiss," Kara added. "But if you stay in this town long enough, you'll see that just about everything unexplained is attributed to angels." She paused, giving Jenna a thoughtful look. "Some people think you're an angel because you saved that girl last night."

Jenna laughed. "I'm definitely not an angel."

"Maybe not, but you still did something very brave. I don't think I would have done it. I would have called 9-1-1, but I wouldn't have jumped in the water."

"You're pregnant. You have a baby to think about."

"You had your daughter to think about."

"Like I said, I didn't even think. If I had, I probably wouldn't have jumped." She paused. "Well, I'd better go. I have an errand to run before Lexie's class gets out." The desire to go home and look through the manila envelope one more time was overwhelming. Maybe there was something she'd missed in it, something important.

"See you later," Kara called out.

Jenna gave her a wave as she hurried out of the shop. Unfortunately, when she reached the sidewalk she found Reid Tanner barring her way.

He gave her a wary smile and held up his hands. "I come unarmed. No camera."

"Are you following me?" Suddenly she wondered if Reid Tanner really was a reporter. Maybe he was a detective sent to find her by Brad. He seemed much more interested in her than in the article he was supposedly writing.

"If I'd been following you, you would have seen me on your way over here. You were looking over your shoulder every five minutes."

"And how would you know that if you weren't following me?" Maybe it was *his* gaze she'd felt earlier.

"I was getting off Henry Milton's boat," he explained. "I had a good view of Ocean Avenue and I saw you and Lexie walking over here. Where are you off to now?"

"Nowhere—I'm just waiting for my daughter." She certainly couldn't leave Lexie at the shop now, not when she was so unsure about him.

"Want to get a cup of coffee? Dina's Café is just across the street."

She would come under more speculation from the locals there—not to mention that having an in-depth conversation with a reporter was at the bottom of her list. "No."

"No? That's it?" A smile played at the corner of his lips. "Ouch."

"Look, I've made it clear that I'm not interested in talking to you. So why do you keep asking?"

"A better question would be, why are you afraid of me?" His gaze bored into hers.

Would he ask her that if he were working for Brad? Maybe, if he didn't want her to know why he was really here.

"I think our deal was two questions, and you reached your limit," she said.

"Let's make a new deal."

His intense gaze made her warm, and she really looked at him for the first time. He was tall, six feet plus with broad shoulders. He wore faded jeans and a black knit sweater that was pushed up to the elbows. There was a shadow of beard along his jawline, and his wavy dark brown hair reached down to his collar. His nose was slightly crooked, as if he'd taken a punch or two, and his skin was tan, as if he spent time in the sun. There was arrogance in his stance and an "I don't give a shit" attitude in the set of his mouth, but his brown eyes were filled with shadows. Whoever he was, he had something to hide—which didn't surprise her. Lately, she'd begun to think that everyone had a hidden agenda.

"Are you really a reporter?" she asked abruptly.

"Why would you ask me that?"

"You don't seem like the kind of man who'd be interested in writing about angels."

"I cover what the magazine tells me to cover," he said with a shrug. "It's all about the money."

"Really? You don't care about what you write?"

"Not anymore." There was a hard, bitter note in his voice.

"Why is that?"

"Long story."

A story she found herself wanting to hear . . . but the last thing she needed was to get more involved with this man. He could keep his secrets, and she would keep hers. "I should go back inside."

"Jenna, wait." He put a hand on her wrist.

Heat ran through her like a wildfire, burning her, shocking her, and she jerked her arm away. His gaze narrowed, and she knew she'd overreacted. But there was something about this man that unnerved her, something about him that made her want to flee as fast as she could. Even though she'd told him she was afraid of him, it wasn't fear of physical violence. It was something more intangible, something more dangerously attractive.

"I might be able to help you," Reid said, his gaze fixed on her face.

She tried to clear her expression, worried that she was giving away too much. "I don't need your help."

"Are you sure about that?"

"Positive. And I am not your story, not your puzzle to solve."

"I keep telling myself that, but I find you incredibly—intriguing."

A nervous flutter rippled through her stomach. She hadn't been the focus of a man's intense interest in a long time, and she didn't quite know how to handle it. "I have to go." She turned, reaching for the door of the quilt shop.

"Jenna." He called her back again.

"What?"

"If you wanted to stay hidden, you never should have jumped into the bay to save that girl. That was a mistake."

"I know," she whispered. "But I didn't have a choice."

She let herself into the shop, her heart racing. Reid Tanner saw too much. He was intelligent, perceptive—sexy—God! The last thing she needed was an unexpected attraction to a total stranger. The man could be dangerous to her on so many levels. She took a quick look out the window, wondering what his next move would be. Would he come into the shop? Would he wait for her to come out? Or was she making his interest in her bigger than it was?

Reid had his back to her. As she watched, he pulled out his phone and punched in a number, then walked away. Who was he talking to? Could it possibly be Brad?

Her heart thumped against her chest. She didn't want to believe that Reid was setting her up, but she knew nothing about him. And his last comment about her making a mistake—had he been trying to tell her something?

She had to make sure that he was who he said he was. If he really worked for *Spotlight Magazine*, someone should be able to confirm that.

Since Lexie was still involved in her class, Jenna

slipped back out of the store. Reid had disappeared. She walked across the street to the local newsstand and perused the magazines. She'd been so caught up in her own private hell the last few months, she'd barely paid attention to the world news.

She found *Spotlight Magazine* on the second shelf. It was a glossy magazine, its headlines teasing celebrity babies, divorces, affairs, UFO sightings in New Mexico, a pregnant man in Ohio, and a female psychic claiming she knew where twenty-three bodies were buried. Reid Tanner was an intelligent and sharp man. What was he doing writing for a sensational tabloid? It seemed off—wrong.

Opening to the first page, she ran her finger down the list of editors. Reid's name wasn't there. She flipped through the magazine but didn't see his name on any of the articles. She took the magazine to the counter, paid for it, and then walked back across the street. She glanced around to make sure no one was watching her, then she pulled out her phone and dialed the main office number for *Spotlight*.

When the operator answered, she asked to speak to Reid Tanner. The woman hesitated for a second, then said, "Hold on." A moment later she came back on the line. "I'm sorry. I don't have a record of Mr. Tanner. He might be one of our freelancers. I can have one of the editors call you back if you'd like."

"No, thanks." Jenna's hand shook as she closed the phone. Was Reid a freelance reporter? Or did he have another reason for being in Angel's Bay, a reason that had to do with her? Even if he wasn't working for Brad, his curiosity about her could be very dangerous. If he asked questions of the wrong person, or if—God forbid—he went to the police, she'd be in even more danger than she already was.

FIVE

Joe Silveira sat back in his desk chair, the springs squeaking under his weight. The Angel's Bay Police Department was housed in a two-story, one-hundred-year-old building that had more character than modern conveniences, but Joe liked being tied to the past, liked sitting in the same chair that so many men before him had used. Part of the reason he'd moved to the small town was to feel a sense of connection to the community he served. Unfortunately that community was on hold at the moment, and his personal life was taking center stage.

Checking his watch, he adjusted the phone at his ear as he half-listened to his wife's latest real estate deal. If there was one thing Rachel did better than anyone else, it was talk. He'd known that from the first moment he'd met her during their sophomore year in high school. He'd fallen in love with her before he knew her last name. She was everything he wanted, a raven-haired beauty with perfect skin and a dazzling smile, who was not only beautiful, but kind, compassionate, and at the time perfect. She lived in a two-story house with a front porch swing. Her father was a well-known doctor, and her mother was a housewife who volunteered at the school and organized fund-raisers. Rachel had a life completely different from his own.

Half Mexican, half Irish, he'd grown up one of six kids in a chaotic working class family on the turbulent streets of Los Angeles. His mother had worked as a waitress, his father as a supermarket manager. They'd wanted him to go college, become a lawyer, a doctor, or an engineer. And he'd tried to go that route. He'd graduated with a degree in political science and had been accepted to law school, but deep down he'd always known that he really wanted to be a police officer. That was probably the first crack in his relationship with Rachel. She'd been disappointed when he dropped out of law school; she'd envisioned living in a house like the one she'd grown up in. But she'd come around and supported him when he entered the police academy.

Over the years, things had slowly changed between them. He worked long hours and what he saw on the streets spilled over into their relationship. Rachel started to make plans that didn't include him. She had friends he didn't know. She spent time at her parents' tennis club and seemed to be more interested in working on her serve than on getting pregnant. When it was time to get a house, he'd wanted to buy a small place they could afford. Rachel had talked him into accepting a big house near the club as a gift from her parents.

To this day, he didn't know why the house bothered him so much. It had been an incredibly generous gift and he adored Rachel's parents, who'd welcomed him into their family with open arms. But the house hadn't felt right, and the extra rooms had only seemed to provide more space in which he and Rachel could grow apart: a distance that had deepened to a critical point when he'd decided to quit his job and move up the coast, hours away from their life, their friends, and their families.

"Joe, are you listening?" Rachel demanded, interrupting his thoughts. "You never listen to me anymore."

Maybe because what she talked about now bored him out of his mind. But that wasn't being fair to her. No doubt he'd bored her more than a few times with cop talk. Actually, that wasn't true. One of her biggest complaints was that he didn't share his job with her. She didn't understand that he had to compartmentalize his life or he'd never survive.

"Joe," she repeated with irritation in her voice.

"Sorry," he said quickly. "I'm a little distracted."

"Yeah, I get that."

"It's going to be a busy weekend up here. We have a lot of tourists in town for the summer festival, not to mention fanatical angel seekers camping out on the cliffs. Last night we had an attempted suicide off the pier."

Rachel sighed. "Wow, tourists, angel seekers, and a jumper—sounds like a hotbed for police activity."

When had she become so sarcastic? Ignoring her comment, he asked, "When are you coming home?"

A heavy silence followed his question, and he knew the answer before she gave it. Ever since she'd gotten her real estate license three years ago, she'd become consumed with her career and the next big deal that was always just around the corner.

"I can't make it up there this weekend, Joe. I have to cover an open house on Sunday."

"Rachel—you promised you'd start tying things up in L.A. We need to be together."

"I know that, but it's busy here, too. And I'm making a lot of money right now, money for us, for our future. I'm making more than you. It would really be better if you just quit that job and came home. I ran into Mitchell the other night. He said the department would take you back in a second."

"That's not what I want and my home, our home, is here."

"What if I need you to come back for me?" she asked.

"What if I need you here?" he countered. "This is a good town, with great people, and there's plenty of real estate to sell up and down this coast."

"You're wasted there, Joe. You're too good, too smart, to be a small town chief. I know you needed a break, and maybe going back to the department isn't a good idea. But there are cities closer to my business than Angel's Bay."

"This isn't a break for me. It's where I want to be." He'd known that the second he'd walked into the small two-bedroom house his Uncle Carlos had left him. For the first time, he'd felt like he belonged somewhere. He'd told Rachel that more times than he could count, but it never seemed to sink in. She didn't understand how he could want to live in an isolated town that was miles away from everything familiar.

"It's where you want to be right now," Rachel said. "But that will change. I know you, Joe. You crave excitement, danger. You can't bury that side of yourself, no matter how hard you try. You're going to want more."

"I know I'm asking a lot of you, but I think if you gave Angel's Bay a chance, you'd really like it here. This place is beautiful. It's a great community in which to raise a family. We can make this work."

"I want to make it work, Joe," she said, her voice softening. "I do. I just don't know how right now."

"I don't, either," he admitted. "But I know we can't do it if we're apart. I'd really like it if you could get up here for at least part of the weekend. A lot of people have been asking about you. They want to meet you. I've received a dozen invitations to dinner that I've been stalling on. If you give this place a chance, I think you'll like it."

"I'll try. But I have to go now. I'll speak to you later."

He heard the click before he had a chance to say good-bye, to tell her he loved her. There had been fewer and fewer of those moments since they'd moved to Angel's Bay. Actually, he'd really been the one to move. Rachel had only spent a half dozen nights or so in their home overlooking the ocean. Perhaps he needed to consider the fact that one of them was going to have to give in, and it might have to be him.

He looked up as a tentative knock came at his door. "Come in." He was surprised when Charlotte Adams walked in, and a little rattled as well. He was attracted to the beautiful doctor with the honey gold hair, intriguing light blue eyes, and sun-kissed skin. It was an attraction he was hoping would go away. He certainly didn't intend to do anything about it; he was married to Rachel. And despite their problems, he intended to stay that way.

"Sorry to bother you," Charlotte began, "but I'm concerned about Annie. Have you gotten any more information on her family situation?"

"Have a seat." He waved her toward the chair by his desk and picked up the fax he'd received a few minutes earlier. "Annie's father is Carl Dupont. He's an ex-marine, did a couple of tours in Afghanistan, had half his hand blown off in an ambush, and is on permanent disability."

"That's horrible," Charlotte said, compassion filling her eyes.

"I was about to head up the mountain to speak to him. I have a new address for him, at least it's the one where his disability checks have been going."

"I'd like to go with you," Charlotte said.

He was taken aback by her request. "I don't think so."

She straightened in her chair, and he saw a look of stubborn purpose enter her eyes.

"I'm concerned about my patient's well-being," she said briskly.

"This is police business, Dr. Adams."

"It's also my business as her doctor. I want to see where she's been living, and if the conditions will be good for her and her baby to return there."

"It's not up to you where she goes when she leaves the hospital. Annie is eighteen. She doesn't have to go back if she doesn't want to."

"She's also pregnant, with barely enough income to buy food, and how long her employment will last, considering her suicide attempt and her pregnancy, is anyone's guess. She will need help. She may not have any other alternative but to return home."

"Do you always get this involved with your patients?" he asked curiously.

"Annie might legally be an adult, but she is also a young girl who is so scared of something or someone that she tried to kill herself and her baby. The more I know about her background, the more I'll be able to help her."

"You didn't answer my question."

Charlotte sighed. "No, I don't always get this involved, but Annie is different."

"How so?"

She hesitated and then shrugged. "Her case just means something to me. So can I go with you to meet her father?"

Joe knew it was a bad idea for a lot of reasons, but somehow he heard himself say yes, and Charlotte's answering smile made him want to say yes to anything else she asked of him. Shoving that idea out of his head, he got up from his chair and waved her toward the door. "Let's go. I need to get back before the festival starts."

Charlotte followed him out to his squad car. She buckled her seat belt while he turned the key in the ignition, acutely aware of how close she was sitting to him. He cleared his throat and told himself to get a grip. This was business, not personal.

"Thanks for this," Charlotte said. "I know it's not protocol."

"I appreciate your concern for your patient," he said as he pulled out of the parking lot.

They didn't speak for a few minutes. He had a lot of things he wanted to say, wanted to ask her, but every question seemed to lead down the dangerous path of getting to know her better.

"You know, I haven't met your wife yet," Charlotte said, breaking the silence between them.

His hands tightened on the steering wheel. "Rachel has been in and out of town. She's still wrapping up our life in Los Angeles."

"You must miss her."

"I do," he said quickly and emphatically.

"How long have you been married?"

"Nine years, but we've been together since we were fifteen."

"High school sweethearts?" Charlotte asked. "That's amazing. You must know each other so well."

"I thought we did." As soon as he said the words, he regretted them. "I'm sure you'll meet her soon enough." He paused. "What about you?"

"I'm not married, if that's what you're asking. I left this town when I was eighteen to go to college, and then it was on to medical school, internship, and residency. Suddenly, I realized it had been thirteen years since I'd been home for more than a weekend or two." She took a breath. "It's both familiar and strange to be back here now."

"I understand your father was the local minister for what—thirty years?"

"Thirty-four. He died in February."

"Right. I heard that. I'm sorry."

"Thanks."

"Is that why you came back?"

"Yes, though I didn't make it in time. I was planning to move down the following weekend, and he took a turn for the worse. He passed on before I got here." She gazed out the window. "We never had that last conversation, never said good-bye, but maybe it was better that way. Some things are better left unsaid."

He was curious about what those things were, but decided not to ask. "I'm sure your mother must appreciate having you around."

His words brought a rueful smile to her lips. "I wouldn't say that. I'm her least favorite child, but unfortunately for her, I'm the only one available. My older sister, Doreen, and her husband just moved to San Francisco, and my younger brother, Jamie, is in the army in the Middle East, so there's no one around but me."

"I can't imagine you being anyone's least favorite."

Her smile broadened. "That's nice of you to say, but you don't know me very well."

"I know you're a good doctor, and a very caring, involved one. I'm sure your mother must be proud."

"You'd think, but we have a complicated relationship." Charlotte paused for a moment. "My family always had high expectations. My father was the spiritual guide for many people. My mother was his more-than-able partner, who supported him and the congregation in every possible way. I was the preacher's kid, and I was supposed to follow along, be above reproach, but I did some things I shouldn't have when I was a teenager. I let my mother down. I don't think she's ever forgiven me."

"Isn't forgiveness what your father preached?"

"My father, yes. My mother, not so much." Charlotte picked at a piece of lint on her skirt. "I wasn't close to my father. My mother always stood between us. She wasn't the kind of parent who said, 'Wait until your father gets home.' She was his protector. She kept all the problems away from him. She wanted him to be focused on her and the church—in that order, I think, although she pretended otherwise. She loved him fiercely, but that fierceness made her do some things that were . . ."

"Unforgivable?" Joe queried.

She gave him a quick look. "What have you heard?"

"What do you mean?" he returned.

She stared at him for a long moment. "Nothing. Anyway, it's all in the past. I'm here now, although I'm not sure how long I'll stay. Some days, I think my mother would be happier to see me go. Then I talk to my sister, who convinces me that my mother needs someone here, that she's not as strong as she pretends to be, because she not only lost my dad, but her beloved son is in a war zone. I guess that someone has to be me."

It bothered Joe to think that Charlotte might move. He liked seeing her about town, eating waffles at the counter of Dina's Café, picking up a newspaper at the newsstand, running along the waterfront in the early evening just before sunset. He suddenly realized just how often he looked for her when he was out. That had to stop.

"So you're not thinking of staying here forever," he said briskly. "That's too bad. The town needs good doctors like you."

"Well, we'll see. Right now I'm just dealing with what is, not what might be down the road. And speaking of roads . . ." She grabbed on to the armrest as the car hit a big bump. "Are we still on one?"

"You wouldn't know it, but yes." He slowed the car down as they hit another pothole. They'd left the paved county road a mile back. He suspected they were getting close to the Dupont property because of the number of warning signs posted along the way that included *No Trespassing, Pass at Your Own Risk,* and *Dog on Property*. His instincts told him that Carl

Dupont would not greet them with open arms and a pitcher of lemonade. "I shouldn't have brought you here," he muttered.

"I'm sure it will be fine. You're the chief. What's he going to do?"

He could have told her numerous stories about people who were too strung out, too crazy, or too angry to give a damn that he had on a uniform.

"We just want to talk to him," Charlotte added.

"Shit!" Joe hit the brakes as a man suddenly appeared out of the trees, wearing army fatigues and a helmet. He had a rifle in his hands, the barrel of the gun pointed directly at their car. "I don't think he wants to talk to us." Joe threw the car into park and punched the radio button to call his dispatcher for backup. Unfortunately, there was no signal. They were out of range. "Stay in the car, Charlotte."

He opened the door slowly and stepped out, keeping his body behind the door. "Mr. Dupont, I'm Chief Silveira. You need to put down the gun. I've just come to talk to you about your daughter, Annie."

"Got no daughter," the man yelled back, but he lowered his weapon. "And you're on private property."

"Annie is in the hospital," Joe said, relieved that the man had put down the gun. "She tried to kill herself last night. She jumped into the bay. A good Samaritan went in after her. She's lucky to be alive."

"I told you. I don't have a daughter anymore."

Before Joe could say anything, he heard Charlotte's door open. As she stepped out the man raised his gun again, this time pointing it at Charlotte. Joe's heart skipped a beat. He never should have brought her with him.

"Mr. Dupont? I'm Annie's doctor," Charlotte said. "I'm sure you must be worried about your daughter."

"My daughter is a whore. She deserves whatever she gets. She shamed me. She shamed the Lord. Now get off my property and don't come back."

"Get in the car, Charlotte," Joe ordered. "And Mr. Dupont, put down that gun before I arrest you."

The other man lowered his gun, obviously not crazy enough to completely test authority.

Charlotte slipped back into her seat and shut the door. Joe followed suit. He started the car and backed it down the narrow road until he could find a place to turn around. When he was heading down the mountain, he looked in his rearview mirror. Carl Dupont was watching them leave. He probably wouldn't move until he was sure they were gone.

"You shouldn't have gotten out of the car," he said sharply. He'd put Charlotte in danger; that was inexcusable.

"I'm sorry."

"He could have shot you!" Joe said. "Are you always so impulsive? Do you think before you act?"

"I said I was sorry," Charlotte returned.

"Right, forget it. It was my fault. I shouldn't have brought you." He ran a hand through his hair as he headed toward the main road.

"I was trying to help," Charlotte said, "but I was wrong. And to answer your question, my impulsiveness does sometimes get me into trouble. I'm working on it."

He cast a quick look in her direction, seeing an apologetic smile on her pretty mouth. She was certainly different from any doctor he'd ever worked with before. She cared way too much about her patients. She was so determined to help a teenage girl, she barely knew that she'd put herself in front of a gun. He was both pissed off and deeply admiring, but he didn't intend to let her see that.

"You need to work harder," he told her.

"Got it. So, what are we going to do now? Annie can't go home. Even if her father did take her back, who knows what kind of hell he'd put her through?"

"She's an adult, Charlotte."

"Which means . . ."

"That there's nothing I can do. She needs to talk to a social worker, find out what programs are available to her. Her father has no legal obligation to support her after the age of eighteen."

"That man is crazy. And he has a gun. He's dangerous. Can't you do something about him?"

"I'll look into the situation, see if he has permits, but arresting Mr. Dupont won't help Annie."

"That's true," she said with a sigh. "I feel so sorry for her. I wonder if she has any other relatives who can help her."

"You'll have to talk to her again and find out."

"I will," Charlotte agreed. "Can you imagine what it must have been like, living with that man for her father? I just don't understand how people can turn their backs on their children when they're in trouble. It's wrong. Inexcusable."

Joe gave her a thoughtful look. "We're not talking about Annie anymore, are we?"

"Of course we are," she said quickly.

He didn't believe her for a second.

"I'll find a way to help Annie," Charlotte vowed.

"Because no one helped you?" he guessed.

She shot him a look that told him to mind his own business.

He smiled back at her. "I don't scare off that easily."

"And I don't share my life history with people I barely know."

"So we'll get to be friends."

"I don't think that's a good idea, Chief."

"Probably not," he muttered.

"Definitely not," she agreed, crossing her arms in front of her chest as she stared out the window. "So tell me more about your wife."

Six

Jenna hurried Lexie home from the quilt shop, eager to explore the ideas running through her head. She'd been so busy establishing a life where Lexie could thrive that she hadn't really examined the reasons why they'd been sent to this town. She'd always thought it was random—a community that wasn't easy to get to, and was located on the other side of the country. But maybe there was more to it than that.

After sending Lexie down the hall to change her clothes and wash up, Jenna went into her small bedroom and shut the door. The envelope was on the top shelf of her closet, hidden under a stack of sweaters. She pulled it out and took it over to the bed. Though she'd looked through the enclosed materials several times, she now wondered if there was something she'd missed: some reason that she'd been sent to the place where, more than a century ago, a small child with the same birthmark as Lexie had been saved by the town. It seemed far too big a coincidence.

Inside the envelope were copies of birth certificates, identification cards, and Social Security numbers under their new names. Also enclosed were the directions to Angel's Bay, the telephone number of the real estate firm where Kara Lynch worked, a bank card, and an account at the local bank. She had been given a prepaid cell phone for emergencies. All the things she had needed to disappear from her life had been provided for her. But what was she missing? Why had she been sent here?

There was nothing in the envelope that could answer that question.

Were there clues in the house?

The furniture had come with the rental, along with the pictures on the walls and the curtains at the windows. They had simply walked in the door and started their new life.

Jenna walked over to the window and looked out. Her street was on one of Angel's Bay's many hills, providing ocean and town views from different parts of the house. From her bedroom, she could see the pier from which she'd jumped the night before. It was strange to think that even here in this room, she might have seen that poor girl leap into the bay. It was as if she'd been meant to save her, meant to see her, meant to be in this place.

A shiver ran down her spine. Was she imagining the connection? Maybe she was just getting caught up in the angel folklore, the idea that there was something at work that no one could see or understand. Or maybe she *should* listen to her instincts that were telling her to pay attention, to look deeper.

Turning away from the window, she picked up the phone on the nightstand. Digging into the drawer, she pulled out Kara Lynch's business card, which listed both her home and business numbers. When Jenna had left the quilt shop, Kara had been headed home as well. She hoped she was already there.

The phone rang twice, then Kara answered with a cheerful, "Hello."

"Hi, Kara, this is Jenna Davies."

"Hey, Jenna. Twice in one day, what a treat."

"I forgot to ask you earlier, but I've been wondering—who owns this house that I'm renting? Is it someone local? I had a question about the furniture."

"I hope it's all satisfactory."

"Oh, it is. I was just wondering whether one of the pieces was an antique," she said.

"I'm sure they're all antiques, but you could check with Janice Pelovsky. She runs Aunt Mary's Antiques on Grove Street."

"Is Janice the owner of this house?"

"Oh, no. The house is actually owned by my real estate company. My boss's aunt lived there, Rose Littleton. She died two years ago. My boss has been renting out the place ever since. Is there anything else I can help you with?" Kara asked.

"No, that's all, thanks."

"Great, I'll see you at the festival."

"Yes, see you there." Jenna hung up the phone.

Rose Littleton. She was sure she'd never heard that name. She reached for her purse, took out her cell phone, and hit redial. Paula didn't answer, and she chose not to leave a message.

She had just returned the manila envelope to the closet when Lexie came skipping into the room in a pair of blue jeans and a T-shirt covered by a pink sweatshirt, pink being her favorite color.

"I'm ready," Lexie proclaimed, an eager smile on her face.

Lexie had two new front teeth, but one of her baby teeth on the side was dangling by a thread. Every time Jenna saw it she felt a wave of guilt. "Maybe we should pull that tooth out," Jenna said halfheartedly. She didn't really want to do it. She hated the thought of causing Lexie any more pain, but it seemed like a motherly responsibility, and one she needed to address.

Lexie snapped her mouth shut, a defiant look coming into her eyes. "No," she said through tight lips.

"Doesn't it bother you, hanging like that?"

Lexie gave a vigorous shake of her head.

"Okay then, it stays in until it comes out on its own." Jenna wished all of her problems would resolve that easily.

"It can't come out now, because the tooth fairy won't be able to find me," Lexie said.

Jenna's heart turned over and unexpected moisture blurred her eyes. That Lexie could even believe in the tooth fairy and angels seemed like a miracle.

"It can't come out until we go home," Lexie added, breaking Jenna's heart a little more. "It has to go under the special pillow."

Jenna blinked back the tears. Lexie had had to deal with so much in her seven years. It wasn't fair to ask so much of her. She was missing her childhood. But at least she was alive. That was all that was important.

Jenna grabbed her sweater out of the closet, then smiled and said, "We better go to the festival before Kimmy eats all the pizza."

"Can we see the angels tonight?" Lexie asked as they left the room. "They're supposed to come out, because it's the town's birthday."

"Let's see how the carnival goes."

"You never want to take me to see the angels," Lexie complained. "It's not fair."

"Honey, no one has seen the angels, and it gets cold out there on the cliffs." There were also too many strangers around. "What kind of pizza do you want tonight?"

Lexie's face brightened as she contemplated the question. "Pepperoni," she said, as she skipped onto the porch. "I'm starving."

At least that was one thing she could fix, Jenna thought as they headed down the street.

Reid stared at his computer screen as the video played again. He'd watched the angel video a dozen times already, but he wanted to look at it again now that he'd actually been to the cliffs. The airy white shapes, with what appeared to be wings, flew around the rocks, sometimes at a blurring speed. They couldn't possibly be angels, so what were they? Or were they anything?

A few special effects could easily create angel shapes. But while hundreds of skeptics had posted online that the video was a hoax, thousands more claimed that it was proof that angels did exist.

After turning off the video, Reid uploaded the digital images he'd taken from Henry's boat. He zoomed in on the cliff, and as he stared at the lines, the picture in front of him seemed to change. He didn't see Allison's face. He saw someone else's: a child's face, big brown eyes, pug nose, curly hair . . . A wave of nausea swept through him.

Reid closed his eyes. He didn't want to see Cameron's face. Why would he see that image now? Maybe Henry was right—the angels showed you what you needed to see. But he didn't need to see Cameron or Allison's face on some rock wall; they were branded in his brain forever.

Opening his eyes, he shut down the picture gallery and clicked on his word processing program. He'd written two paragraphs for his article, and they were total crap. He had no factual information, no photos of angels, just scratches on a bunch of rocks that could be anything. He had nothing but anecdotal stories from people who probably hoped to increase tourism to the town with their tales of angels, shipwrecks, and missing treasure. Nothing newsworthy to report.

But this wasn't about the news. And though he'd been telling himself that he could handle writing fluff pieces for cash, he couldn't stomach putting his name on a piece of garbage. It felt—wrong.

He leaned back in his chair and stretched his arms overhead, wondering why he gave a damn. It didn't matter what he wrote now. His real career had ended eleven months ago. He should give the readers what they wanted to read: fantastical tales about angels, miracles, hope, love, and all that other shit.

But as he set his hands on the keyboard, the words wouldn't come. Somewhere deep inside, some part of his soul was still alive and kicking back, reminding him that he'd once loved the news, lived for it, in fact. He should be working toward getting back what he'd lost. What he was doing now was the biggest sellout of his life.

It had all started with the damn paper route. He'd lost his parents young. He'd gone into foster care and as he grew up, he'd always been looking for a way to make a buck, so when the older brother of a friend asked him to pitch newspapers out the side of his van every day, he'd jumped in.

Those newspapers had changed his life. He could still smell the paper, see the ink smeared on his fingers, feel the weight of the paper as he tossed it onto the porch of an expensive house in a suburban neighborhood. His friends hadn't taken the job seriously at all. They'd laughed when the papers landed in the sprinklers or in someone's bushes, but he'd always tried to put them on the porch—because somehow even then he'd known that what was in those papers mattered, that people needed a voice, someone to shed light on what was being hidden, on who was being hurt. And he'd wanted to be that person.

He'd had to clear a lot of hurdles to get to the top. It hadn't been easy getting through college. He'd had to work two, sometimes three side jobs to cover his tuition and rent. And he'd spent most of his twenties paying back his student loans. But eventually, everything had come together. All his dreams lined up exactly the way he'd planned. Breaking the big story had been the most important thing to him, nothing else had mattered—including *how* he got the story. The means always justified the end . . . until he realized that it didn't.

As he contemplated the article before him now, his cell phone rang. It was Pete McAvoy, his editor and an old friend, the one who'd gotten him this writing gig. He debated not taking the call, but he knew Pete would hound him until he answered. He'd already called three times in the last two days.

Flipping open the phone, he said, "Hello, Pete."

"So you're talking to me again?"

"I wasn't avoiding you. I've been busy tracking down angels. They're very difficult to arrange interviews with."

"Funny. So what's the status?"

"The boys who filmed the video haven't come back to town yet. I need to talk to them before I can give you a story."

"I'm not looking for Pulitzer Prize–winning material here," Pete said.

"And you're not going to get it, so don't worry. This is all bullshit—you know that."

"It's a paycheck, Reid. Last I heard, you weren't exactly rolling in cash."

"That's what not working for a year will do."

"You're working now."

"If you can call it that." Reid debated whether to give voice to the idea that had been running through his brain all day. "What if I stumbled across a more interesting story?" The words came out before he could stop them.

"What kind of story are we talking about?"

"I'm not sure yet, but my instincts tell me that I'm on to something."

"I thought you'd drowned those instincts in beer and tequila."

"Miraculously, they seem to have survived." He just wasn't completely sure he wanted those instincts back.

"Are we talking hard news? Are you ready to do that kind of story?" Pete asked.

"I don't know. Maybe . . . maybe not."

"You always used to know. You always used to be ready. You were a good reporter, Reid; too good to quit." Pete paused. "Is it really a news story that makes you want to stay in Angel's Bay, or are you hiding out there? I know this must be a rough time of the year for you. It has been almost a year."

"If I wanted to hide out, it wouldn't be here in the land of love and miracles. I'll get the angel story to you by early next week."

"Reid, if you come up with something big, do it. Trust your instincts. There is nothing that would please me more than seeing you do what you do best, and that's hard-hitting news stories that make people think. In the meantime I've got space to fill, so find me some angels and do it soon."

"Yeah, yeah. Don't call me; I'll call you." Reid closed his phone, then shut down his computer, and walked over to the window.

From his room at the Seagull Inn, he could see that the festival was in full swing. Lights had been strung up along Ocean Avenue and at the center of the carnival was a tall Ferris wheel. He couldn't remember the last time he'd ridden the Ferris wheel.

Actually, he could. The memory began to play in his mind, and as much as he wanted to stop it, it kept on coming . . .

As their chair rounded the top of the Ferris wheel, he could see the entire carnival. The town of Williamsville was celebrating its centennial with a fireworks celebration, and Reid was enjoying a rare moment away from work with one of his closest friends.

Reid glanced over at Allison's face. Her red hair glowed in the moonlight, and her eyes were lit up with a joy he hadn't seen in a very long time.

He didn't know what was going on between Allison and her husband, Brian. The two of them had been inseparable since they'd all met sophomore year in college. They'd been a trio before and after Allison and Brian hooked up. Reid had been there for all the important events in their lives: the engagement, the drunken bachelor party, and the wedding in Florida, where the reception tent had sprung a leak and drenched the guests in an intense summer shower. Alli and Brian hadn't cared. Their love had been palpable. He'd seen that love grow stronger when Cameron was born. Reid had waited with Brian when Allison had been rushed to the hospital for an emergency C-section. He'd seen Brian sweat out the minutes of terror, and he'd rejoiced with him when Cameron had been declared perfectly healthy.

Over the years he'd started to drift away—his fault. They were an enclosed family unit, and as much as they cared about him, he felt he didn't belong. As a foster kid, he'd changed homes and schools as often as he changed his shirts. He was used to being on the outside and didn't really know how to get any closer. But now, he was starting to realize that by staying away to give them their privacy, he hadn't been much of a friend.

He knew something was wrong. Brian had begged off on this trip to the carnival, claiming he had to work late. He'd seen the strain in Allison's eyes when she'd heard Brian's excuse, and he'd seen the disappointment in Cameron's face when his father said he wasn't coming.

Now Reid glanced down at the little boy who was clinging to the railing so hard his knuckles were turning white. Reid was a poor substitute for Brian, but he could try. Reid covered Cameron's hands with his. "Don't worry, buddy, everything is okay."

"It's too high up here." Cameron's voice wavered. "It's scary."

"I won't let anything happen to you."

Reid smiled at Allison.

"Thanks," she whispered. "It's been a rough week."

"Are you ever going to tell me what's going on?"

"I was going to ask you the same question. Why are you here, Reid?"

"To see my friends," he prevaricated.

She shook her head. "You haven't been in touch in months. I think you want something. Why don't you just ask?"

"You know me too well." He took a breath. "I'm doing a story on counterfeit drugs being sold to local hospitals."

Her eyes widened. "At Glen Oak Memorial?" she asked. The hospital where she worked as a nurse.

"It's one of three I'm investigating. You haven't heard anything?"

"A few rumors, nothing specific."

"I need someone on the inside to help me."

"And that's me," she said with an understanding nod. "Now I get it."

"If it puts you in an awkward position . . ."

"It will." She met his gaze. "But I'll do it for you."

"You should think about it," he said quickly, already having second thoughts about involving her. But he'd been running into roadblock after roadblock, and people were dying because they weren't getting the right strength of medication thanks to watered-down doses and pure placebos. He had some evidence, but he needed more. He wanted to get it before someone else did, and he was so close.

The Ferris wheel came to a halt, and they stepped out. Cameron ran over to join a group of friends while Allison and Reid stopped a few feet away.

"I don't need to think about it." Allison put her hand on his arm. "I trust you, Reid. I know this is important or you wouldn't ask me. I'm glad you finally asked me for something. Sometimes it's difficult to be the one who always takes."

"That doesn't describe you," he said, surprised by her words.

"It does with you. You give so much to me and Brian and Cameron, but you never let us give anything back. You're in our life, but you don't let us into yours. We care about you. But you always keep us at a distance."

"I didn't realize I was doing that."

"Because you've been doing it your entire life. You learned how to walk away before people walked away from you. I get that. But we're not going anywhere, so you better get that, *too. Since you've given me a chance to be in your life, I'm going to take it. And you'll just say thank you. It's good to learn how to receive."*

He grinned. "Fine. I'll let you buy me an ice cream, too."

"Hey, don't get greedy," she said with a laugh.

Reid was relieved that they were back on an even keel. He'd never meant to hurt her by keeping her at a distance. "Since we're sharing, are you and Brian okay?"

A shadow passed through her eyes. "We will be."

"Now who's being vague?"

"We'll be fine. Come on, let's get that ice cream."

Reid opened his eyes, unable to bear seeing her image in his mind, hearing the sound of her voice in his head. He shouldn't have let her into his life. And she shouldn't have trusted him. If he could relive one moment in his life, it would be that one. Because that's when it had started, and if it had never started, it never would have ended so terribly.

Turning away from the window, he picked up his wallet and grabbed his room key. He needed to get away from the memories. The problem was, no matter where he ran, they seemed to find him.

Seven

The idea had been brewing ever since she'd come down the mountain, but as Charlotte walked into her mother's house, she wondered if she was completely out of her mind. If she was, her mother would certainly say so. Monica Adams was not one to mince words, especially with her ever-disappointing middle child.

As Charlotte made her way through the house she was puzzled to see a stack of empty boxes in the hallway. Had her mother finally decided it was time to go through her father's things? In the three and a half months since her father had passed away, her mother hadn't moved a thing. His clothes still hung in the bedroom closet, his magazines lined the coffee table. Even his keys still rested on the side table from the last time he'd entered the house. It was almost spooky, but Charlotte had given up trying to convince her mother to make changes. Actually, she'd given up trying to make her mother do anything a long time ago, which was why her new idea was incredibly foolish. But she'd give it a shot, because she was desperate.

The house was quiet, nothing like it had been when her father was alive. Growing up, Charlotte had always come home to a house filled with the smell of dinner cooking in the oven, the sound of conversation in the kitchen, and the nightly news on in the den where her father caught up on the events of the day. Her brother, Jamie, was usually running some automated car down the hardwood floor in the hall, and her sister, Doreen, was almost always on the phone. Sometimes the house had been filled with people from the church: bible groups, the ladies' auxiliary, or people just wanting to speak to her father. Their house had been the center of the action.

Now it felt as if she were living in an old theater, with only the ghostly sounds of the past echoing through the quiet rooms. Everything had changed, and yet in some ways it hadn't changed at all. Her relationship with her mother was as rocky as ever—maybe even more so without any buffers between them.

Charlotte found her mother sitting on the back porch staring out at the night. A sweater hung loosely over her shoulders. Monica Adams had lost at least ten pounds in the past few months and her posture, normally upright and ready to do battle, was defeated. The warrior had lost her biggest battle. She'd lost her husband.

As Charlotte paused in the doorway, she thought

again how wrong it was for her mother to be sitting on the wicker loveseat all alone. For as long as she could remember, her parents had retired to the deck every night after dinner. On warm summer evenings she'd heard their hushed voices late into the night, the occasional giggle, the sudden silence when she'd imagined them sharing a kiss. There had never been any doubt in her mind that her parents loved each other madly.

In many ways her parents had lived in a world separate from their children. They'd had a flock to tend; her father as the minister, her mother as the minister's wife who supported him and the community in every possible way. Their children were supposed to fit in wherever they could, and always represent the family with honor and integrity. Doreen and Jamie had done their part. She was the only one who had screwed up, who had marred the perfect family picture her mother had strived to create from the first minute of her marriage. But her mother had painted over her mistakes as if they'd never occurred, as if it were all just a bad dream, never to be talked about again.

"Don't hover, Charlotte," her mother said abruptly.

Charlotte started. "I'm sorry."

"You're late."

"I had a patient to deal with."

"You sound like your father." Monica finally turned her head to look at her. "But he always called to let me know he'd be late so I wouldn't worry."

Charlotte accepted the criticism without comment. She walked onto the porch and took a seat in the chair next to her mother. This was not how she'd hoped the conversation would go, but it was pointless to wait for a better time. "I need a favor, Mother."

Monica raised a surprised eyebrow. "From me?"

"Yes. I don't know if you heard about the girl who jumped off the pier last night, but—"

"Of course I heard, Charlotte. She's pregnant and no one knows who the father of her child is, although there is certainly a great deal of speculation going on about errant husbands. I had three calls before lunchtime."

"Right." Charlotte should have anticipated that her mother's network of friends would have filled her in. Gossip had always run rampant in Angel's Bay.

"So what do you need from me?" Monica asked.

"Annie—that's the girl's name—is eighteen years old. She has nowhere to go, and I have to release her from the hospital tomorrow." Charlotte took a deep breath. "I'd like to bring her here."

Her mother arched a disbelieving eyebrow. "You want me to take in this girl?"

"It's not as if you haven't helped people before."

Her mother frowned, and her lips tightened. "Those days are gone, Charlotte. They ended when your father died."

"She's a girl in trouble. She doesn't have anyone to help her. I just need a room to put her in temporarily. I'll accept all responsibility for her; you won't have to do a thing."

"You accept responsibility? That would be a first."

Charlotte felt her temper flare, but she knew there was nothing to gain by arguing with her mother over the past. Since her father's death, she'd become even more of a whipping post for her mother. She hoped that eventually her mother would ease up, that the grief would lessen, and they'd find some way to communicate with each other, because right now they were all they had.

"It will just be for a few days," Charlotte continued, ignoring her mother's comment, "until I can find a more permanent solution for Annie."

"I can't help you."

"You can—you just won't," Charlotte said in frustration.

"No, I can't." Monica picked up a letter from her lap and handed it to Charlotte.

"What's this?" Charlotte asked, skimming quickly.

"It's an eviction notice. The church says I have to be out of this house in thirty days."

"What? That's crazy," Charlotte said, shocked by the news.

"No, it's just true."

The letter, while worded far more diplomatically, did indeed request that they vacate the property. "You've lived in this house for thirty-four years," Charlotte said. "It's your home."

"Technically, it's not. It belongs to the church. It's the home for the Angel's Bay minister and his family, and the minister is no longer here." Monica drew in a tremulous breath. "I have to find somewhere else to live. Somewhere else—I can't imagine where." She shook her head, staring out at the darkness. "It would have been easier if I had died first. Then everything would have gone on the way it was supposed to."

Charlotte had no idea how to respond to her mother's statement. She'd never been able to hold a conversation with her mother, nor had she ever been privy to her mother's deepest thoughts. But one thing she did know for certain was that leaving this house would be incredibly difficult for Monica Adams. Her whole life was in these walls.

"There has to be a way for you to stay here," Charlotte said.

"There isn't. Reverend McConnell, who has been filling in from the church in Montgomery, is weary of making the trek here every week, and he was only intended to be a temporary replacement. The new minister starts this Sunday, and he will be officially moving in at the end of the month. Apparently he became available quite suddenly, and the church decided to hire him and put him up in an apartment in town until I can move out."

"Oh, Mom, I'm sorry."

"Are you? You always hated this house."

"That's not true."

"You couldn't wait to leave it."

"All children want to leave home—that's the way it is." Charlotte was glossing over a painful period in her life but she didn't see the point of having that conversation now, or perhaps ever. Some things were best left in the past.

Monica drilled her with a sharp look. "You think I don't know how I disappointed you?"

"I was the one who disappointed you," Charlotte countered.

"Well, that's true. You did disappoint me. You still do. And the sad thing is, you don't even know why."

"Oh, I know why." But even as she said the words, Charlotte saw some odd emotion flit through her mother's eyes. *Did* she know why? Suddenly she wasn't certain.

Monica stood up, walked to the back door, then paused. "That girl has nowhere else to go?"

"No."

"All right. You can bring her here for a week or so. I know your father wouldn't have wanted me to turn her away, even during this painful time in my own life."

"Thank you," Charlotte said quietly. "But Mom—what are you going to do about the house?"

"I suppose I'll find somewhere else to live."

"I can't imagine you not living here."

"Neither can I, Charlotte. But then I couldn't imagine living without your father, and here I am. By the way, the new minister is your friend, Andrew Schilling."

Charlotte's heart stopped. Andrew Schilling was back in Angel's Bay? Her former boyfriend was going to be the new minister? She hadn't seen Andrew in thirteen years, and had hoped never to see him again.

"I guess Gwen finally won," Monica said, referring to a long-running competition she'd had with her friend Gwen Schilling over their children and everything else in their lives. "She always thought her kids were better than mine. She always wanted what I had, including this house, my husband—"

"What are you talking about?" Charlotte interrupted. "She didn't want Dad."

"Yes, she did. Gwen and your father dated before we married, but he picked me. He picked *me*," her mother said fiercely. "He loved me, only me."

"Of course he did. No one could ever doubt that." She'd had no idea that the basis of her mother's rivalry with Gwen Schilling was her father.

"I did everything for your father. I lived my whole life for him," her mother added with a confused shake of her head. "What am I supposed to do now?"

Charlotte didn't know what to say. But it didn't matter, because her mother had already gone inside.

Strands of white lights and hanging lanterns lit up the picnic area of the carnival as night descended in Angel's Bay. A barbershop quartet had been entertaining them the past few minutes; next up was the middle school choral group. The festival was certainly a family affair. Jenna and Lexie were sitting with Kimmy's family: her mother, Robin, her father, Steve, and baby brother, Jonathan, who was almost two.

Robin Cooper was a short, curly-haired brunette, who looked more than a little tired. She was a stay-at-home mom. Steve worked as a lawyer doing estate planning and family trusts. According to Robin, Steve spent long hours at the office, and this was the first time in a long time they'd been out together as a family. Steve was currently standing ten feet away, talking to two other men, and had been in that conversation for the past hour. Robin seemed put-out, especially since she'd been wrestling with a squirmy toddler for the past thirty minutes.

"Can we get a balloon animal?" Lexie asked, pointing to the man making elephants out of balloons at the next table.

"Sure," Jenna said, as Lexie and Kimmy got up from the table.

"Take your brother with you," Robin told Kimmy. "Hold tight to his hand."

"He won't stay," Kimmy complained.

"Well, I'm here if you have a problem." Robin sighed as Kimmy took Jonathan to the next picnic table. "Thank God, two minutes of relief. You must think I'm a terrible mother."

"More like an exhausted one," Jenna said gently.

"That's kind of you. Steve always tells me that his mother raised five children without breaking a sweat. She also cooked four-course dinners every night, cleaned the house, sewed their clothes, and basically performed all superhuman tasks."

"Sounds like a tough act to follow."

"She's a lovely woman," Robin said without much

conviction. She gave Jenna a halfhearted smile. "I do mean that. It's just that I'm tired of being compared to her. What was your mother-in-law like?"

"Nothing like that, thank goodness."

"You were lucky. Well, I guess you weren't lucky," she stuttered. "Sorry, I don't know if you want to talk about him or not—your husband, I mean."

"I really don't," Jenna said. "No offense. It's just painful."

"Sure, of course. I understand."

As Robin fell silent, Jenna noticed a man sitting alone at a nearby table, looking their way. He wore jeans and a blue T-shirt, and a tattoo peeked out from under his sleeve. He frowned when he caught her staring back, then stood abruptly and walked away. Jenna didn't like men who disappeared on eye contact. "Who's that?"

"Who?" Robin asked.

"That man over by the popcorn machine, in the T-shirt," she said.

"Oh, that's Shane Murray. He's a local fisherman."

"I've never seen him around."

"He's a loner. Not much for social gatherings. My husband says he's a cool guy. With that body, half the single women in town are in love with him. He's often a Monday night hot topic."

"A what?" Jenna asked in confusion.

"At quilting night," Robin explained with a laugh. "He's a popular topic, except when his grandmother, Fiona, or his sister Kara is listening in. You know Kara, don't you?"

"Yes, she rented my house to me. I didn't realize he was one of the Murrays."

"There are a lot of them; it's hard to keep track. His brother Michael runs the Irish pub. Patrick doesn't live here anymore. Then there's Kara and Dee. Dee works with her father, Finn, running a charter boat service." Robin paused. "You should come to quilting night. You'll meet people, have fun. I'm sure this Monday night everyone will be talking about that girl, Annie, and her baby—and who the father might be." Robin's gaze traveled to her husband again.

Was Robin worried about Steve? It was obvious there was some tension in their marriage. "I'm sure the father is a teenage boy," she said, hoping to reassure Robin. "She's very young."

"I'm not sure that matters when a pretty young girl is willing and available. My father cheated on my mother more than once," Robin added bitterly. "I guess that makes me worry that my husband could cheat on me. Not that I think it's him. My God, of course I don't. Forget I ever said that. It's just that things have been kind of off lately between us," Robin continued, obviously needing to vent. "Ever since I had Jonathan, I haven't been all that interested in—you know—sex." She blushed furiously. "Sorry. I don't know why I'm telling you all this, you must think I'm crazy."

"I don't," Jenna said quickly, even though she was a little taken aback. She and Robin were barely acquaintances.

"I'm just so exhausted I can't think straight. Some days I feel like I don't even have time to brush my teeth, and then Steve comes home and wants to know where dinner is and why I didn't pay the bills and what did I do all day besides watch the kids. As if watching a two-year-old isn't a full time job! Yesterday Jonathan climbed into the dryer. He could have suffocated in there and it would have been my fault. Sometimes I think I wasn't meant to be a mother. I'm not very good at it."

"Motherhood is a tough job. I never realized until I had a child just how difficult and overwhelming and worrying it is, and I only have one kid."

Robin gave her a grateful smile. "Thanks for being so nice. I hope we can get to know each other better. Kimmy and Lexie have formed such a good friendship, maybe we can, too."

"I'd like that," Jenna said, feeling bad that she couldn't be as honest with Robin as Robin was being with her. She looked up as the kids returned with their balloon animals.

"Mommy, can we play skee ball now?" Kimmy asked.

"Can we?" Lexie echoed.

Before Jenna could answer, Kara Lynch stopped by the table.

"Hey there," Kara said. "Sorry to interrupt. I was hoping to see you here, Jenna. Do you have a minute?"

"Well," Jenna began, "I think we're off to skee ball."

"It's okay, I'll take the kids," Robin offered as she

got to her feet. "Jonathan isn't going to sit still another second anyway. You can join us when you're done."

Jenna hesitated. She hated to let Lexie out of her sight, but the skee ball game was just around the corner. "Okay, but stay with Kimmy and her mom," she told Lexie.

"I will," Lexie promised.

Kara sat down on the bench as Lexie left with the Coopers.

"So what's up?" Jenna asked curiously.

"I have more information on Rose Littleton, if you're interested."

"I am interested."

"I spoke to my boss, Ben Farraday. He's Rose's nephew and he told me a little about the family. Apparently Rose was one of four girls. She and her sister Martha never married, and they lived in the house until first Martha died, then Rose a year later. The other two girls got married. Cornelia was Ben's mother. Thelma moved to South Carolina and had several children, and Ben doesn't know where she is now. But what I thought you might find interesting is that Rose was a piano teacher, just like you. Ben said that his aunt was very good. She used to play at church every Sunday. Isn't that funny? In fact, that's her piano you're giving lessons on."

A shiver ran down Jenna's spine. Another coincidence? She didn't think so. Something was going on that she didn't understand, and right now anything that she didn't understand could potentially be very, very dangerous.

"Ben said his aunt Rose was convinced that she was descended from baby Gabriella, who was rescued by the town after the wreck. Apparently she had a birthmark just like the one Gabriella had, the angel's wing that you saw on the quilt, remember?"

"Yes," Jenna said, her heart pounding. Rose had a birthmark the same as Lexie? It seemed unbelievable.

"Ben also told me that his aunt was trying to find out who Gabriella's parents were. I guess the survivor reports were pretty vague. Legend has it that an angel saved the baby and brought her to shore. If you're interested in the history, there are some journals and letters at the library."

"I am interested," Jenna replied. Especially because the town's history seemed to be colliding with her own.

A big, burly guy in a police uniform walked up behind Kara and put his strong hands on her shoulders. Kara smiled up at him. "Hi, honey. This is Jenna Davies. I don't think you two have met. This is my husband, Colin, on duty as usual."

"We haven't officially met," Colin said with a broad smile, "but I did see you on the pier after you rescued the jumper. She owes you a debt of gratitude."

Jenna shrugged uncomfortably. The last thing she wanted to do was get into a conversation with a police officer, but Colin was sliding onto the bench next to Kara. He gave his wife a tender kiss on the cheek.

"Jenna is too modest," Kara said. "She gets embarrassed when people make a big deal about her bravery. I'm sure you don't know what that's like, honey," she added with a laugh and a nudge. "Colin loves being the center of attention. He's a big ham."

"Not true," Colin said. "I'm very shy."

Jenna didn't believe that for a second. She knew a charmer when she saw one. And while she had become very distrustful of anyone in a uniform, she had to admit that Colin Lynch seemed more like a big, huggable teddy bear than a threat to her safety.

"So how do you like Angel's Bay?" Colin asked. "Are you planning on staying?"

"I think so," Jenna said. "Lexie—my daughter—loves the school and her friends."

"It's a great place to raise kids," Colin said. "Kara and I both grew up here. We met in first grade. I tripped her on the playground. She scraped her knee and called me a moron. It was love at first sight."

"You were a moron. And it was not love at first sight," Kara interjected. "I couldn't stand you until at least the fourth grade."

"After that we were inseparable," Colin finished.

"Except when we fought—which was a lot. Colin is stubborn."

"And Kara talks way too much."

"You're the one who is boring Jenna senseless," Kara pointed out.

"No, you're not," Jenna protested, enjoying their teasing exchange. She hadn't been around many happily married couples, but these two were practically glowing.

"Jenna is interested in the history of her house,"

Kara continued. "Do you know anything about the Littleton women who used to live there?" She turned to Jenna. "Colin knows a lot about this town. He's a history fanatic. Oh, and he believes in the angels, too." She rolled her eyes.

"That's right—I saw one once," Colin said.

"Really?" Jenna asked.

"I was fifteen. I was diving by some of the caves around the point. You can only reach them at certain tidal periods, and you have to dive under rocks to get into the caves. I became disoriented and couldn't find my way out. All of a sudden this girl appeared; she was my age. She gave me her hand and the next thing I knew, I was coming up inside the cave."

"You were probably hallucinating from lack of air," Kara told her husband.

Colin shook his head. "It was an angel. She saved me. I would have drowned if she hadn't shown me the way. Miracles happen when you believe."

Jenna wanted to believe in miracles, but how could she? She certainly hadn't seen any sign of angels wanting to help her. "That's really interesting, but I should probably go. I need to catch up with Lexie since I have the quarters for the games." She got to her feet. "I really enjoyed meeting you, Colin. And I'm glad that an angel saved you, because you seem like a good guy."

He smiled at her. "I am. If you ever have any problems, just give me a call."

As much as Jenna liked him, he was the last person she would call, but she simply said, "I will," and left the table. She headed toward the skee ball game, but there was no sign of Lexie, Kimmy, or the rest of Kimmy's family. As she moved through the carnival, her heart began to race. She told herself not to panic, but all of her instincts were screaming that something was very wrong.

Finally she spotted Robin. She was wrestling again with her squirmy toddler and talking somewhat heatedly to her husband, Steve.

"Where are the girls?" Jenna interrupted.

Robin looked startled by the urgency of her question. "Why, they're right over there." She turned her head and pointed toward a water toss game.

Jenna saw Kimmy's ponytail and started to breathe a sigh of relief until she realized that Lexie was nowhere in sight. She ran over to Kimmy and grabbed her by the arm. "Where's Lexie?"

"She went to the bathroom."

"You let her go alone?"

Kimmy's mouth started to tremble, and Jenna realized she was scaring the little girl. "It's okay, honey, I'm sorry. I just need to find Lexie."

"What's wrong?" Robin asked, coming up behind them.

"Lexie went to the bathroom alone. I have to find her." Jenna took off on a run toward the public bathrooms on the other side of the carnival. She couldn't believe Lexie would have gone by herself; they had spoken about never going anywhere alone over and over and over again. She *never* should have left her—not for one second.

She ran into the bathroom and stopped abruptly, staring in disbelief at the empty stalls. She called Lexie's name in desperation, her voice echoing off the cement walls.

"Is she here?" Robin asked, running into the bathroom, Kimmy's hand in hers.

"No," Jenna said, feeling the most intense fear she had ever felt.

"We'll find her," Robin said. "I'm sure she just went back to the games."

"Or to see the angels," Kimmy put in.

Jenna stared at Kimmy. "What did you say?"

"Lexie wants to see the angels. She said she has a question for them."

And suddenly Jenna knew exactly where Lexie had gone.

Eight

Reid drained the beer from his plastic cup and tossed it in a trash can. The carnival was going strong, with happy screams coming from the Tilt-A-Whirl, and laughs and cheers from the game area where kids were throwing basketballs in hoops and aiming darts at balloons. The smells of buttery popcorn, hot pretzels with mustard, and sweet cotton candy were making him restless. Ever since he'd arrived in Angel's Bay, he'd felt as if he'd stepped into a Norman Rockwell painting or a nineteen-fifties movie where everything was wonderful.

He wouldn't have minded growing up like these kids. He could have handled hanging on to his innocence a little longer. He could have been satisfied with having two parents who cared about him, who took him to school and helped him with homework. He would have enjoyed riding on the shoulders of his father, like the three-year-old boy in front of him.

But he'd stopped wanting things he couldn't have

a long time ago. This wasn't his life. He was just passing through, and the sooner he got out of town, the better.

Turning away from the carnival, he crossed a parking lot and headed toward the bluffs that ran above the ocean. About a half mile down, the cement walkway turned into a well-trodden dirt path. The traffic out to the cliffs had been heavy the last few days. At the farthest point, he could see groups of people huddled together, awaiting the appearance of the angels. He hoped he could gather more information.

It was a bright night with a full moon, but the ocean was in a wicked mood, the waves bouncing off the rocks below, sending up a white spray that caught on the wind and put a fine sheen of moisture on his face. He'd never been a beach person, but he was starting to like the taste of salt in the air, and the energy of the sea made his heart beat a little faster in anticipation of something, though he didn't know what.

He was about a hundred yards away from the cluster of people when he saw a small, lone figure standing at the edge of the cliff. As he drew closer, he couldn't believe his eyes. It was Jenna's little girl, Lexie. And nowhere in sight was the ever-protective, ever-watchful Jenna.

As he drew closer, he said, "Hey there," in a soft voice, not wanting to scare her.

Lexie jumped about a foot when she saw him, and he could see her eyes fill with fear. For a split second he was afraid she would take a backward step right over the side of the cliff. While there was a makeshift fence farther down the bluff, here there was nothing between Lexie and the sea below.

He quickly put up a reassuring hand. "It's okay. I'm the man who took your mom's picture the other night. Remember? My name is Reid—Reid Tanner. I'm a reporter. I'm here to report on the angels. And I heard your name is Lexie."

Lexie didn't answer.

"You need to move away from the edge," he added. "It's dangerous to stand that close."

She didn't say anything, but she did take a step away from the cliff, which he found reassuring.

"So where is your mom?" he continued. "I bet she's worried about you being out here all alone. How come you're not at the carnival?"

Lexie's lips drew in a tight line. The little girl was as closemouthed as her mother. But while she didn't seem interested in talking to him, she also didn't appear ready to leave.

"You must be waiting for the angels," he guessed. "I'm hoping to see them myself."

"Do you think they'll come?" she asked, a desperate note in her voice.

"I don't know. What do you think?"

"I hope so. I need to ask them a question. It's important."

"It must be, or you wouldn't be here. Your mom doesn't know you're here, does she?"

"I asked her to bring me, but she wouldn't." Lexie turned her face back toward the ocean. "She always says we'll do it another time, but we never do."

"What do you want to talk to the angels about?"

"I can't tell you." She crossed her arms over her chest, a picture of stubborn defiance.

He smiled, thinking that she reminded him a little of himself as a kid, pretending to be tough when inside he was terrified. But Lexie had a mother who cared about her, who was probably worried out of her mind. He wanted to take Lexie back, but he suspected she wouldn't go easily, and dragging away a screaming child who wasn't his own wouldn't look too good. Maybe he'd just keep her talking until Jenna came, which was sure to be any second.

"It's a secret, huh?" he asked casually.

She nodded her head. "I'm going to wait here until they come."

"Maybe I should wait with you, just to make sure you're okay."

She gave him a quick look. "They might not come if you're here."

"Well, you can't stay here by yourself. The angels would get mad at me if I left you here."

"Angels don't like to talk to grown-ups—only to little kids. That's what Kimmy says."

"Is Kimmy your friend?"

"She saw an angel once. She got lost in the park and she couldn't find her way out, and an angel lady came and took her back to her parents. They're really good at finding parents." Lexie turned to give him a closer look. She might be wary, but she was also curious. "Are you going to take their picture?" she asked. "They might not like it. My mom doesn't like to have her picture taken."

"I've noticed that," he said with a dry smile. "But I don't understand why. She's very pretty. So are you."

"I know. I look like an angel. Everyone says so."

His smile broadened. Lexie was starting to relax, and with a few nicely worded questions, she might even tell him why she and her mother were so scared. But pumping a little child for information didn't sit well. It was also possible that his questions might trigger some sort of traumatic memory. It was clear that Jenna and Lexie were in trouble and hiding from someone. He could imagine half a dozen scenarios, most of them leading back to an abusive husband/father. He had no idea what Lexie knew or didn't know, but he was becoming more interested in finding out with every passing minute. Perhaps he could help them—it was why he'd gotten into news in the first place. But Jenna didn't want his help. She'd begged him to stay out of her life.

"Do you have a kid?" Lexie asked curiously.

He shook his head. "No. Why?"

"Do you want to have a kid?"

"I don't know. I hear they're a lot of work. They run off when they're not supposed to."

She frowned, taking his point. Lexie was smart, and she obviously had a mind of her own. "I had to come here. It's important."

"What do you want to ask the angels?"

"I can't say. I'm not supposed to talk to strangers," she added belatedly. "You need to go away."

"I don't think so. I have a few questions for the angels myself." He sat down on the ground a few feet away from Lexie and stretched out his legs. A moment later Lexie sat down, too, carefully keeping her distance from him.

"What do you want to ask them?" she inquired a moment later.

"I want to know what their wings are made of, and how high they fly."

"Those are silly questions. Angel wings are made of clouds. And they can fly all the way to heaven. Don't you know anything?"

He smiled to himself. "Actually, I don't know much. You're pretty smart for . . . what are you—ten, eleven?"

"I'm seven. Do you think angels are like Santa Claus?" Lexie asked. "You know, how he won't give you presents if you're bad? Do you think that the angels won't talk to you if you're bad?"

"I don't believe it works that way," Reid said slowly, sensing Lexie's need to be reassured. "Did you do something wrong?"

Her eyes were solemn as she nodded. "I didn't go to my room when I was supposed to." Her mouth trembled, and she looked away from him. "Did your daddy ever hit your mommy?"

His gut tightened. "My father went away when I was a baby. I didn't know him. But I do know that it's wrong for anyone to hit. And especially for a man to strike a woman."

"Even if they're bad?"

"No matter what," he said firmly.

"But sometimes when daddies are sick, they get mad, and they accidentally hit someone."

"Did someone hurt your mother, Lexie? Was it your father?" He knew he was pushing, but if someone had hurt this little girl or Jenna, he wanted to make sure that it didn't happen again.

Lexie looked like she really wanted to answer him, but a group of people came down the path, and she drew her knees up to her chest and wrapped her arms around them.

When the group had passed by, she said, "Kimmy says angels can see everything in the world. They can talk to you when you're lonely. They can make you feel better when you're hurt. And sometimes they can find people."

"Is that what you want the angels to do—find someone for you?"

Lexie gave him a steady look. "Do you think they really can?"

"Who do you want to find?"

Lexie started to open her mouth, but they were interrupted by the wild, panicked call of her mother. Lexie scrambled to her feet. Reid got up as well, knowing that Jenna wouldn't be happy to find her daughter with him.

A second later, Jenna swooped in and scooped Lexie into her arms. "You scared the life out of me, Lexie." She wrapped her arms tightly around the little girl.

"I'm sorry," Lexie said. "I wanted to see the angels."

"They're not here." Jenna gave Reid a furious look. "Did you bring her down here?"

"No. I was just walking by and I saw her alone. I didn't want to scare her by trying to take her back. I figured you'd be along any minute. And here you are—as well as half the town."

Jenna looked at the crowd of people who had followed her down the path. "Oh, God," she muttered. "She's fine," Jenna called. "Thanks, everyone. Everything is okay."

"I'm really sorry I didn't watch her better," a woman said. She had a child by her side and another in her arms, and her face was a picture of distress.

"It's all right, Robin. It's not your fault. Lexie, tell Mrs. Cooper that you're sorry that you ran off."

"I'm sorry," Lexie mumbled, her head down, her toe kicking at the dirt.

"It's okay, Lexie. You just scared us," Robin said. "I guess we'll be going home then." She gave Reid a curious look, then glanced back at Jenna. "Do you want to walk back with us?"

"I'll be along in a few minutes," Jenna said.

"Are you sure? Do you know him?" She lowered her voice, although Reid could still hear her.

"He's a reporter," Jenna replied. "We've met a few times. It's fine, but thanks for your concern."

"I still feel horribly guilty. I never should have taken my eyes off of the girls. I couldn't forgive myself if anything had happened."

"But it didn't, and this was Lexie's fault, not yours. Say good-bye to Kimmy, Lexie."

Lexie obediently said good-bye, and Kimmy gave a sad wave as her mother dragged her away.

"For someone who likes her privacy, you're sure finding ways to be the center of attention," Reid said when they were alone.

"Lexie—how did you get here?" Jenna asked, turning to her daughter. "Did he bring you?"

Lexie shook her head. "I came by myself."

"I told you," Reid said.

"Why do you keep showing up wherever we are?" Jenna demanded.

"It's a small town, Jenna. I was on my way to talk to the angel watchers." He tipped his head toward the group still clustered at the point.

"Well, don't let us keep you. We're going home."

"No," Lexie said with a stubborn stomp of her foot. "I have to wait for the angels."

"Lexie, don't argue with me."

"You never let me come here! I want to see the angels. They're going to be here any second. I *know* they are. I have to talk to them."

Reid waited for Jenna to tell Lexie that angels didn't exist, that they were just a fairy tale. But she remained mute, a battle going on in her eyes. Finally, she said, "This isn't the right place or time, Lexie. We'll come back another day."

"I'm not going," Lexie declared.

Reid could see that Jenna was torn between making a scene in front of him and giving in to Lexie's desire to hold her ground.

"She has a stubborn streak, just like you." Reid

nodded toward the horizon. "The fog is coming in. It won't be long before it reaches us."

Jenna took a quick look over her shoulder and then glanced back at him. "You're right. I guess we can wait a few minutes," she told Lexie. "But once the fog rolls in, we won't be able to see any angels. We'll have to do it another day."

"I hope they hurry." Lexie slipped away from Jenna, moving a few feet away, her gaze fixed on the ocean.

"Don't get any closer to the cliff," Jenna warned.

Lexie moved farther down the bluff but kept a good distance from the edge. She obviously thought she'd have a better chance of talking to an angel if she wasn't standing next to them.

"What did she say to you?" Jenna asked him, her voice low.

"She spilled all your secrets."

A spark of fear flashed in her eyes, but she quickly covered it. "No, she didn't."

"No, she didn't," he agreed. "But she told me she's looking for someone. She thinks the angels can find that person." He paused, wondering if Jenna would fill in the blank, but of course she didn't. "I'm guessing if it's an angel she wants to talk to, and her father is dead, then it has something to do with him." Reid moved closer to Jenna. He heard her quick intake of breath, saw her stiffen at his nearness, but she didn't move away. "He's not dead, is he, Jenna?" he whispered.

"Of course he's dead," she said immediately.

"That's why Lexie is looking for angels." She turned her head away, as if she were afraid he'd see something in her eyes.

"I don't believe you," he said quietly. "I think he hurt you, maybe Lexie, too, and that's why you're hiding in Angel's Bay."

"You should stick to the story you're supposed to be writing."

"And you should go to the police. Get their help."

"I don't need anyone's help. Lexie and I aren't hiding. We're—we're mourning. Lexie wants to see the angels, because—because she really needs to believe that heaven exists, and that the person she loved more than anyone else in the world is okay."

"The person you loved, too?" he couldn't help asking.

She looked him straight in the eye. "Yes, the person I loved very, very much."

Her words hit him harder than they should have. He barely knew her; he didn't have any right to care about whom she'd loved, or how much. Maybe her husband wasn't alive, wasn't thc one she was scared of—but he still knew that she was hiding. She was far too skittish.

"It's a funny thing about grief," he commented. "It doesn't make you scared—it makes you brave, because the worst has already happened. When you lose someone you can never get back, it makes you not care what happens to you. But you don't act like that: you act like someone who is terrified of losing, and is fighting as hard as she can to stay alive." He paused. "Or maybe you do still have someone to lose—Lexie. She asked me if it was all right for a man to hit a woman, for a daddy to hit a mommy."

"She didn't ask you that," Jenna said in disbelief, fear in her eyes.

"Yes, she did. Did your husband hit you?" A new image formed in his head. "Did you hit back, Jenna? Did you kill him? Is that why you're on the run? Because the police are after you?"

Her breath quickened. "I didn't kill anyone. You have quite an imagination; you should be writing fiction."

"I could be wrong, but you're lying about something. I'd bet my life that you're on the run."

"It's not *your* life you'd be betting. Just leave us alone. Please."

She moved away from him, walking over to Lexie. She tried to put her arm around the little girl, but Lexie shrugged it off and moved away. Jenna wrapped her arms around her waist, in almost the exact same stance as her daughter, and as Reid watched them stare out into the night, he thought he might be looking at two of the loneliest people in the world.

Make that three . . .

For long minutes he stood there, waiting for the fog to roll in over the bluff, waiting for Lexie and Jenna to turn around and go home, waiting for his feet to move—but he couldn't seem to take a step forward or backward. He was caught in limbo, in a place where he didn't know who he was anymore, or what he was meant to do, what he was supposed to want.

All his life he'd had one focus, one goal, and then it was done. He was no longer the hotshot reporter breaking big stories, but he also wasn't going to be satisfied writing puff pieces for a tabloid. He'd thought he could do it for the money, that he could go on not giving a shit about anything in the world.

But Jenna and Lexie were making him care, making him want to be the old Reid Tanner. Could he go back, even if he wanted to? And *did* he want to?

"Lexie, it's time to leave," Jenna said, interrupting his thoughts.

"The fog isn't all the way in," Lexie returned.

"It's late. We'll come again another day."

"You always say that, but we never do."

"Lexie." Jenna tried to catch Lexie's arm, but the girl jumped away.

"Leave me alone," she cried. "I don't want to go with you. It's not our home, and I don't want to play your stupid games. I don't want to pretend anymore. I want my mommy!" She burst into tears.

Reid stared at them in shock. *Lexie wanted her mommy?*

Jenna swung the sobbing girl into her arms and ran past him. He was too stunned to stop her.

Jenna wasn't Lexie's mother? Then who the hell was she?

Nine

Jenna knew Reid would follow her; she was just surprised it took him an hour to get to the house. She'd been tempted to pack their suitcases and hit the highway as soon as she got Lexie home, but Lexie was hysterical and exhausted, and after crying her eyes out, she'd finally fallen asleep. She looked like a very small angel in her white nightgown, her golden hair spread out like a halo on the pillow behind her head. Her eyelids were puffy and her cheeks red. She was a very sad little angel, and Jenna didn't know how to make it better.

The knock at the front door came again, persistent and determined. She shut Lexie's bedroom door and walked out to the living room. She looked through the peephole, relieved to see Reid was alone. At least he hadn't called the cops.

She opened the door and stepped back.

He entered without a word.

They stared at each other for a long, silent minute.

"What took you so long?" she finally asked. "Did you go to the police?"

"Should I have?" he challenged.

"No."

His gaze held steady. "Who are you?"

"Do you already know the answer to that question?" she countered. "Are you really in Angel's Bay looking for angels, or were you sent here to look for me?"

"Is someone after you?"

"Yes. Someone who wants to hurt me and Lexie."

"I'm not working for that person, whoever he is."

"I'd like to believe that. But I called *Spotlight Magazine* and the receptionist never heard of you."

"That's because I've never been inside the building. I'm a freelancer. But I'm not here to talk about me, and you know that." His gaze drilled into hers. "You're not Lexie's mother, are you?"

She drew in a long breath and blew it out.

When she didn't reply, he said, "Maybe I should just ask the police," and headed toward the door.

"Wait." She would have to give him some part of the truth. "All right. I'm not her mother."

He turned back around. "Keep going."

"You'd better sit down." She would have to find a way to get Reid Tanner to keep her secret, and that would take more than a minute.

She walked into the living room and sat down in an armchair. Reid took a seat on the couch, his dark eyes never leaving her face. He had the most intense gaze of anyone she'd ever met, and it rattled her even more. She stared down at the hardwood floor, trying to collect her thoughts.

"Did you kidnap Lexie?" Reid asked abruptly.

Her head came up in shock. "God, no! How could you think that?"

"She said she was tired of pretending you were her mother. She said she wanted to go home."

"I'm her aunt. Lexie is my sister's child. My older sister, Kelly."

"And where is Kelly?"

Jenna drew in a breath for strength. "She's dead. She died a little over two months ago." Saying it aloud made it even more horribly real. She'd been so busy protecting Lexie that she hadn't given herself a minute to grieve, and she couldn't do that now. She had to keep her wits about her.

"Why the pretense? Why ask a seven-year-old to go along with such a deception?"

"It's complicated."

"If you tell me the truth, maybe I can help you."

"Or maybe you won't want to."

He considered that, a thoughtful tilt to his head. "Try me."

"I can't tell you everything. But I can say that my sister was a beautiful, kind, gentle person. She was murdered, and the person who killed her will kill me and Lexie if he finds us."

"Why?"

"I can't go into it."

Reid shook his head. "Why don't you go to the

police and ask for protection? If your sister was murdered, they must be looking for her killer."

"They're looking in the wrong place. They've been sent to look in the wrong place."

"By the killer?"

"Yes."

Reid stared at her with a sharp intelligence that made her worry. He was a smart man. If she gave him enough pieces to the puzzle, he would put it together, and she couldn't let that happen.

"Where do the police think Lexie is?" he asked.

"I'm not sure."

"I know you're talking about Lexie's father. He's the murderer, right? Lexie already suggested to me that she saw her father hit her mother. It doesn't take a huge leap to guess that the violence escalated."

Jenna was shocked by his statement. "Did Lexie really tell you that?"

"In a manner of speaking. Is that what happened? Did your brother-in-law kill your sister?"

"No one seems to think that he did it." Jenna paused. "I don't know exactly what Lexie remembers, and she never ever talks about it. I can't believe she said something like that to you. You're a stranger."

"I'm a good listener. Come on, Jenna, give me his name."

She bit down on her lip to stop herself from saying too much. Reid *was* a good listener. His warm gaze invited her to confess all, but she had too much to lose. "I can't. The more you know, the more danger you put Lexie in."

"Maybe I'll be protecting her," he argued. "All I have is your word for what happened. You might have stolen Lexie from the supermarket or the schoolyard, made up a story, asked her to pretend to be your daughter, told her that her father killed her mother."

"It didn't happen that way," she said quickly. "I am Lexie's aunt. You have to believe me." Reid's theories worried her, and what he'd do about those theories terrified her even more.

He remained unconvinced. "I don't know what to believe."

"You've seen me with Lexie. You know I love her, that I'd do anything for her," she said passionately, desperate to convince him. "I'm not hurting Lexie in any way—I'm protecting her. And this isn't your business. You don't live here. You're not a cop. You're a reporter, who's supposed to be writing a story about angels." Suddenly it was all clear to her. "That's it. You want a bigger story, and you think I'm it! That's why you're so interested in me and in Lexie."

"That might be part of it," he admitted.

His agreement stung. "How dare you poke your nose into my business? Press is the last thing I need."

"It's not about what you need. It's about the truth."

"The truth? The truth is that the little girl who wants the angels to bring her mother back to her is in danger. And media attention will only bring that danger closer."

"Again, I only have your version of the story."

"It's *not* a story." His cool attitude made her crazy. He had no idea what was at stake. To him it was just a news article, but to her it was literally life or death. "You need to back off," she said flatly. "Sometimes the truth hurts the wrong person."

"Lies hurt people, too," he said with a ruthless note in his voice. "As well as cover-ups, pretenses, and betrayals. You wouldn't be the first person who gave me the wrong version of a story, pleading her case with sad, earnest eyes, while lying every second."

There was bitterness in his voice now, and the darkness she'd seen in him earlier came back in full force.

"Who are you talking about?" she asked.

"It doesn't matter." He abruptly stood up.

She jumped to her feet, not sure what he intended to do, not sure what she wanted him to do. She put a hand on his arm. "Don't. Please."

"Don't what?"

"Don't tell anyone I'm not Lexie's mother. Don't use me to get a story. Just leave me alone and forget you ever heard what Lexie said tonight. Walk away. Please."

He stared at her for a long moment, but instead of moving away, he took a step closer. His eyes were filled with shadows, and she had no idea what he was thinking.

"I'd like to walk away," he said finally. "I spent the past hour trying to talk myself out of coming over here. I quit hard news almost a year ago. I told myself I was done digging into other people's lives. I was done with giving a damn about the truth. And then I met you—a woman who jumped into the bay to save a stranger's life, not only at the risk of her own, but also at the risk of her secrets being discovered."

Reid shook his head. "I thought I could walk away from you and Lexie and pretend that whatever was happening was none of my business, but it turns out that I can't." He reached out and ran his finger down the side of her cheek.

She caught her breath at the intimate caress. Things had suddenly become very personal.

"And it has nothing to do with my journalistic ambition," he continued. "I can't stop thinking about you. I have no idea who you really are—an accomplished liar, or a desperate woman in terrible trouble."

His finger moved to her lips, then he cupped her chin, tilting her face up to his. Her blood ran hot. Her nipples tightened. A wave of unexpected and reckless desire shot through her body. She caught her bottom lip between her teeth, knowing that she should move, because nothing could happen between them. But when his gaze traveled to her mouth, her lips tingled in anticipation. He lowered his head so slowly that she had plenty of time to move, yet she couldn't take a step.

She wanted to feel his mouth on hers. She wanted him to wrap his strong arms around her and pull her into his hard body. She wanted to lose herself in him for just a minute . . . a minute when she didn't have to be strong and protective and fierce.

She leaned into the kiss, her mouth opening under his. His tongue swept inside her mouth, tangling with hers. His hands fell to her waist, pulling her up against his hips. She pressed her breasts against his chest, and the spark that had flared at their first meeting turned into raging desire.

She'd never felt so needy, so wanton. She ran her hands up under his shirt, feeling the power of his muscles, the heat of his skin. She wanted to strip off her clothes and do the same with Reid's. She wanted to make love to him. It was foolish, reckless, dangerous. Impossible.

In the end it was Reid who pulled away. His breath came sharp and quick as he gazed down at her. His fingers burned into the bare skin between her shirt and her jeans. He looked like he wanted to let her go, but couldn't. She felt the same way. He was the wrong man at the wrong time. She couldn't allow him into her life.

"Let go," she whispered.

"I'm trying," he said, a husky note in his voice. "What the hell was that?"

"Craziness." She put her hands over his and slowly disengaged them from her body. "That shouldn't have happened. I don't usually act so impulsively."

"Why start now?"

"I'm attracted to you," she admitted. "I don't want to be."

"I'm not thrilled with the idea, either."

She drew in a deep breath as silence fell between them. "So what now? What are you going to do?"

Reid gave her a long, hard look. She didn't know what he was thinking, but his gaze grew cool as the seconds ticked by. Finally he said, "Did you think kissing me would put me on your side? That I would no longer question you? That I wouldn't go to the police? Was it just another move in whatever game you're playing?"

His suggestion infuriated her. "I'm not playing a game. But maybe I should ask you the same question. Did you think kissing me would make me want to tell you my story? Did you think it was your way into hearing my deepest and darkest secrets?"

Reid didn't answer, his ragged breath matching the quickened tempo of her pulse. Then he abruptly turned on his heel and left.

For sixty seconds, she stood frozen in place. What was he going to do next? Would he go to the police? Would he start digging into her life? Or would he let it go? She fought the urge to run after him. She couldn't leave the house; Lexie was asleep in her bed.

Jenna sank down on the couch, touching her lips with her fingers. One taste of Reid wasn't nearly enough. She couldn't remember the last time she'd lost her head so completely, been swept off her feet by a touch, a kiss. And by a man she didn't even trust—a man who didn't trust her. What a foolish, impetuous thing she'd done. She had to find a way to fix things, but how? Reid was like a dog with a bone. He wasn't going to give up.

For a moment she considered the thought that maybe she didn't want him to. Maybe he could help her. But Kelly's instructions had been so clear. She'd begged her not to tell anyone, not to trust, not to believe that anyone was a friend. Kelly had known what she was dealing with. Jenna still didn't know. All she knew was that she had to do what her sister had asked her to do.

She looked up in surprise as Lexie padded into the room, rubbing her sleepy eyes. "Hey, what are you doing up?"

"I'm thirsty," Lexie said, climbing into her lap.

"I'll get you some water," Jenna replied, glad that Lexie hadn't walked into the room a few minutes earlier. "Do you want to get back into bed, and I'll bring it to you?"

Lexie hesitated, her mouth trembling. "I'm sorry I told the truth."

"I know, honey." Jenna sighed. How messed up was Lexie going to be, when she had to feel bad about telling the truth? But she was alive. She was safe. That's all that mattered for the moment.

"Maybe Mr. Tanner won't tell anybody," Lexie offered.

"Maybe not." Jenna brushed the hair off Lexie's face, tucking it behind her ear.

"I miss Mommy," Lexie said sadly.

Jenna felt a wave of pain. "Me, too."

"I wanted to ask the angels if Mommy was okay,

if she could maybe come back with them and see us sometime. Heaven is so far away."

"Yes, it is." Jenna gathered Lexie close. "But your mommy can see you no matter where you are, and she will love you forever. When she's looking down from heaven, she'll want to see you playing with your friends, learning things in school, and having a great life. She'll want to see you laughing, having fun. That's what she wants for you, honey."

Jenna could hardly get the words out as she thought of how many moments her sister would miss—Lexie buying her first bra, having her first real kiss, getting her heart broken. Kelly would miss seeing Lexie graduate from high school and college. She wouldn't be at Lexie's wedding, wouldn't get to hold her grandchild in her arms, wouldn't get to share in her daughter's life. It was so hideously unfair. Kelly should still be alive. Lexie should still have her mother. This was *wrong*—so wrong.

"If I smile, Mommy might think I don't miss her," Lexie said worriedly.

The lump in Jenna's throat grew bigger. "She wants you to be happy, honey. She wants to see smiles, not tears."

"I don't feel like smiling."

"I know," Jenna whispered.

Lexie's bottom lip trembled. "I just want to see Mommy one more time. I want to say I'm sorry for not staying in my room like she told me to."

"Oh, Lexie, she's not mad at you."

"But I didn't say good-bye. I didn't tell her I loved

her." Lexie looked at her with earnest eyes. "She doesn't know. She went to heaven and she doesn't know."

Jenna's heart broke in two. She hadn't said good-bye, either. She hadn't told her sister that she loved her, that she was sorry for all the years of distance, all the resentment, and that she felt terribly guilty for being completely unaware that Kelly's life was crumbling.

Why hadn't she been more involved? Why hadn't she stepped out of her own world and called her sister? Why hadn't she seen the signs, noticed that her sister was in pain? If only she could go back in time, she would change so many things.

But she couldn't go back. And looking at Lexie now, who was the spitting image of her mother, Jenna knew the only thing she could do was take care of Lexie, give Lexie the love, the devotion, and the security that Kelly would have wanted her to have.

"Your mommy knows everything you're thinking, honey. She knows that you love her, that you're feeling bad that you didn't get to say good-bye. But she doesn't want you to be sad." Jenna put her hand over Lexie's heart. "Your mommy is here, in your heart, and she'll be with you always. Whenever you want to see her, just close your eyes. And there she'll be."

Lexie closed her eyes. "I do see her," she whispered after a moment. "And she's smiling."

A tear slipped down Jenna's cheek, and she

brushed it away. If she broke down now, she was afraid she wouldn't be able to go on. And the one thing she knew for sure was that she had to keep going.

Reid downed two shots of tequila in rapid succession and ordered a third. The Giants were playing the Dodgers on the TV over the bar, but he wasn't paying attention to the ball game. He was thinking about Jenna, and what the hell he was going to do about her. Part of him wanted to go back to her house and finish what they'd started. He hadn't felt so restless or off balance in a long time. He didn't know what to do with the mix of lust and adrenaline running through his body. Sex would have been his first choice, but having sex with Jenna would only complicate things. He needed to think, to consider the facts.

While everything Jenna told him might have been a lie, his gut told him she'd been honest with the few details she'd given. From there he could fill in the blanks. Jenna and Lexie were on the run, probably from Lexie's father. Lexie's mother had been murdered, probably by Lexie's father. According to Jenna, the police were looking for the wrong person. So if the perpetrator was Lexie's father, then he had a great alibi or enough power to influence a police investigation, because the police always looked at the husband when the wife died under suspicious circumstances.

The real question was—what was he going to do?

He could find out exactly who Jenna was and who Lexie's parents were; he had contacts in law enforcement. Hell, he could go to the local police station and tell them he had reason to believe that Lexie was not Jenna's daughter. He could break a solid news story and get his career going again.

He could also get Lexie killed, and maybe Jenna, too. He needed to know more about their situation before he involved the police. He'd already made one mistake by kissing Jenna. God, she'd tasted good. Her response had been so much more than he expected. Under her quiet exterior beat the heart of an emotional, passionate woman. He should have expected the fire. He'd felt her music rip through his soul—why hadn't he expected that the same would happen with her kiss? Why hadn't he realized that one taste, one touch, and he'd want to get her naked, take her to bed, and never get up again?

But Jenna was scared, and wanted to get him on her side. Who knew her true motives for kissing him? For a woman who'd said she was scared of him, she'd sure gotten over her fear fast. He didn't want to believe she'd faked the passion, but could he really trust her? It was easier to suspect the worst and never be surprised than to hope for the best and always be disappointed.

The bartender, Michael Murray, set the shot in front of him. "Should I bring the bottle?" he drawled, a knowing gleam in his eyes. Reid had already exchanged small talk with him, knowing that bartenders in small towns were usually a well of information, especially bartenders who were part of the town's most prominent family.

"Maybe," Reid replied, downing the shot in one quick, burning swallow.

"Gotta be a woman," Michael said with a grin. He poured Reid another shot and set it in front of him. "Last time I broke up with my girlfriend, I got so drunk I puked my guts out for two days. I'm telling you, man, it's not worth it."

"Thanks for the tip," Reid said, staring at the fourth shot.

"So who is she?"

"A mess of trouble," Reid replied.

"Aren't they all?"

"Good point." Reid downed the fourth shot as Michael moved away to tend to another customer. The place was crowded, standing room only. The festival had shut down and most of the action had moved to Murray's.

"You look lonely," a woman said, sliding in next to him. She had on a low-cut top and her hair was light blond. She appeared to be in her early thirties, and from the seductive smile she gave him, she was looking for a hook-up. She was pretty in a thin, brittle, bar scene kind of way, reminding him a little of his mother. She probably wouldn't be happy to hear that. "Buy me a drink?" she asked.

He was about to say sure, when he heard Allison's voice in his head. "*She's not good enough for you, Reid. You always go after women who won't ask enough of you. You deserve more. Stop selling yourself so short.*

Stop going for easy. You know what you really want, and it's not her."

He shook Allison's voice out of his head. He'd obviously had too much tequila. But then he caught a glimpse of a woman sitting at the far end of the bar. She was in the shadows, but he could see the sparkle of red hair, the hint of a knowing smile. His gut tightened. Her face turned into the light, and for a second he thought it was Allison. She was dressed in the same black dress he'd seen her in that last day. She raised the necklace she was wearing to her lips and kissed the gold heart that hung from it. He'd given her that heart when she'd had Cameron. He got to his feet, stunned. She had to be an illusion, but she seemed so real, so vibrant, so alive. Not at all like she'd looked the last time he'd seen her—her body cold, her skin a bloodless white.

"Where are you going?" the woman next to him asked. "I thought we were getting acquainted."

He didn't reply; he had one goal and one goal only. Someone blocked his way. He shoved the person aside, intent on getting to the other end of the bar. He sensed Allison was slipping away.

"Hey, watch it," a man protested.

"Get out of my way," Reid said abruptly.

"You need to learn some manners," the man replied, the strong scent of whiskey coming from his mouth.

Reid tried to step past him, but the man grabbed his arm. Reid pulled away and stumbled into someone else. That guy shoved him back, and suddenly fists were flying. Reid took a shot to the face and felt blood spurt from his nose.

"Fuck," he roared, swinging back in retaliation. All the pain of the last year surged to the surface, begging to be released. It felt good to hit someone, to hit something, to let the anger out. He wasn't just fighting to get across the room anymore; he was fighting to get his life back. And it felt damn good.

Joe Silveira looked at the bloodied, bruised faces of the three men who sat in lockup. Two of his officers, Colin Lynch and Henry Markham, had broken up the fight and brought the men back to the station. Joe had let them stew in the cell for the past hour, but he felt like getting home now. As bar fights went, this one had been pretty tame. It had been broken up almost as soon as it started, with minimal damage to the bar.

He recognized the Harlan brothers, Roger and Bill. They ran the hardware store in town. The third was a stranger, a reporter by the name of Reid Tanner, apparently in town to report on the angels.

Joe didn't usually handle the Friday night bar fights. He left that for his officers, but he'd sent Colin and Henry home. The men had wives, families, and he didn't. At least no one who was here, which was why he'd decided to work late. The loneliness of his life was beginning to get to him. He liked his house, the town, and his job, but there was a big hole in the personal department. He missed Rachel.

He missed sleeping with her, talking to her, even listening to her chatter about her damn job. But he was here and she wasn't, and he didn't know when that would change.

"Chief, it was his fault," Roger Harlan said, pointing to Tanner. "He hit me first."

The reporter didn't bother to argue, but then he hadn't had much to say for himself since he'd been brought in.

"That's right, and he damn near knocked me over," Bill slurred, backing up his brother.

"You got anything to say?" Joe asked Reid.

"Nope."

"Great." He considered his options. The Harlan brothers had been drinking heavily since their mother had passed on a month earlier. He suspected they'd probably started the fight, since Roger had a short fuse, especially after some drinks. "One of you elbowed my officer in the face," he stated. "Assaulting a police officer is a serious crime."

Roger frowned. "That was an accident. I wouldn't hit Colin on purpose; he's like a brother. I grew up with him. You know that."

Joe did know that. He also knew that Colin wasn't interested in pressing charges against a longtime fishing buddy, nor did any of the men seem inclined to press charges against one another, which made his job a lot easier.

"All right," he said. "Here's the deal. You'll all pay for the damages to Murray's. And on Sunday, the beach patrol could use some volunteers to clean up after the festival breaks down. I'll expect to see the three of you out there."

The men all gave a nod.

"Good. Now if any of you so much as spit in the street, I'll haul your asses back in here on all sorts of charges." He opened the door. "Roger, Bill, your wives are waiting out front. Go home and stay out of trouble."

The Harlan brothers left. As Reid Tanner got up, Joe stepped in front of him. "Why don't you hang on a sec?"

Reid gave him a hard look. "Special treatment for the out-of-towners, Chief?"

"Just thought we'd have a little conversation," Joe said. "What's a former hotshot reporter for the *Washington D.C. Journal* doing here in Angel's Bay?"

"You did your homework."

"I like to know who's in town. You seem to have a reputation for stirring up trouble. The last story you wrote got you fired."

"Actually, I quit. And I'm not looking for trouble, just for angels—like everyone else."

"Did you see any at Murray's Bar?"

"Nope. Just a fucking ghost," Reid replied sharply, anger still simmering in his eyes.

"Tequila will do that to you."

"You're probably right about that. Can I go?"

"In a minute. What have you discovered about the angel video?"

Reid frowned. "Not a hell of a lot. Why?"

"I've been wondering what's going on down at

the cliff myself. I've had officers patrolling the area to see if anyone is attempting to deface the front of the cliff, but no one has seen a thing. Yet every day there appears to be some new mark, usually seen after the fog lifts. I can't imagine how anyone could get up or down that cliff in the foggy darkness, but I have no other explanation."

"Neither do I, Chief."

"But you'll let me know if you get one. Before I read about it in your magazine." It was a statement, not a question.

"If it's not the work of angels, I'll certainly let you know."

"Do you need a ride to your hotel?" Joe wasn't normally in the habit of offering rides to people he'd locked up, but it might be a good idea to keep an eye on Tanner. It struck him as wrong that a reporter of Reid's caliber would be working on a piece about angels. It made him think the man had another reason for being in town.

"I'd rather walk," Reid said.

"Think you can make it back without getting into any more fights?"

"I didn't start the last one."

"But you didn't turn away." Joe gave Reid a speculative look. "Sometimes it feels good to fight back, doesn't it?"

"What would you know about that, Chief?"

"More than I can say. You might want to put some ice on your face. You're going to have a hell of a shiner in the morning. I'm betting it's not your first."

"Not by a long shot."

"Don't make me sorry I let you go with just a warning," Joe said as Reid headed out the door.

After Reid left, Joe walked back to his office and shut down his computer. He turned off the lights, closed up the office, said good-bye to the night dispatcher, then headed for home. He wasn't looking forward to his cold house or his empty bed, but maybe he was finally tired enough now to sleep. For a married man, he spent a hell of a lot of nights alone.

Ten

Kara watched her husband sleep. She didn't like the look of the small bruise under his eye. Fortunately for the Harlan brothers, Colin was an easygoing guy who didn't feel like bringing old friends up on assault charges. Kara didn't feel nearly so charitable; she hated it when Colin got hurt. Actually, she hated whenever he had to do anything remotely dangerous. Thankfully, Angel's Bay was a peaceful town, but deep in her heart she was terrified far more than she should be every time her husband left the house.

It had gotten worse since she'd become pregnant; she kept thinking of all the things that could go wrong. What if the fight Colin had broken up had turned deadly? What if someone had pulled out a knife or a gun? What would she have done if something had happened to him? She couldn't bear the thought. She put her hand on his arm, reassured by the solid muscle. She knew that Colin was more than capable of taking care of himself. And he'd taken great care of her for most of her life. He had a heart as big as the ocean, with so much love inside, and he'd always wanted to give that love to her, even when she hadn't wanted to take it.

She slipped out of bed, threw on her robe, and left the room. It was four o'clock in the morning, but she felt too keyed up to sleep. Moving down the hall, she opened the door to the baby's room. Colin had put up new wallpaper last weekend, with balloons and circus animals, but no clowns, because she'd always thought they were more scary than funny.

She smiled as she crossed the room to look at the crib her mother had given her. Most of the Murray children had slept in that crib, including her older brothers, Shane and Patrick, her younger sister, Dee, and her younger brother, Michael. The idea that her baby would be sleeping there, too, seemed exactly right. The Murrays had always been about family, which was why they'd taken in the baby, Gabriella, so long ago.

She hadn't thought about their history in ages, but talking to Jenna had reminded her of the deep connection she had to the place where she'd lived her entire life and planned to stay forever. Thank goodness Colin felt the same way. His childhood had been far rockier than hers. His parents had split when he was young. His father had moved to San Diego, and Colin had spent many summers going back and forth between his mom and dad. Then both of his parents had remarried and started other families, and

Colin had gotten lost in the shuffle. But he'd always been welcome at her house, always been welcome in her heart. And now they would have a baby to share their love.

They'd wanted a baby forever, and she'd almost lost hope. The rockiest part of their marriage had been the year before the pregnancy test had come back positive. For months, the struggle to conceive had put tension between them, and for a while she'd wondered if she'd lose Colin over it. But as her grandmother had told her more than once, she had to keep the faith that things would work out, and they had.

She touched the mobile that hung over the crib, watching the tiny angels swing back and forth. It was a gift from one of her grandmother's friends, and soon her baby would have an Angel's Bay quilt made by all the women in town with love and care. She couldn't wait to see what they came up with.

"Hey, what are you doing in here?" Colin asked from the doorway. He ran a hand through his hair as he looked at her in concern. "Is something wrong?"

"Not really. I just feel a little—off." Her body had been tight all day, and now her abdomen felt crampy. A wave of terror followed that thought, and she quickly put her hand to her stomach.

Colin was at her side in a second. "Is it the baby?"

"I—I don't know."

He led her over to the rocking chair and she sat down. He knelt by her side. "I'll call the doctor."

"It's the middle of the night."

"I don't care."

"Wait. It's gone." She let out a breath, feeling the discomfort subside. "Probably just gas."

He didn't look convinced. "I think I should take you to the hospital, or at least call Charlotte."

"But—" She started to protest but Colin was already gone. A second later, she heard him on the phone. He came back and handed her the receiver.

"I'm so sorry, Charlotte," she said. "I told Colin not to call you."

"It's okay. Tell me what happened," Charlotte said in a sleepy voice.

"Nothing, really. I just felt a little cramp for a minute, but it's gone now."

"Any bleeding?"

"I don't think so. Should I be worried? I'm not going to lose the baby, am I?" She couldn't bear to think of losing the baby now. But even as the thought passed through her head, she felt the baby kick, as if to reassure her. She put a hand to her abdomen and let out a breath. "I feel the baby moving."

"That's a very good sign, Kara. What I would suggest is that you get back in bed and try to sleep. Call me in the morning, or before that if you have any other problems."

"Thanks. Sorry again, Charlotte," she added, and hung up.

Colin was already on his knees in front of her, his hand on her stomach, his green eyes relieved. "Thank God."

She put her hand over his. "I didn't mean to scare you."

"No more middle of the night trips without me by your side, okay?"

"I just came down the hall. I couldn't sleep."

"Next time wake me up. I don't care how tired you think I am," he added, knowing what she'd been about to say. "There is nothing more important to me than you and our child."

"I feel the same way about you, Colin." Her eyes blurred with unexpected tears, and she gave a little sniff and a sheepish smile. "Hormones."

"Yeah? So what's my excuse?" he said gruffly, as he took her by the hand and led her back to bed.

It was barely dawn when Annie Dupont got out of bed and walked over to the hospital window. Her room faced a grove of redwood trees. Through the early morning light, she could make out the tops of some of the buildings in town. To the east were the mountains—the mountains where her father lived, where she'd spent her whole life.

She wished she had a room facing the ocean, so she could watch for the angels. She knew they existed; one had rescued her from the icy cold water of the bay. Everyone had told her that the woman who saved her wasn't an angel, just a good Samaritan, but she'd heard the angel voices telling her where to swim. She'd seen more than one hand reaching out for her, bringing her back to the surface when she thought she might drown. And when she'd looked into the angel's eyes, she was sure she'd seen her mother's face looking back at her.

Her mother had believed in angels. She supposed her father did, too, although his religious beliefs focused more on the fires of hell and Satan trying to possess human souls. Her mother had once told her that her father hadn't always been crazy and obsessed, that he'd been gentle and kind, a good man. But when he'd come back from tours of duty with the army, he'd changed. He'd seen his friends die and had almost lost his own life. After that he became cold, withdrawn, paranoid. That was the father she knew, the one who wore fatigues and patrolled whatever shack they were living in as if it were a palace filled with gold. He carried his guns wherever he went, and sometimes in the middle of the night he would wake her and her mother up, make them leave, go farther up the mountain where no one could find them.

They'd lived off the land, mostly. Her mother had occasionally gone into town to pick up sewing jobs. And for a while she'd been allowed to go to school, until her father got worse, then it was homeschool. After her mother died, it was no schooling. Her only relief had come when her father let her take a job with Myra's Cleaning Service. He'd allowed her to go down the mountain on an old motorbike as long as she was home each day before dark and promised never to speak to anyone in town.

But she'd longed for human contact, and on the

days she'd come to town, she'd lingered as long as possible.

Then she'd met him—her baby's father, a man who had made her feel like she belonged in the real world, not her father's world. But she couldn't tell him about the baby. She'd already ruined her own life; she couldn't ruin his.

When her father had found her throwing up one morning, he'd guessed instantly that she was pregnant. He'd told her that it was the devil's work, that she had a demon child growing inside of her and that she must go and ask for forgiveness, and if she was worthy, maybe—just maybe—the angels would save her.

And they had.

Or maybe she'd just gotten lucky.

She knew she'd done a really stupid thing, but the last few days with her father taunting her incessantly, she'd gone a little crazy. Now she knew she couldn't go back up the mountain. She had to find somewhere else to live. Not just for herself, but for her baby. But where would she go? She had no money and her job didn't pay much—if Myra would even let her keep it now. What kind of a life could she possibly give a child when she wasn't sure she could take care of herself?

As she stared out the window, she wondered if the angels had made a mistake.

Jenna had always been a morning person. She loved the quiet of the early day, the sound of the town waking up, the smell of coffee, the storekeepers opening their doors, moving displays of fresh fruit out onto the sidewalk, the rustle of newspapers being opened, the smells of the fish coming back on the boats from the early morning runs. The summer sun was already heating up the air. It was going to be a beautiful day.

Normally, after dropping Lexie at the library for Saturday morning children's hour, she got coffee and sat down to read the local paper. But this morning she had other things on her mind, namely Reid Tanner.

She'd spent a sleepless night wondering what he would do. Would he go to the police, turn her in as a possible kidnapper? Would he start digging into her life on his own? Or miracle of miracles, would he let it go? Somehow she doubted Reid had ever let anything go in his life.

Her breath caught in her chest as a police car turned the corner and came toward her, cruising slowly. Was he looking for her? The car came to a halt next to her. The window was rolled down; then she heard Colin Lynch's voice.

"Morning, Jenna," he said. "You're out early."

Her heart was beating a mile a minute, but Colin just seemed to be making conversation. "You, too," she said lightly. "Don't they ever give you a day off? You were working last night, weren't you?"

"It's a busy weekend. Too many people drinking way too much."

"I'm sure."

"Have a good day now."

She let out a sigh of relief as he drove on. Maybe Reid hadn't told anyone her secret. She had to find out for sure. It was probably a mistake to go to see him, but not knowing was making her crazy, so she turned the corner at the next street and headed to the Seagull Inn.

Reid took a minute to answer her knock, and when he opened the door he looked like he'd just gotten out of bed. He was barefoot, wearing jeans and a slightly wrinkled maroon T-shirt. His hair was curly and completely wild, but it wasn't his hair that made Jenna's jaw drop—it was the black eye and the bruises on his face.

"What happened to you?" she asked in surprise.

He scowled. "I ran into someone's fist."

"Looks like more than one fist."

"What do you want, Jenna?" he asked, his voice less than welcoming.

For the first time, she was the one pursuing him. It was nice to be proactive instead of reactive for a change. "We need to talk."

"Are you actually going to talk?" he challenged.

"Well, not unless you let me in." She certainly didn't intend to have a conversation with him in the hall.

He stepped back, waving her inside. Reid's room had a masculine feel, with dark wood paneling, heavy, weathered antique furniture, and pictures of seascapes and fishing boats adorning the walls. A small black suitcase stood against one wall, and she spotted his shirts hanging neatly in the closet. The sheets and blankets on the king-size bed were tangled, and there was a smear of what looked like blood on the pillowcase—probably from his nose, which appeared a bit more crooked than it had the day before.

"Who did you fight?" she asked.

"A couple of guys at Murray's Bar."

"Over what?"

"A simple misunderstanding."

She tilted her head. "A simple misunderstanding that left you looking like a boxer who just went ten rounds in the ring?"

"You should see the other guys," he said with a cocky grin.

"Guys—as in more than one?"

"Apparently brothers—the Harlan brothers." As she waited for him to go on, he sighed. "I thought I saw someone I knew at the bar. I got up to check it out and some drunken asshole thought I shoved him. He pushed me. I ended up knocking into his brother, and the next thing I knew we were being hauled off to jail, where we sat for a couple of hours until the chief decided to let us go. That's the story."

She had a feeling he'd glossed over a few details. "Does your face hurt?"

"Do you really care?"

She was surprised at how much she did care. She was also very aware of just how alone they were and just how close the bed was. It wouldn't take much to tumble onto those sheets with Reid and forget all about why she'd come here.

"It wasn't that difficult a question," Reid said.

She realized he was still waiting for an answer. "I was being polite."

"I'm fine. Now it's your turn." He folded his arms in front of him. "What's up? You tell me to stay away from you last night, and here you are first thing this morning. What exactly did you come here for? Conversation? Or something else?"

She ignored the challenging look in his eyes. "I have to know if you're planning to tell the police that I'm not Lexie's mother."

He stared at her for a long moment, his gaze completely unreadable. "I haven't decided. I need more information."

"All you need to know is that by keeping my secret, you'll be protecting Lexie, an innocent little girl."

"I only have your word for that, Jenna, and since I don't know you, I have no idea if your word is good. If you want my cooperation, tell me something about yourself."

"I can't, Reid. I can't trust you. If it were just me, maybe I could, because you seem like you might be a decent person."

"What a compliment. I'm stunned."

"But it's not just me. I have Lexie to consider, and she is the most precious thing in the world to me."

He frowned. "I believe you care about her, but it could be a crazy, obsessive kind of love."

"It's not. Lexie is my niece, and I have good reasons for the deception." How could she convince him? She had no concrete proof to wave in front of his face. She paced back and forth in front of the bed, searching for something to say that would give him enough information to trust her, but not so much that he could cause more problems.

"You're in way over your head, aren't you, Jenna?" Reid asked.

"More than you can imagine," she admitted, pausing in front of him.

"Who else knows that you have Lexie?"

"Only one person. The person who helped me start over."

"And you trust this person?"

"So far it's worked out. It can keep working out if you pretend you didn't hear anything last night."

He shook his head, his gaze softening. "Jenna, Lexie is a seven-year-old child. She's going to crack again. She'll tell someone else, probably one of her friends. They'll tell their parents. This whole thing is bound to explode in your face."

"Down the road, perhaps, but right now I just need a little time." The longer she kept the secret, the more opportunities she would have to figure out her next move. For two months her only goal had been to make it from one day to the next. She couldn't think any further into the future than that. "Well? What do you say?"

"I'll think about it."

She shook her head. "I need an answer now, Reid. I didn't sleep all night, worrying about what you were planning to do. Just tell me you'll keep the secret."

He stepped toward her, and she instinctively took

a step back. He frowned. "You're not really scared of me, are you?"

She could lie and say yes, but for some reason she wanted to tell the truth about this. "I'm more scared of me. I shouldn't have kissed you last night. I am in no position to get involved with anyone, and I shouldn't have acted on impulse." She took a breath, knowing she had to finish it. "I did not kiss you to seduce you into keeping my secrets."

"And I didn't kiss you to get the story," he said, his gaze clinging to hers.

She saw the honesty in his eyes and took a quick breath as another jolt of electricity swept through her. "To be completely truthful, I might have kissed you to cover up, or to get you on my side, if I'd thought of it. I know that doesn't make me a very good person, and you probably won't believe this, but deception used to be a foreign concept to me. Growing up, I always told the truth. Now everything has changed. Some days I wonder if the lies will get so complicated that I won't remember who I really am."

"That could happen. It's difficult to lead a life of pretense. At some point, the truth always comes out."

She sighed. "That's not what I want to hear."

"If your sister was murdered, you should go to the police and tell them who you suspect of killing her. They can protect you and Lexie."

"In other circumstances I would agree with you, but the person who killed my sister has extensive connections in law enforcement. I can in no way be certain that Lexie or I could be protected. And there's a possibility that . . ." She hesitated. Was she insane to tell him as much as she was? If he got an inkling of who was involved, he wouldn't be able to let the story go.

"A possibility that what?" he prodded.

"That the police might think that I took Lexie. They might try to return her to someone who shouldn't have her."

"If you're truly her aunt, I'm sure you'd be a good candidate to take care of her, especially if it's her father who is under suspicion, which I'm guessing is the case. Are there grandparents available?"

"No, not really."

"Not really isn't no."

"Then we'll just leave it at no," she said, waving a frustrated hand in the air.

"Jenna—I grew up in a lot of tough neighborhoods. I was a foster kid. I saw my share of women getting knocked around by men. I've also been writing about crime for more than a decade. If everything you've told me is true—if your sister was killed, and her murderer wants to kill you, too—then you will never be safe. You can't hide forever. Someday, sometime, something will happen, and he'll find you."

"If you're trying to scare me—"

"I'm trying to wake you up. What are you doing to actually protect yourself besides hiding?"

"There's nothing else I *can* do."

"What about trying to find some evidence against the killer?"

"I can't do that and stay here to protect Lexie. My sister was killed on the other side of the country."

"You'd be surprised what you can do if you know how to do it."

She stared at him, feeling a tiny seed of hope begin to grow inside of her. "Are you telling me that you can help me?"

"I'm good at digging up facts."

But what if his investigation became known? What if his questions set Brad off, gave Brad a trail to follow? "I can't take the risk," she said slowly.

"You can't afford not to. Someone who has killed once won't be afraid to do it again."

"If I do nothing but lay low, maybe he'll just forget about us."

"Forget about his only child? Come on, Jenna. You know better than that. You won't be doing Lexie or yourself any favors by pretending that the problem will go away. It won't. Talk to me, Jenna. Talk to me before it's too late."

Eleven

Jenna knew that Reid was right. She couldn't stand still forever. She couldn't just hope they'd be safe; she had to take action to make sure of it. Trusting a reporter was a huge leap of faith, but Reid already knew so much. He wouldn't stop digging even if she refused to talk to him. If she let him go off on his own, who knew what he would come up with, what alarm bells he would trip?

"If I tell you my story," she said finally, "will you promise me that you won't go to the police and that you won't write anything about me or Lexie until it's all over? Until we're truly safe and the murderer has been caught? That's the deal."

"I agree."

She searched his eyes for the truth. He didn't look away. Her gut told her that Reid was a man whose word was good, but that's all she had—her gut. "I hope I'm not making a mistake."

"You're not." He took a seat in the chair by the desk, waiting for her to begin.

Jenna sat on the bed and clasped her hands together. "Okay, here goes. The truth is that I don't really know what happened between my sister and her husband. Kelly and I were not close. For the past five years I spent most of my time in Europe, where I toured as a concert pianist. A couple of months ago I had a crisis in my career, and I came back to the States. I needed some time away from the pressure to regroup. I went to see Kelly, who lived outside of Boston. I got a hotel room near her house, because I wasn't sure she'd be happy to see me. It had been a long time since we'd talked.

"When Kelly came to the hotel, I was shocked at her appearance. She was very thin, and there were bruises on her arms and one on her neck. She told me that she was in trouble and that she had been for a while, but she hadn't realized just how much trouble." Jenna's voice caught in her throat as she remembered the panic in Kelly's voice, the terror in her eyes. Why hadn't she made Kelly stay with her that day? If she had, Kelly might still be alive.

"Take your time," Reid said quietly. "Do you want some water?"

She drew in a deep breath and slowly let it out. "No, I'm all right."

"Your brother-in-law was abusing your sister," Reid said. "That's what you found out, right?"

"Yes, but I don't think that was all of it. I've

been going over in my mind the last two conversations that we had. Kelly told me that she'd met with someone about three weeks before I arrived. A man had told her some horrible things about Brad that she didn't want to believe, but now she thought they were true."

"What kind of things?"

"She wouldn't elaborate. She told me she was going to leave Brad, but she had to make sure that everything was set before she did."

"What was the man's name?" Reid interrupted.

"She didn't say. I suggested that we pick up Lexie from school that minute and leave town. Kelly refused. She convinced me to wait until the next day. She asked me not to call or come by the house, because she didn't want Brad to know I was in town. She had one last thing to do. Before Kelly left, she gave me an envelope and asked me to meet her and Lexie at the park by her house the next day. If anything happened to her, I was to find Lexie and follow the instructions in the envelope. I was to keep Lexie safe, no matter what. Most important, I could not let Brad have Lexie."

Jenna looked over at Reid. "Kelly said that everything would be fine as long as she kept pretending."

"Did you ask her why she didn't go to the police?" Reid queried.

"I didn't have to ask. My brother-in-law is a cop."

His lips tightened. "Got it."

"The next day, I went to the park as scheduled. I saw police cars on Kelly's street on my way over there, and I had a horrible feeling, but I went to the park anyway. At first I didn't think anyone was there; then I heard crying. I found Lexie hiding inside one of those round tubes in the playground. She was sobbing her heart out, and she had blood on her shoes."

Jenna swallowed back a choking knot of emotion. "Lexie said that her daddy hurt her mommy, and that her mommy told her to run to the park and find me. I don't know exactly what Lexie saw that day. Sometimes it sounds like she was hiding and saw them fighting, but her father didn't see her. Then it sounds like Brad went looking for her, and while he was out of the room, she went to her mom and Kelly told her to run, which means that Kelly was still alive at that point." Jenna's voice broke as she thought of her sister wounded, dying, desperate and so very alone. Had Brad come back and stabbed her again? Had Kelly suffered even more after Lexie left?

Jenna's hands began to shake, and she couldn't get any breath into her lungs. Her muscles were so tight; she felt as if she was about to snap.

The next thing she knew, Reid was sitting next to her, pulling her into his embrace. She resisted, afraid to accept the help. She'd been operating on her own for a long time, desperately trying to keep every potential for danger away. But as Reid's arms tightened around her, she couldn't resist his solid strength, his intense warmth, the comfort he offered. She was exhausted from carrying the weight of Kelly's murder and Lexie's safety on her shoulders, worn out from the unrelenting fear of being discovered.

She finally slid her arms around his waist and rested her face against his chest just for a minute to pull herself together—then she could go on again. But emotion still welled up inside her, threatening to swamp her. She bit down on her bottom lip and squeezed her eyes tight, afraid she was going to lose it. She *couldn't* lose it. She had to be strong.

"It's okay, Jenna. You can let go," Reid whispered against her hair. His hand stroked her back. "You're safe here. You're safe with me. You're not alone anymore."

A sob escaped her, then another, and Jenna cried for the first time since her sister had died. She cried for the future she would never have with Kelly. She cried for the wasted past, the harsh words, the misunderstandings, the pettiness, and most of all, the regret she would carry her entire life.

She'd never imagined she would lose her sister. She'd never believed that they wouldn't some day have an opportunity to be close. She'd told herself a million times that next Thanksgiving or next Christmas or next summer, she'd spend time with Kelly.

She'd always thought she had tomorrow, and what she'd put off for too many years could never be regained now. The sister who had once shared her bedroom, shared her confidences, shared her life, was gone. And she was never, ever, coming back.

Her tears soaked Reid's shirt, but he just held her until the storm passed. When her sobs turned into gulps, and she struggled to breathe, he handed her a box of tissues from the side table. She blew her nose, aware of her puffy eyes and teary face. "Sorry," she muttered. "I don't know why I did that."

"You were due." His gaze was warm and understanding.

"I was weak." She never indulged in tears. Her father had always told her that emotion must be saved for the music. *Don't cry it, play it.* Now she felt completely naked and vulnerable. She'd never meant to let Reid all the way in, but somehow that's where he'd ended up.

"Weak doesn't describe you, Jenna. You're one of the most courageous women I've ever met," he said softly.

"You don't know me that well."

"I know you're hard on yourself."

"Most people don't think I'm hard enough."

His gaze narrowed. "Most people being . . ."

"It's not important. Thanks for the shoulder. You might need to change your wet shirt." Her gaze drifted across his broad chest, and she had to fight the urge to help him take that shirt off. It would feel so good to give in to desire, to lose herself in the wonderful, mindless oblivion of—

"Jenna," he said sharply.

She met his eyes and saw the same flare of desire there.

"Don't look at me like that," he warned.

Embarrassed, she said, "I—I don't know what you mean—"

"Yes, you do." He jumped to his feet and returned to his chair. "You need to finish the story so that I can help you. Let's get back on track. You picked up Lexie at the park. What happened next?"

She drew in a deep breath and let it out. It took her a minute to regroup. "I wanted to go to the house to see if Kelly was all right, but I had her voice in my head, telling me to take Lexie and keep her safe. I knew the police were at the house, so I did what Kelly had asked. I drove for the next four hours and I stopped in a motel a couple hundred miles away. I had my laptop with me, so I went on the Internet. That's where I learned that Kelly had been stabbed to death during an alleged burglary.

"They showed a picture of Brad sobbing, pleading for someone to find his wife's killer. He had bandages on his hands, self-defense wounds, supposedly. He was also flanked by his brothers in blue, and he was so good, I almost thought his grief was real. Then I remembered what Lexie had said, and the bruises on Kelly's arms, the terror in her eyes. Brad killed my sister. I'm sure of it." She met Reid's gaze. "If I hadn't had Lexie to keep safe, I would have gone after him. I would have made sure he paid."

"I know you would have," Reid assured her. "Where was Lexie supposed to have been during this burglary?"

"The news report said that fortunately the couple's young daughter had been staying with relatives in another state and wasn't home at the time of the burglary, which of course was a lie. I don't know why Brad gave that story."

"It certainly wouldn't have been difficult to dispute with a simple investigation."

"No one was looking for Lexie because Brad told them she was safe."

"Why didn't he say she was missing?" Reid pondered. "That doesn't make sense."

"Maybe he knew I had her."

"Maybe. Go on."

"The envelope that Kelly had given me had detailed instructions on setting up a new life. Apparently she had been planning to leave for a long time. She'd contacted a group that could get abused women out of dangerous situations. The group created a new identity for her and for Lexie, so I simply took Kelly's place. I was sent here to Angel's Bay and provided with identification. There was a bank account waiting for me, a house to rent, a new life, everything I needed to start over."

Jenna paused. "The thing is—Lexie barely knew me. I was this distant aunt who played the piano and lived far away and sent her nice presents. She didn't understand why I was taking her away from her home. The first few days were really difficult. At first she didn't talk at all. It was almost as if she was in a trance, as if she'd put herself in a place where there wasn't any pain. Then she started to cry, to scream. She hit me, yelled at me to take her home."

"That must have been tough."

"I didn't know what I was going to do. Lexie kept asking me where her mother was, when were we going home. I finally had to tell her that her mother was dead, that she was an angel in heaven. For some reason, that explanation calmed her down. I think on some level she already knew that her mother was dead; she just needed it confirmed. Eventually she stopped crying. I told her about the safety plan that Kelly had devised and how we had to pretend to be mother and daughter. She went along with it, and most days she's remarkably good at keeping up the pretense."

Jenna drew in a breath. "I know that Lexie is still confused and in pain. She's just hiding from it—perhaps the same way we're hiding from her father. It's all become a game, a pretense. Maybe she thinks that one day when the game is over, everything will go back to the way it was. Or perhaps she's come to believe that her mother is in heaven. I'm not sure."

"That's why Lexie wants to talk to the angels," Reid said heavily. "She wants to find her mother. She wants to ask her if she's all right."

"Yes," Jenna said with a nod. "And it breaks my heart, but what can I do? Lexie didn't have closure. She didn't see the funeral or the casket. And her father—I don't know what she thinks about him. Sometimes her dad is the bad guy. Other times she's so confused, she says a bad guy came into the house and killed her mother. I'm sure she's in desperate need of therapy, but I've been afraid to take her to see anyone. It's too risky. I keep thinking if enough time passes, Brad will just give up, and I can get Lexie help and somehow this will all work out."

"That seems overly hopeful. What do you think

Brad's intentions are regarding Lexie? Abusive husbands don't always abuse their kids. Does he love Lexie? Does he want her back? Or does he want to hurt her?"

"I don't know. It's possible that Lexie could pin the murder on him. Maybe her testimony could put Brad away. But she never tells the same story twice."

"The defense attorneys would rip her testimony to shreds," Reid said. "You need more evidence. You need to know what your sister knew about her husband."

"How on earth am I going to figure that out?"

"You can start by giving me his last name."

One last lick of doubt made her hesitate. But she'd gone this far; she might as well go all the way. "Winters. Brad Winters." A light sparked in Reid's eyes and she jumped up, putting a hand on his arm. "Reid, you have to be careful. Brad is a very smart man and a cop. If you start making inquiries about him, you'll lead him to us."

"That won't happen," he said firmly. "But the only way you'll ever be truly safe is if we find a way to take Brad down."

"We, huh?" She liked the sound of a partnership. Reid's strength, his confidence, was already making her feel like she had some power in her corner.

"That's right. Now, the best way to defeat an enemy is to find out everything you can about him," Reid continued. "Your sister discovered something about her husband. If we can figure out what that something was, we'll have ammunition to go after him. You can only retreat for so long, Jenna. At some point you hit a wall, and the only way to battle is to fight back."

She nodded, beginning to feel better. "Okay, I'm ready to fight. But I should point out that this isn't your war. If you get involved, you could be in danger, Reid. Even if your investigation doesn't trigger something to bring Brad here, he might still be able to find me on his own. If you're helping me, your life could be on the line."

"I can take care of myself."

"And you want to do all this just to get a story?" she queried.

"That's right," he said quickly.

He started to pull away, but she tightened her grip on his arm. "I don't believe you. I think—I think you want to help me."

"Maybe a little," he admitted.

"I wouldn't have figured you for a knight in shining armor."

His expression turned grim. "Don't ever mistake me for that, Jenna. I'm no knight, believe me."

"Now who's too hard on himself?"

He shook his head. "You have enough to figure out, Jenna. Don't worry about me." He glanced down at her hand on his arm. "And . . . you should let go."

She should, but the heat of his body was deliciously warm and the air between them filled with electricity. It was the same charge she felt before she took the stage, the delicious and terrifying sensation that something amazing could happen if she just let it. Her stomach danced with butterflies and as she looked into Reid's dark gaze, she knew that he felt it, too.

He put his hands on her hips and pulled her up against him. "Remember that I told you to let go," he said, before his mouth came down on hers.

The kiss started out hard and a little angry, as if Reid were pissed at himself for wanting her. But as her mouth softened under his, the anger turned to passion. He kissed her as if he couldn't get enough of her, as if he were dying of thirst and she was his salvation.

Suddenly her legs were hitting the edge of the bed and she went down onto the mattress with a soft *swoosh.* Reid followed, his body covering hers, his mouth seeking the soft curve of her neck, his hand caressing her breast, his leg parting her thighs.

She ran her hands through his hair and moved restlessly under him, desperate to get closer. She wanted to feel his hands and his mouth on her bare skin. She yearned to ease the reckless, aching point of desire that was tightening every nerve.

Then the clock chimed. It didn't make sense at first. She was so caught up in Reid, she'd lost track of where she was. It chimed again and again.

"Goddamn clock," Reid ground out as he lifted his head. "Who puts a grandfather clock in a hotel room?"

The clock chimed ten times, and Jenna sat up in shock. "Oh, my God, I'm late. I have to pick up Lexie at the library!" She shoved Reid off her and stumbled to her feet, catching a glimpse of herself in the wall mirror. Her hair was tangled from Reid's impatient hands, her lips soft and kissed, her eyes dark and smoky. "I look like a mess."

"You look beautiful," Reid said. "But you should go."

"Yes. And we can't do that again. This is the wrong time, the wrong place, the wrong everything."

"Then why does it feel so right?" Reid asked.

Jenna grabbed her purse and headed out the door, having absolutely no answer.

TWELVE

As Charlotte opened the door to her mother's house and encouraged a reluctant Annie to enter, she hoped she was doing the right thing. Annie had been released from the clinic after several lengthy sessions with a psychiatrist, who had come to the conclusion that Annie was no longer a danger to herself or to her baby. Annie had admitted that jumping off the pier had been a momentarily stupid impulse, and one she had no intention of repeating. She'd felt desperate and alone, and her father's extreme behavior had driven her to the edge, but she very much wanted to live and to make a life for herself and her baby.

Charlotte had spent enough time talking to Annie to believe her, but she still intended to keep a close eye on her, at least for the immediate future. Annie would face many difficulties in the days and weeks to come, and she would need support to deal with them.

"Are you sure it's okay?" Annie whispered, her face pale, her light brown eyes worried.

"Yes," Charlotte said reassuringly. "My mother is very happy to have you stay here for a few days until we can find a more permanent place for you to live."

"She doesn't think I'm bad, that I'm a—sinner?"

Charlotte suspected her mother had a lot of negative thoughts about Annie and her teen pregnancy, but she hoped her mother would wear her minister's wife face, not the condemning face she'd shown Charlotte so many years ago. "Don't worry, it will be fine." She surreptitiously crossed her fingers, hoping that would be the case.

As they moved farther into the house, Charlotte was surprised by the delicious aroma coming from the kitchen. When she'd left the house in the early morning her mother had still been asleep, and she was usually in no hurry to get up and face the day. Apparently something had changed.

"Finally, you're here," her mother said as they entered the kitchen. She had an apron on over her black slacks and gray sweater, and there was a rosy glow to her cheeks. She actually smiled when she saw them. "You must be Annie. I'm Monica Adams. I hope you like oatmeal raisin cookies."

"I—yes," Annie stumbled.

"Good. Lunch first. I've made a chicken salad and I picked up some fresh strawberries at the farmer's market this morning," Monica went on. "Why don't you wash up and we'll eat? The bathroom is down the hall on the left."

"Okay." Annie cast Charlotte a quick look and then left the room.

"Wow, you've really gone all out," Charlotte said in amazement. The bright-eyed woman facing her today was not the woman she'd had a conversation with last night or any of the nights in the last several months. "Thank you."

"I'm not doing it for you. I'm doing it for your father. I had a dream last night. Your father told me that I needed to move on, to be strong for him, to keep his legacy alive, and to make him proud." Her eyes misted. "He appeared so handsome, so alive, and smiling—not like he looked those last few weeks when he was in so much pain." She cleared her throat. "I intend to honor your father in every possible way."

"Great," Charlotte said warily, not sure where her mother's new attitude would take them, but it was a welcome change from the half-dead woman she'd been living with.

"Although I could have used your help this morning," her mother continued. "I had to change Jamie's sheets and tidy up his room—so much for your taking complete responsibility."

Apparently her mother wasn't that different after all. "I had to go into the hospital. Kara Lynch had a cramp scare last night and I wanted to check on her, but she's fine."

"Thank goodness. Kara is a lovely girl, not like that brother of hers, Shane, who is always so sullen. And those tattoos on his arm—who knows what they mean? I cross the street whenever I see him coming."

"Shane isn't a bad guy."

"Please don't defend Shane Murray to me," her mother said, "or any of those other boys you ran with in high school. You were always drawn to young men with questionable values. The only one of your boyfriends I ever liked was Andrew, and heaven knows why you stopped seeing him." Her mother gave her a sly look. "Now that he's coming back, maybe the two of you will find you have more in common these days."

"I don't think so."

"How would you know? You haven't seen him in years, have you?"

"No, but I can't see myself dating a minister."

Her mother's mouth drew into a tight line. "Like me, right? You can't see yourself as the minister's wife, because you think my life is a waste."

"I don't think that at all."

"I'm not stupid, Charlotte. I know you believe that being someone's wife, tending to their needs, isn't enough. You're a career woman. You're a doctor and so very important. You bring new life into the world. How could a minister's wife who bakes cookies and takes soup to the sick compare to a doctor?"

Charlotte stared at her mother in amazement, not realizing just how much pent-up anger her mother had toward her, and it wasn't even true. "I don't think what you've done with your life is unimportant," she said slowly. "You've helped a lot of people."

"I've seen the disdain in your eyes many times. Do you think I don't know how disappointed you were to have me as a mother?"

Charlotte met her mother's gaze. "What you've seen in my eyes didn't have anything to do with your role as a minister's wife. It had to do with the choices you made for me, not for yourself. Do you really want to talk about what happened?" She held her breath, because she wasn't quite sure she was ready to have it all out now.

After a moment, her mother shook her head. "There's nothing to discuss. The past is the past. We can't change any of it." Monica walked over to the oven and pulled out a tray of golden brown oatmeal raisin cookies. Those were her sister Doreen's favorite; Charlotte hated raisins. And her mother knew that. "I still think you should give Andrew a chance," her mother said as she slipped the cookies onto a plate.

"I'm sure all the single women in the church will be after him," Charlotte said lightly. "I hope he likes baked goods and homemade quilts. He'll be getting a lot of them."

"See, there you go, making fun of our town traditions."

Charlotte sighed. "I really wasn't doing that. I just meant that Andrew will be at the top of the eligible men list, and a lot of single women will be interested."

"You can compete."

"Excuse me?"

Her mother raised an eyebrow. "What? I'm not allowed to acknowledge that you're pretty? You are my daughter, after all." She paused, glancing toward the door. "Why don't you find Annie? She seems to have gotten lost."

Charlotte was more than happy to end her conversation with her mother. She found Annie down the hall in her brother's room. Annie was staring at the photographs on Jamie's desk and in her hand was the most recent one, taken right before her brother shipped off on his first deployment. He was in uniform, his once long hair cut very short, his boyish face looking very adult, very determined.

Annie stared at her with accusing eyes. "I can't stay here," she said flatly.

"What's wrong?" Charlotte asked in surprise.

Annie pointed to the photo. "This is a soldier's room."

Charlotte remembered Annie's father, dressed in fatigues, aiming a shotgun at them.

"The army makes people crazy," Annie continued. "When they come home they don't know who they are anymore."

"Is that what happened to your dad? Did he change after he came home?"

Annie nodded. "My mom used to be able to talk him down when he'd get really upset, but when she died, he went over the edge. I didn't know how to bring him back. He's fighting his own war up on the mountain. Sometimes I used to think I was his hostage, his POW. But then other days he'd be almost normal again. I never knew who he'd be when I woke up in the morning." She swallowed. "He only let me go to town to work so I could buy food for us." Giving Charlotte a worried look, she added, "I don't know what will happen to him now. He grows vegetables and he has some chickens, but not much else. He told me not to come back. I don't know what to do."

"You need to stay here, rest, and take care of your baby. We'll sort it all out, Annie. Maybe we can get your father some help, make sure he has enough to eat, but I don't want you to go back there alone. You have to think not only of yourself, but also about your baby. All right?"

"Okay," Annie agreed, appearing relieved.

"I think you might be more comfortable in my room," Charlotte said. "Come with me; you're going to love this room. My sister, Doreen, decorated it when we were teenagers, and she's a real girly girl."

"Oh, wow," Annie said, breathing in the sight of the all-pink room, the fluffy pillows on the double bed, the stuffed animals on the loveseat by the window, and the shelves and shelves of books.

"We used to have twin beds until I moved out after high school, then Doreen took over the room. The books are mine; she was the makeup girl." Charlotte pointed to the dressing table where there were still rows of bottles of nail polish, as well as a hand mirror, a couple of hairbrushes, and a drawer full of discarded makeup.

"It's so pretty," Annie said, her eyes lighting up.

Annie might be eighteen and pregnant, but she was still a little girl in so many ways—a beautiful little girl with her light blond hair and brown eyes that were a mix of innocence and sadness. Annie had seen some bad things in her life, but she also had no idea what the rest of the world had to offer her.

Charlotte couldn't help wondering who had taken Annie's innocence. Another young kid? Or someone older, who should have known better? She had asked whether Annie had been forced into having sex, and Annie had told her no. Other than that she'd provided no other information about the father. Charlotte very much hoped the girl wasn't lying, but she knew firsthand that teenage girls could get into all kinds of sexual trouble.

Annie caressed the fluffy comforter. "It's like a fairy-tale room. You were so lucky to grow up here."

"I didn't see it that way when I was younger." Looking at the room through Annie's eyes, Charlotte realized just how privileged she'd been. But she'd always felt like the room was Doreen's, and the house was her mother's, and she'd never really fit in anywhere. She started at the sound of the doorbell.

"Would you get that, Charlotte?" her mother called.

"I'll be right back," Charlotte told Annie. "Feel free to look around."

She headed to the front door as the bell rang again. She threw it open, expecting one of the ladies from the church dropping off yet another casserole—and her welcoming smile turned to shock at the sight of the man on her porch, holding a bouquet of flowers. His once blond hair had turned darker, but he still had blue eyes, a cleft in his chin, and a beautiful mouth. Her heart did a backflip. For a second she went back in time to the moment when she'd opened her door to find the high school star baseball player,

Andrew Schilling, holding a handful of wildflowers that he'd picked on the way over to her house. He'd asked her to go for a ride in his car, and she'd taken his hand, and then . . .

"Charlie?" he asked, his eyes widening in surprise. "Is it really you?"

She swallowed hard. She couldn't let him see how unsettled she was. "It's me. What—what are you doing here?"

"I'm going to be the new minister."

"Yes, my mother told me that yesterday. I didn't realize you'd be here so soon." She wasn't ready to see him, to talk to him. But here he was, wearing dark brown slacks, a cream-colored button-down shirt, and a brown blazer. He looked handsome and conservative, older. She couldn't help wishing she was dressed in something a little more exciting than gray capri pants and a black sweater, with her hair pulled back in a ponytail.

"It's been a long time," Andrew said, clearing his throat. "I heard you're a doctor. That's very impressive."

"Yes. And you're a minister."

"I think we've established that," he said with a small smile.

"So what can I do for you?"

"I came to talk to your mother. Look, I don't want to put you and your family out of your home. You've been here forever. It doesn't feel right. I can keep an apartment in town."

"You'll do nothing of the sort," Monica Adams said, coming up behind Charlotte. "Hello, Andrew."

"Mrs. Adams. These are for you," he added, handing her mother the flowers.

"They're beautiful, and it was very thoughtful of you to bring them. You're the new minister now, and this will be your house, a place for you to bring your wife and your children."

"I'm not married," Andrew said quickly.

"Well, I'm sure you will be at some point."

"But I don't need this house right now, and I don't want to push you and your family out of it. It's been your home for so long."

"Yes, it has been my home. I will miss it more than I can say, but my husband would want you to be here. This is where you belong. I'm glad it's you and not a stranger," she added. "Would you like some lunch? We were just about to sit down. There's plenty to go around, and I'm sure you and Charlotte would like to catch up. I remember how close you were before she took up with that other boy."

Andrew looked decidedly uncomfortable, and Charlotte willed him to say no. She could *not* have their first conversation in thirteen years take place in front of her mother.

"I'm sorry, I can't," he said. "I have a meeting at the church."

"Of course. Another time."

"I'll look forward to it," Andrew said.

As her mother walked away, Charlotte started to close the door, but Andrew put up a hand.

"Do you want to get a cup of coffee later?" he asked.

She hesitated. "I'm busy today. Sorry."

He nodded, a rueful smile on his lips. "I probably deserve that. I think I said the same thing to you the last time you wanted to talk."

He had, and she remembered every word as if it had been branded into her head. "It was a long time ago, and really not a big deal. I'm sure I'll see you around."

"Charlie?"

"What?" she asked, feeling a desperate need to close the door on him and her past.

"I'm happy you're here. That we're both here at the same time."

"I'm not sure I'm staying."

His gaze held hers. "I hope you do."

She drew in a quick breath and closed the front door, then leaned against it for a long minute. Andrew Schilling had once been the star of her teenage fantasies, but she wasn't that girl anymore, and he wasn't that boy. They couldn't go back; the past was gone. Now she had the present to worry about—and there were some things she didn't want Andrew to ever find out about.

Thirteen

Opening the door that led from the kitchen into the basement, Jenna paused on the landing to flip on the light switch and then slowly descended. She'd been down here once before when she'd first rented the place to make sure there was no outside access. A few six-inch-long windows ran along one wall, but they were far too small to allow anyone to climb in. At the moment, she was looking for any clues to the owner to figure out why she and Lexie had been sent to this particular house.

"What are you doing?" Lexie asked from the doorway above.

"Just looking around. Careful," she added, as Lexie came down the stairs after her.

"This place is spooky," Lexie declared.

Jenna turned on a light, relieved to see some of the shadows disappear. Like Lexie, she was not a fan of spooky, especially after the last two months.

There wasn't much in the basement: a bureau, a

desk, two old lamps, and a large trunk that looked about a hundred years old, along with a water heater and some rusted lawn furniture.

"Whose stuff is this?" Lexie asked.

"I'm not sure," Jenna said. "It might have belonged to the woman who used to own this house. Her name was Rose Littleton."

"Rose. That's a pretty name," Lexie murmured, her tiny brows pulling into a frown. "Mommy talked about someone named Rose."

"She did?" Jenna was becoming more and more convinced that Angel's Bay had not been a random choice in which to relocate. "What did your mommy say about Rose?"

"I don't remember. Oh, wait, Rose is an angel," Lexie said, her face brightening.

Great.

"And she had an angel's kiss, just like me and Mommy."

Jenna stared at Lexie. "You mean Rose had the same mark on her heel as you and your mother? How would your mother know that?"

Lexie shrugged. "How come you don't have an angel's kiss?"

"I don't know." Jenna had never considered the birthmark on Kelly's heel anything special. She didn't think her mother had had one, but she honestly couldn't remember. Some days she could barely remember her mother's face. And most of her memories were a blur, a mix of her own thoughts and what people had told her about her mother. She wondered what Lexie would remember about Kelly twenty or thirty years from now. Probably not much.

Lexie moved over to the trunk. "What's in here?" She pulled on the lid, but it wouldn't budge.

Jenna yanked up on the handle and in a sputter of dust, the lid opened. She coughed and waved her hand in the air to dissipate the dust.

"Clothes," Lexie squealed, kneeling down next to the trunk. "We can play dress-up like me and Mommy used to play." She pulled out a dress that seemed to go on and on, a white dress with old, faded lace. "Is this an angel's dress?"

"No, honey, I think it's a wedding dress." That was odd, since Kara had told her that Rose had never married. Maybe the dress had belonged to Rose's sister.

Lexie dug deeper into the trunk, pulling out a veil, a pair of yellowed elbow-length gloves, a tarnished silver comb and brush. The pile grew higher and higher, capped off by a small leather-bound black journal. While Lexie put the veil on her head, Jenna opened the journal and sat down on the floor. The first page had an inscription.

"My dearest Rose," Jenna read aloud, *"for the times when you feel alone, know that you are not. If you listen to your heart, you will hear the whispers of those who have gone before you. You are an angel, and one day you will fly again. Love, Mother."*

"I told you she was an angel," Lexie said, sitting next to Jenna.

"Yes, you did," Jenna murmured as she turned the page.

"What else does it say?" Lexie asked.

The first diary entry was dated June 8, 1950. *"We buried Mitchell today,"* Jenna continued. *"Yesterday was supposed to be our wedding day, but instead I buried my fiancé in the hard, cold ground. I threw roses on his casket. I listened to Reverend Jacobs talk about Mitchell's life. I know he's gone, but I still can't believe it's true. I feel so alone. Mother and the girls have tried to make me feel better, but my heart is broken. I don't know how I can go on. How can I live without him? All of our dreams, all of our plans gone—just like that. When I came home, I sat at the piano and tried to play. Music has always been my comfort, but I can't even escape there now. Nothing will ever be the same again."*

Jenna looked at the wedding dress again. "I guess that was her dress."

"She never got to wear it," Lexie said. "That's sad. What else did she write?"

Jenna turned the page. The next date was a month later, July 14, 1950. *"I have been trying to pass the time since Mitchell's death by researching the shipwreck. I know that Mother and I share the same birthmark on our heel as Gabriella, the lost baby of the wreck. It appears that every first daughter descended from Gabriella shares the mark. Legend has it that an angel grabbed Gabriella from the swirling ocean waters by her foot and carried Gabriella to safety, laying her gently on the shore. The mark on her heel is the mark of her angel. But what the legend doesn't tell me is what happened to Gabriella's parents. Who were they? How did they die? How did a small baby come to be separated from her mother?*

"My mother says that every woman born with the mark has tried to find those answers, but no accounts from the wreck mention Gabriella's parents. In fact, most of the survivors swore they never saw the baby until the morning after the ship wrecked. How could that be, when they were on that ship for nearly two weeks? Was Gabriella an angel sent to earth to start over? Some people think so, but it seems like a fanciful thought. It's hard for me to believe in the angels anymore. I can't understand why God would take Mitchell so young. But I am trying to pass the time.

"I went to the library today and did some more research. I found an entry in a journal written by Samuel Martin, one of the sailors from the ship. He heard a terrible fight in the minutes before the ship crashed into the rocks, a gunshot, and a baby's cry. Unfortunately, none of the bodies that washed ashore had bullet wounds, so he can't be sure of what occurred. I think something happened on that ship before it went down, something that had to do with Gabriella's parents, my ancestors. But will we ever know?"

Jenna turned the page, expecting the story to continue. But there was a new date, two months later, September 9, 1950. *"A lot has happened since I last wrote. Mother became ill with a terrible fever. At night I would bathe her forehead with cool water and listen to her ramble about joining my father in heaven. I tried to make her fight, to stay with me and my sisters, but she got weaker, and last night she passed. We're all alone now. I have three younger sisters to raise, as well as the baby growing inside of me. How can I possibly do it all?"*

"She had a baby?" Lexie asked.

"It looks that way," Jenna said in surprise. She turned to the next page, dated March 10, 1951. *"I gave away my child today. I had only a few moments to hold her in my arms and say good-bye. The woman who took her assured me that my baby will be raised by a kind and loving family, who can give her everything I cannot. It was the most difficult decision I have ever made, but I don't have enough money to take care of my sisters and a baby. I hope one day I will find her again. I am comforted by the thought that I will know she is mine by the birthmark on her heel, the one that matches my own. No matter how far apart we'll be, we'll always be connected by the angel's kiss. I also tucked the locket that Mitchell gave me into her blanket, so she will have a piece of her parents with her forever. I hope she will forgive me for letting her go. Perhaps someday she will come back to me."*

Jenna flipped through the rest of the pages, but they were empty. She looked over at Lexie, realizing the little girl had gone unusually quiet, and there was a confused look on her face. "What's wrong, honey?"

"Mommy had a locket. It opened up, and she said she was going to put my picture in it. Do you think it was Rose's locket?"

"I don't know how it could have been," Jenna said slowly, not sure at all. If Rose had a birthmark and she gave away a daughter, who had the same mark as Kelly and Lexie . . .

Jenna went back to the passage in the journal, and the date suddenly jumped out at her. "Oh, my God," she whispered. Her mother, Crystal Bennett, had been born on March 10, 1951, the same date as the baby born to Rose. But Jenna had never heard that her mother was adopted. Had her mother known? Had Kelly?

Kelly must have known, must have traced their family tree back to Angel's Bay. That's why they'd been sent here to Rose's house—*to her grandmother's house.*

Her pulse tripled in time. It hardly seemed possible, but all the facts were pointing in one direction. Even if she could dismiss the dates as coincidence, Lexie's birthmark was undeniable.

Rose Littleton was her grandmother. And she and Lexie were connected to this town by the blood of their ancestors. Kelly had wanted to start over where she had a past, where their mother had been born, had been given away. A shiver ran down Jenna's spine at the connections. She could almost hear Rose's voice in her head, the sound of her sobs as she gave away her child. She could feel her desperate need to one day see her baby again.

But Rose hadn't seen her child, as far as Jenna knew. And Rose had died two years ago, probably before Kelly had made her plans to run. Yet somehow they'd ended up here.

Lexie stood up and sneezed, bringing Jenna back to the present.

"Can we go to the carnival now?" Lexie asked.

While Jenna was still caught up in the past, Lexie was already moving on, which was probably a good thing.

Jenna set the book down and stood up, knowing that she had to address something very important. "After what happened last night, Lexie, I think we should stay home."

Lexie's face fell. "I'll be good. I'll stay with you, and I'll call you Mommy. I promise," Lexie said with an earnestness that made Jenna feel like crying. "I won't forget. Kimmy said there's a bonfire on the beach tonight, and everyone roasts marshmallows. There are going to be fireworks, too. Please, we *have* to go."

"What about the angels?" Jenna asked. "Are you going to run off and look for them again?"

"They won't come during the fireworks, because it will be too loud," Lexie said with an authoritativeness that made Jenna smile.

"What about before or after the fireworks?"

Jenna could see the indecision in Lexie's eyes. "I won't look for them, but if they find me, I'm going to ask them about Mommy," she said stubbornly.

"Honey, it doesn't work that way."

"You don't know how it works. You're not in heaven, and you don't know anything about angels. If the angels are going to talk to anyone, it will be me, because I have the angel's kiss on my foot."

Jenna could hardly argue with that. "All right, but no angel hunting without me. Deal?"

"Deal," Lexie said happily, skipping away before Jenna could change her mind.

Jenna slowly followed. At the top of the stairs, she gave the basement a last look, then flipped off the light and shut the door. She'd come back later and look for more clues to the past. In the living room, the old piano called to her. She crossed the room and sat down at the bench, imagining another woman sitting on this very seat, her hands resting on the same keys. Jenna remembered Rose's words about turning to the piano for comfort. Music had played through their family for generations. She hadn't inherited the angel kiss birthmark, but she had inherited a gift for music.

Jenna rested her fingers lightly on the keys and, without conscious thought, began to play. She didn't know the tune, didn't know where the notes came from. When she stopped, she shivered. Turning her head quickly, she felt a slight breeze coming from somewhere, but the windows were closed. She had the oddest feeling that Rose had just played a song for her. That was crazy—Rose was dead. But as she got up and left the room, a tiny voice reminded her that many people believed music was the voice of the angels.

Jogging was Charlotte's stress reducer, but there were too many people out and about today and she didn't want to risk another encounter with Andrew, so she'd hopped on her bike instead. While she usually enjoyed chatting with her friends and neighbors, there were a lot of things she wasn't in the mood to gossip about today—like Annie's baby, Andrew's return, and her mother's eviction, all topics that were no doubt being discussed all over town.

She needed some time to herself to figure out how to deal with Andrew. Not that she intended to have any sort of relationship with him, but their paths would cross. Her mother expected her to go to church on Sundays, and if Andrew was moving into their house, she would no doubt have to deal with him about those issues.

Turning down one street, she headed for the next hill, feeling her thighs begin to burn, but it was a good pain, and one she knew how to fix. The pain from her youth had never healed, just scarred over her heart.

Seeing Andrew again had brought back a lot of memories, both good and bad, and she didn't particularly want to remember that time in her life. She'd moved on, and she was terribly afraid that Andrew would ask her questions she didn't want to answer. Mostly she was afraid that she'd start to feel something again for him, and that was the last thing she wanted.

She pedaled harder, her lungs straining as she reached the top of the last hill. She turned down the street, her pulse slowing as the street leveled out. She knew her mother would try to push her and Andrew together. She had already seen the wheels spinning in her mother's head at the thought of a potential marriage between her daughter and the new minister—as if history would repeat itself, that she would lead her mother's life. That was not going to happen. She didn't want that life for herself, nor did she want to be Andrew's wife anymore. Too much water under that bridge.

Pushing Andrew out of her head, she tried to appreciate the ride. Now that she was back, she was beginning to realize how much she'd missed this town: the crisp, clean air, the ocean views from just about every part of town, the smell of the sea, the sense of community. Like it or not, she was a local girl and always would be.

She was almost to the end of the street when a pickup truck passed her and turned into the driveway of the last house. She recognized Joe Silveira as soon as he got out of the truck. He wore faded jeans and a long-sleeve rugby shirt. Her stomach did a little flip. She was considering a quick U-turn, but she was too late. He saw her and waved.

She coasted down the street and stopped her bike in front of him. "Hi, Chief."

"Dr. Adams," he said with a smile. "I usually see you jogging. I didn't know you were a biker."

"I needed some hill work." She felt a little dazzled by his warm gaze. He had the darkest, sexiest eyes.

"I'm impressed. I get tired just driving up that hill."

"You must do more than drive. You're in good shape." She bit down on her lip. Great, give away the fact that she'd been checking out his body. That was completely inappropriate.

Joe didn't seem to mind. His smile broadened. "Thanks. So are you."

She cleared her throat, feeling a desperate need to change the subject. There was something about Joe Silveira that always made her feel off balance.

She was also wishing that she'd put on some lip gloss, maybe some blush, but instead she was sweaty, and heaven knew what her hair looked like sticking out from under her bike helmet, which she always wore since she'd done a stint in the ER.

"I brought Annie home with me—to my mother's house, that is," she said, uncomfortable with the silence between them. "She's going to stay there for a week or two until we can find a more permanent solution."

A gleam of surprise entered his eyes. "That's very generous of you and your mother."

"Annie is alone and in trouble. She needs help. I couldn't look the other way."

"A lot of people could."

She knew he was right; she'd met many cold, impersonal, burned-out health-care workers in the past. But she hoped never to become someone who didn't give a damn. "As my mother would tell you, I've always had the bad habit of wanting to take home strays. After two dogs and four cats, my mother put her foot down and insisted that I find other homes for the animals. I was a little surprised she agreed to let Annie stay there, but I took her up on it before she had a chance to change her mind."

"If I can help, let me know."

"I'll do that. So are you going to the bonfire tonight?"

"I'll be on duty later. What about you?"

"I'm not sure if I'll go." She shrugged. "I've seen it all before."

"I bet you have, but not for a while. Things change."

"Not in Angel's Bay," she said with a laugh. "I went into Dina's Café to grab a cup of coffee, and I swear that Rudy and Will were having the same argument about who caught the biggest fish that they've had every year of their lives."

"And I understand they're both terrible fishermen," Joe said with a grin. "So, how much farther are you riding today?"

"This was my last hill. I'm looking forward to going down on the way back."

"Sounds like a good time for a drink. Do you want to come in? You look thirsty."

"Well . . ." She hesitated, knowing that the right answer was no, but heard herself say, "Thanks, that would be nice."

She walked her bike to Joe's front door and leaned it against his porch railing, then took off her bike helmet and shook out her hair. It fell in tangles about her shoulders.

Joe opened the front door and a barking golden retriever raced out, jumping first on Joe, then on Charlotte.

"Rufus, down," Joe ordered, but the dog seemed far more interested in licking Charlotte's face with absolute joy and excitement.

"You're a honey," she said, leaning over to scratch the dog's head.

"Sorry," Joe said, grabbing Rufus by the collar.

"Don't be. I love dogs. Where did you get him?"

"He came with the house. Rufus was my uncle's

dog. The neighbors had him after my uncle died, and I didn't even know about him until two weeks ago, when he dug his way under the fence and came over. Since then he hasn't been inclined to leave. The neighbors are older and apparently quite happy that Rufus decided to move out, because the next thing I knew, there was a big bag of dog food on my porch."

"You don't look too unhappy about it," Charlotte commented. It was nice to see Joe relaxed and carefree. In the past, she'd only seen him on duty.

"I always wanted a dog when I was a kid, but my mother said she had enough to do raising six children. When Rufus came over, I couldn't send him back. I figured this was really more his home than mine."

"I understand."

"You would," he said, meeting her gaze. "Come on inside."

Charlotte entered the house, curious to see where Joe lived. The home was older, with probably two or three bedrooms. The living and dining rooms had hardwood floors and were sparsely furnished. From the living room, sliding glass doors opened onto a redwood deck.

"Water? Iced tea? Soda? Beer?" Joe asked. "What's your pleasure?"

"I should say water, but to tell you the truth, I'd love a cold beer."

"A woman after my own heart," he said with a grin. "Glass or bottle?"

"Bottle is great."

"I'll be right back. Just shove Rufus away if he gets too friendly." He let go of the dog's collar, but instead of running toward Charlotte, the dog followed Joe into the kitchen.

While Joe was getting the beers, Charlotte opened the sliding glass door and stepped out onto the deck. The view was incredible. She could see Ocean Avenue, the wharf area, and the wide blue ocean. There was no hint of fog on the horizon, just a few wispy white clouds in the summer sky.

Joe came out a moment later and handed her a beer. She took a swig, enjoying the cool slide of the liquid down her throat. Then she waved her hand at the view. "This is—wow."

"I know. I walked into this house, onto this deck, and I didn't want to leave." He set his beer down on the railing. "My uncle left me this place in his will, maybe because I was the only one of his nieces and nephews who came up here and went fishing with him. I think I was twelve at the time, and my mother was trying to get me out of the house for the summer. Uncle Carlos was a fishing fanatic. We spent three days on the water and caught more fish than I could count. I guess he figured I would appreciate the house and the town.

"Originally I came up here to put the house up for sale, but once I saw it, I knew I couldn't sell it. Suddenly I found myself walking into the police station, asking if they had any openings. Chief Robinson was just about to retire, so I was in the right place at the right time."

"To get the top job, you must have had some impressive credentials."

He leaned his forearms on the rail, looking out at the view. "I spent twelve years in the LAPD. I started there when I was twenty-three years old, right after I got out of the academy. I worked patrol, gangs, vice. I saw it all."

Judging by his tone, a lot of what he'd seen had been bad. "Angel's Bay must seem a little boring after Los Angeles," she ventured.

"No, it's perfect." He turned to look at her. "I was ready to leave L.A. In fact, I had quit my job the month before I got this house. I wasn't sure what I was going to do with my life; I just knew that things had to change. I was turning into someone I didn't recognize. I had to get out."

"Did something in particular happen?" He didn't answer right away, and she felt certain she'd overstepped her bounds. "It's none of my business. I shouldn't have asked."

Joe sighed. "I was arresting someone and he attacked me. I fought back. He was a sick bastard, and I wanted to kill him for what he'd done. My partner pulled me off. If he hadn't, I don't know how far I would have gone. I turned in my resignation the next day, thinking I would never be a cop again. But the weeks passed and my head began to clear. When I came to Angel's Bay, it was like the light inside of me went back on. I like it here. There isn't much crime, and what there is I enjoy handling. I loved being a cop; I just needed to be a cop somewhere away from

L.A. The people here are mostly good and they care about each other." He ran a hand through his hair. "Sorry, you asked?"

She was thrilled she'd asked and more than a little pleased that he'd confided in her. "No, I understand where you're coming from. Working in the medical center here allows me to get to know my patients, to be a part of a community, and I like that."

"I thought you weren't sure you were going to stay," he said with a quirk of his eyebrow. "Sounds like you're enjoying your job."

"I do like my job. I love a lot of things about this town, but my mother and I have a complicated relationship, and there are some parts of my past I'd like to forget. Since my past is here, that's not easy to do."

"You can't escape your past no matter where you go," Joe said. "Maybe it's time to stop running away and just face it."

"Says the man who just admitted to running away," she pointed out.

He inclined his head. "True, but I wasn't running away from the past. More like running away from a future of more of the same."

"Well, right now I'm just trying to help my mother deal with her life and my father's death." Charlotte paused, wanting to change the subject. "What was your uncle's name? I wonder if I knew him, if he came to our church."

"His name was Carlos Ramirez. He was my mother's brother. He believed that he was descended from a man named Juan Carlos Ramirez, who was allegedly on the ship when it went down a couple hundred years ago."

"That's interesting."

He shrugged. "What about you? No connections to the wreck?"

"No. My parents came here when my father was assigned to the church. They both grew up in San Diego and most of our relatives are still there. I thought my mother might consider moving back, but this town is her life. My father is buried in the cemetery here, so I suspect she'll stay forever." She took another long drink. "Do you really think this town will be enough for you long term? I can see needing a change, but permanently?"

He shot her a quick look. "You sound like my wife."

His wife—right. She'd almost forgotten.

"Rachel is convinced I will be bored in six months," Joe continued, "and that I'll want to return to L.A., but she's wrong. I feel at home here. This is a place I was looking for, only I didn't know I was looking until I got here—if that makes sense."

"You didn't know what you were missing until you found it. I get it."

"Yes," he said softly, his gaze on her face. "It's funny how you can think you have everything you ever wanted, only to find out you don't."

She had no idea what he was talking about now. She was far too distracted by the way he was looking at her, and far too aware of how close he was and how alone they were.

Then a door inside the house slammed, followed by a female voice. "Joe," the woman called. "Where are you?" A moment later she stepped out on the deck.

The woman was beautiful, with black hair, pale skin, dark eyes, and she was very, very thin. She looked like a very sophisticated model, dressed in a short black dress, her feet encased in stiletto heels. She frowned when she saw Charlotte.

"Rachel," Joe said. "I can't believe you're here."

"I can see that," she said sharply. "Are you going to introduce me to your—friend?"

"This is Charlotte Adams, Dr. Adams," he amended, clearing his throat. "This is my wife, Rachel."

"It's so nice to meet you." Charlotte extended her hand. Rachel gave it a brief shake, her expression cool.

"I thought you couldn't get away this weekend, Rachel," Joe said.

"It seemed important to you that I did," she replied. "But it looks like you're doing just fine without me."

"No, I'm not." Joe gave his wife a pointed look. "Charlotte just happened by. She was taking a bike ride, and we ran into each other."

"That's right, and I should be going. Thanks for the beer, and for your advice about Annie," Charlotte said, wanting to give him an excuse, since his wife was obviously upset about her presence.

"I'll walk you out," Joe offered.

"It's okay. I can find my way. I hope to see you again, Mrs. Silveira," she said. "Good-bye, Chief."

She moved quickly through the house, grabbed her helmet and bike, and headed down the street. She had a feeling Joe was going to be on the hot seat. Maybe he deserved to be, for looking at her the way he had. It was a good thing Rachel had come home. Joe was married, and she needed to remember that. Maybe he did, too.

FOURTEEN

"Nothing is going on," Joe told Rachel. Her eyes were smoking, and he felt absurdly pleased that she was jealous. He hadn't gotten such a strong reaction out of her in a long time.

"You're alone in the house with an attractive woman. That's not nothing."

"Charlotte is a doctor. She's treating a young woman who tried to commit suicide the other night. We're barely more than acquaintances."

"You looked like a lot more than acquaintances when I walked in."

"Come here," he said, holding out his hand.

Rachel ignored him, crossing her arms in front of her chest, and tapping her foot on the ground. "I should have stayed in L.A."

"Don't be like that. I'm glad you're here. Actually, I'm thrilled you're here," he amended. Now he had a chance to show her Angel's Bay at its best. The festival was in full swing; the town was hopping. It wouldn't look like the sleepy backwater she had in her head.

Since Rachel seemed to have no intention of moving, he walked over to her and put his arms around her, pulling her into his embrace. She smelled like Chanel, and for some reason the expensive scent bothered him. He shrugged it off. After a moment Rachel slid her arms around his waist and lifted her head to look at him.

"Did you really miss me?" she asked.

"A lot. I'm glad you came. What changed your mind?"

"You." She gazed at him with confusion in her eyes. "I don't know what to do about us, but I know we need to spend some time together to figure it out. So here I am."

"Here you are," he echoed, kissing her on the mouth.

She pulled away after one kiss. "Do you want to grab my suitcase for me? I have to make a call. I had to get a replacement for my open house tomorrow, and I want to make sure it's all set. I tried to call from the car, but I couldn't get reception."

"No problem."

Before he could move, Rufus came bounding out, and with his usual exuberance pounced on Rachel.

She gave a startled yelp, knocked Rufus sideways with her flailing arm and dropped her phone. Joe watched in dismay as her cell phone went skidding off the deck.

"Goddammit," she yelled as she ran to the rail.

He followed more slowly, knowing that it was

doubtful her phone would survive the twenty-foot drop down a rocky hillside.

"I need my phone." Anger blazed in her eyes as she turned to look at him. "My life is on that phone. Where the hell did this dog come from?"

Rufus laid down at her feet, hanging his head at her tone.

"He's Uncle Carlos's dog."

"He wasn't here before."

"The neighbors were taking care of him, but they aren't anymore."

"Why not?"

He cleared his throat, dreading the reaction he knew was coming. "Because I am."

"No. No way. We are not taking care of a dog."

"This was his home for the last seven years. He dug a hole under the fence to get back here. He's a good dog. Very friendly. You'll like him when you get to know him."

"I don't want to get to know him. I'm not an animal person."

"I'll take care of him. He won't bother you."

"He already cost me my phone."

"He was happy to see you. As happy as I am to see you."

Rachel frowned. "Don't try to be all sweet to me, Joe. You're not keeping that dog."

"Let's talk about it later. You know what you need? A glass of wine. You can change your clothes, get comfortable, and we'll watch the sun set. I don't have to go on duty until eight."

"You're working tonight?"

"The festival is on; it's a busy night. There's a big bonfire on the beach and fireworks. It will be fun. I'll introduce you to some people."

Rachel gave him an uncertain look, and for a moment he had the feeling she might head straight to her car and drive back to Los Angeles. He couldn't let her do that.

"Just give it a chance, Rachel. You've only spent a couple of weekends here, and you've never really met anyone."

"It's all so hokey, Joe. Bonfires, barbecues, carnivals—do you really like this?"

"I do." He met her gaze. "I know it's not fair to you. I know you think that I changed our lives without asking you, without caring about your feelings. I do care. I love you. I've loved you for a long time. But I was suffocating in L.A."

"This is such a drastic change. We could have moved out to one of the suburbs, the west side of town, Pacific Palisades, Beverly Hills, Malibu. Here, we're four hours away from everyone in our lives. And I have a career, Joe. I'm good at selling real estate. It took me a long time to find something I do well. Now you want me to throw it all away."

"There's real estate here, and new developments going up along the coastline just south of here. Vacation homes being built on the bluffs. You can be good here. And so can I."

She shook her head. "You always talk me into things."

It had been the other way around for most of

their life together, but since she was starting to smile, he decided not to press the point.

"Fine, I'll take a glass of wine, and your cell phone. I still need to make a call. And take this dog with you," she said.

"Come on, Rufus." Joe grabbed the reluctant dog by the collar. "Let's go inside." As he shut the deck door, he glanced down at the dog, who made him feel guilty as hell for dragging him inside. Rufus and he had been sharing the last few sunsets together. "It's going to be okay, buddy. She'll like you eventually. Rachel is a good woman, and we want her to stay. So you have to behave yourself."

Rufus gave a little bark.

"Exactly." Joe went into the kitchen, hoping he actually had a bottle of wine. Since Rachel's visits had been few and far between, he hadn't picked up her favorite bottle in a long time. He'd always preferred a cold beer . . . like Charlotte did.

He'd been a fool to invite Charlotte in for a drink, but he couldn't quite bring himself to regret it. Nothing had happened. Maybe there had been a brief moment when he'd felt like kissing her, but he hadn't acted on it, because he wasn't going to cheat on his wife. And Charlotte wasn't the kind of woman to get involved with a married man. So they'd just be friends. It would all work out.

Timothy Milton and James Holt were best friends and the infamous filmmakers of the Internet angel video. Reid had finally managed to get an interview courtesy of Henry Milton, who'd set up the meeting on his boat. Reid was far more interested in researching Jenna's past, but Henry's call had reminded him that he still had a story to write on the angels. He'd get that out of the way and then he could concentrate on Jenna's story.

"Can you tell me exactly what you saw that day?" Reid asked.

Timothy, a lanky boy with sandy blond hair and an earnest smile, nodded. "It was early in the morning, about five o'clock and still dark. We were heading out for a deep-sea fishing trip. When we came out of the harbor and around the bluff, there they were. It was the most incredible thing. There appeared to be two or maybe three angels, I'm not sure. But we could see their wings and their hair. One of them had long, golden blond hair. She was beautiful."

"What were they doing?"

"They were flying around the cliff. One seemed to have something in her hand, like a wand, and she looked like she was painting on the rock wall."

"It was my idea to take the video," James interjected. He was as dark as Timothy was blond, with intense eyes and a lot of energy. He tapped his foot as he spoke. "I knew people were going to go crazy when they saw it."

"How long did you watch the angels?"

"Only a couple of minutes, because one of them saw us," James replied. "She flew right at us. Then it seemed like there were a dozen of them, not just two or three. They smothered us with their wings. We couldn't see. We could barely breathe. When we finally got clear, we'd been blown a hundred yards away and everything was black again."

"That's quite a story. How come we don't see the angels flying toward you on the video?"

"It happened so fast, dude, I couldn't get it," James said. "I think I dropped the camera when they covered us with their wings."

"Lucky for you that it didn't break," Reid said. "So was there any evidence of this angel attack on your boat?"

"What do you mean?"

"You were smothered in wings. Seems like maybe some feathers would have come off?"

"Yeah, that would have been cool," James said. "But no, there weren't any feathers."

"You don't believe us, do you?" Timothy cut in. "You think we're making it up."

"A lot of people make up videos to gain Internet fame," Reid said, studying Timothy's face. The boy appeared to be sincere. His gaze moved to James, whose gaze wasn't nearly as easy to read.

"We didn't fake it," James said defensively. "It happened just the way we said."

"So what do you think the angels drew on the cliff?" Reid continued.

"A map," Timothy answered. "To the shipwreck."

"Everyone knows that ship went down with gold on it," James added. "The angels are trying to tell us where it is."

"Why now?" Reid asked. "It's been a hundred and fifty years."

"Because it's time," Henry interjected, coming on deck to join them. "Everything has a season."

"Why is it time now?" Reid repeated. "What changed?"

"Well, you're here, for one," Henry said.

"The angels came here before I did."

"But they got you here, didn't they?"

"Actually it was your grandson and his friend who got me here."

Henry shrugged. "Result is the same."

"I'm not a fortune hunter, or a shipwreck diver. If the angels are drawing a map to some long lost treasure, I won't be the one to find it," Reid said.

"I don't think it's a map. But I do think they're sending a message, and it's up to you to figure it out," Henry said. "You can't take things so literally. Sometimes you have to read between the lines."

Reid sat back on the bench, annoyed with Henry's riddle. "I'm a journalist. I report the facts and let the readers interpret them."

Henry grinned at him. "The teacher becomes the student. It happens to all of us at some point."

"Are we done? Because we have to go," James said abruptly. He stood up and hopped off the boat onto the dock, motioning for Timothy to follow.

"See you, Grandpa," Timothy said as he followed his friend.

"So you got your story," Henry said when they were alone.

"Yeah, I guess I did." He had photos of the two boys, their eyewitness account, and the video evidence. Unless the angels made an unexpected appearance by Monday, he would file his story and call it a day. "Not much of one, though," he added. "Do you believe them?"

"Timothy is a good boy. So is James. They saw something; I'd bet my life on that. As for your question, why now . . . I believe something occurred; something changed in this town. You just have to figure out what it was. What's new around here? What's different?"

"How would I know? I'm not from around here. Maybe you should answer your own questions."

Henry stroked his chin. "I've been thinking a lot about it, this weekend being the anniversary of the town's founding and all. That could be the reason. Or it could be something else."

"Just what I like—a definitive opinion."

Henry grinned. "I know you like your facts, but sometimes you have to follow your instincts."

"I've done that, and it got me into a lot of trouble."

"Was it your instincts that did that—or your ambition?"

Reid gave him a half smile. "Are you sure you're not a shrink, Henry? Every time I sit down with you, I feel like I'm getting therapy. You should put a couch on this boat."

"My granddaddy used to tell me that the best place to see your reflection is in someone else's eyes. That's the true mirror."

Reid looked at the old man, seeing encouragement in his eyes but nothing more. Was encouragement what he was supposed to see? The idea that someone believed in him, even if he didn't believe in himself?

"You'll figure it out," Henry said confidently. "You're a smart man." He started to cough, a deep hacking sound that seemed to come from his soul.

"Can I get you some water?" Reid asked, a little worried by Henry's sudden pallor.

"I'm—I'm all right," Henry said, clearing his throat. "Used to be a smoker. Even with the cough, I still miss it. My wife made me quit. She was dying, and I made the mistake of telling her I'd do whatever I could to make her happy. That woman always knew how to get me to do the right thing."

Reid stared at the old man, a question buzzing around in his head that he really should not ask, because it was ridiculous and there was no point. But somehow the words came out of his mouth anyway. "Did you ever see your wife—after she passed?"

Henry's eyes widened. "Now that's not what I was expecting you to ask." He let out a sigh. "Never did. Wanted to. Thing is, Mary and I, we had a lot of years together. We said our good-byes. We knew what was coming. We didn't have any unfinished business. Why do you ask?"

"No reason."

"You saw something when we were on the boat. I did, too—the shape of a woman. I didn't recognize her, but I'm betting you did," Henry said.

"That was a shadow passing in front of the sun."

"Who died, Mr. Tanner?"

Reid caught his breath. He didn't want to answer, but he knew Henry wouldn't let it go. "Someone I was very close to," he said slowly. "Her name was Allison. I've been trying to forget what happened to her for almost a year. I thought I was getting close, but then I came here. Now I keep seeing her in my head."

"Just in your head?"

"I thought I saw a woman who looked like her at Murray's Bar, but she disappeared before I could get across the room. I got into a fight."

"Heard you were rumbling with the Harlan boys," Henry said with a nod. "Figured a woman was involved."

"Well, this wasn't a real woman. Just an illusion fueled by too much tequila."

"You feel guilty about your friend's death?"

"It's not a matter of feeling. I am guilty. I'm the reason she's dead. And if she's back, then she's a ghost, not an angel. She's haunting me. Though what the hell is the difference anyway?"

"Some think that ghosts are spirits trapped between this world and the next, with unfinished business. Others believe that all who die go to heaven and become angels. Sometimes they come back because the people they love need something from them: a message, a sign, guidance." Henry shrugged. "Who's to say?"

"It's all a lot of nonsense," Reid said, knowing he

was trying to convince himself as much as he was the old man.

"If you thought that, you wouldn't still be talking to me."

"Well, I'm done," Reid said as he got to his feet. "Thanks for setting me up with your grandson."

"You're welcome. You know, Mr. Tanner, maybe the story you're meant to tell isn't the one you're chasing."

Reid had had the same thought. Maybe he was seeing Allison because she wanted him to make amends by saving another woman the way he couldn't save her.

Maybe that's what he wanted to do, too.

FIFTEEN

As Jenna walked into the town square with Lexie in the late afternoon, her connection to Rose Littleton made her view the town a little differently. If her suspicions were true about her mother being Rose Littleton's child, then Angel's Bay was where her grandmother had spent all of her life. It might have been where her mother would have lived if she hadn't been adopted.

It still bothered Jenna that she didn't know what her mother had known about her birth. But those answers would have to wait until they were free of Brad, until she had an opportunity to speak to her father and to other relatives who might be able to fill in the blanks. In the meantime . . .

She glanced around the square. A community quilting bee was in full swing. Five large frames had been set up with groups of women seated around the edges, working on various quilts. Lexie was called over to join a kid's table by one of her friends, while Jenna saw Kara Lynch waving her over.

She said hello, and the next thing she knew, someone was getting up and she was being urged to take the seat next to Kara's.

"I shouldn't be sitting here," Jenna said quickly. "I don't know how to quilt."

"So you'll learn." Kara handed her a needle and thread. "We'll start with the basics. See the little hole in the needle? Put the thread through there."

Jenna grinned. "Well, I know how to do that." Kelly had gone through an embroidery phase and had occasionally let Jenna hold the hoop and put some stitches in.

"Good," Kara said with a smile. "Do that, and then I'll show you the next step."

"I don't want to mess this up," Jenna said. "Aren't these quilts going to be on sale?"

"Yes, they are. Every year, in honor of the town's birthday, we remake the original quilt. We also make five other designs that are part of the Angel's Bay quilt line and sold all over the world."

"Which is why I need to give up my seat to someone who knows what they're doing." Jenna started to rise, but Kara put her hand on her arm and smiled.

"The quilting bee is about more than just making quilts. It's community and tradition. It's what connects us to each other, and to the past and the future."

Kara's words rang through Jenna's heart, reminding her of the link she'd never expected to find and which now seemed to appear wherever she went. Kara's family traced their family tree back to the shipwreck. How odd to think that Jenna's family tree might go back just as far, perhaps even to the central figure of the wreck, the baby Gabriella.

Jenna's gaze drifted to the center of the quilt, to the white fabric square symbolizing the baby's bonnet, to the angel wing design representing the baby's birthmark, the miracle of her survival. Had Kelly known the legend? Had she believed that somehow Angel's Bay would save her and Lexie as well? It was a fanciful thought, but one Jenna couldn't discount, now that she was starting to believe that her bloodline ran straight back to this town, to this quilt, to this pattern of connecting squares that linked all of the survivors together with one story—a story that had yet to be fully told.

"Are you all right, Jenna?" Kara asked. "You seem lost in thought."

"Just thinking about the history of this town. I always lived in a big city, where people didn't know their neighbors and didn't care. It's strange to think of how so many of you are tied to each other and to those who came before you, and how it's all represented here in this quilt." She fought back the urge to share her own personal link. She couldn't reveal her connection to Rose Littleton while she was living a lie.

Kara smiled at her. "I think you're getting hooked, Jenna. This quilt always works its magic on whoever sits down with it. It draws you into the world and won't let go. Don't be surprised if once you start quilting, you don't want to stop. Quilting gets in your blood."

"That's right, dear," an older woman on Jenna's other side said. "I remember when I first came to Angel's Bay forty-two years ago. I was twenty years old at the time. I'd never done a stitch in my life, but I fell in love with quilting." She gave Jenna a wrinkly smile. "I'm Dolores Cunningham."

"She fell in love with Preston Cunningham, too," an older woman from across the table interjected. "Dolores wanted to impress Preston's mother by making her a quilt. That's why she worked so hard to learn how to do it. I'm Margaret Hill, by the way. My friends call me Maggie."

"It worked, too," Dolores told Jenna. "Preston's mother didn't like me at first. She thought I was a big-city girl out to seduce her son. I won her over with that quilt. I convinced her I was planning to stay, and that I'd fit in perfectly with the family. Preston asked me to marry him the next day, and I said yes."

"But she divorced him three years later," Maggie put in. "You always leave that out, Dolores."

"True, but I still love quilting," Dolores said with a laugh. She gave Jenna a mischievous smile. "Men come and go. Quilts are forever. That's what I always say."

As Jenna listened to the two older women chat, she wondered if they'd known Rose Littleton, if they'd been friends with her grandmother. She wanted to ask them questions, wanted to know everything. But if she started talking about Rose being her grandmother, she'd draw too much attention to herself.

Jenna focused her attention back on the needle in her hand. She finished threading it and then held it up, feeling a very minor triumph. "You're not going to actually make me do something with this now, are you, Kara?"

"Yes, you're going to hand stitch the back and front of the quilt together."

Jenna gave her a dubious look. "Sure I am."

Kara laughed. "It's easy. You just put the needle through here, then pull it up again, like so," she said, demonstrating. "Now you try it."

Jenna did as Kara instructed, pleased when the stitches began to take shape in an even manner. Maybe she could do this. She concentrated hard with each insertion of the needle, praying that she wouldn't screw up.

"Don't worry so much," Kara said with a laugh. "Good grief. You're holding the needle so tightly your hand is turning white."

Jenna lifted her gaze to Kara's. "This is way out of my comfort zone."

"That's a good thing. Quilts aren't about perfection," Kara said. "They're made with love."

"But these will be sold. The customers expect perfection, or they'll want their money back."

"Hand stitching is never perfect. It's human. Maybe that sounds silly and old-fashioned, but my grandmother taught me that each stitch is a personal mark, a piece of history passed along from one generation to the next. People who buy handmade quilts enjoy knowing that they were made in a personal way by humans, not machines."

Jenna couldn't quite grasp the idea that perfection wasn't important. Perfection had been the goal she'd strived for her entire life. She'd spent ten hours a day practicing the piano in her quest to be perfect. And it wasn't just her own expectations she'd had to meet, but those of her father, and her teachers, and later the audience and the reviewers. The concept of imperfection being acceptable seemed completely wrong. But she did relax her fingers as she pulled the needle through the fabric.

"That's better," Kara encouraged.

"Thanks. You're a patient teacher," Jenna said. "I suspect you'll be a great mother."

A pleased light entered Kara's eyes. "I hope so. I had a little scare last night, and it made me realize again how very, very much I want this baby to be born healthy." She put a hand to her abdomen and gave a caressing stroke.

"Is everything okay?" Jenna asked with concern.

"Charlotte—Dr. Adams said I'm fine. The baby is the right size, the heartbeat is strong and steady, so it's all good. It was probably just a cramp." Kara paused, her expression contemplative. "Do you ever get the feeling when things are really good that something bad is about to happen, because you're just not that lucky?"

"I think it's normal to be nervous when you're pregnant," Jenna answered.

"Were you nervous when you had Lexie?"

Jenna hated lying to Kara; the people in Angel's Bay were so nice, so generous with their friendship. "I think we always worry about our kids being all right, even if they're in the womb. Are you sure I'm doing this right?" Jenna asked, pointing to her stitches.

"Yes, that's exactly right. And thanks for the reassurance. I hate sounding so paranoid. I've had this weird feeling lately. It's silly. I don't know how Colin puts up with me, but he's been great. He's an incredible man. I know he'll be a wonderful father." She shook her head with a little laugh. "So my nerves are probably just hormones, right?"

"Probably," Jenna agreed, but as she gazed around the square, she couldn't shake her own bad feelings. There were so many strangers in town. If someone was watching her, she wouldn't have any idea. Then again, there was safety in numbers. No one could hurt her or Lexie here in the middle of a quilting bee. It was when she was home alone that she really had to worry.

She knew that Reid was right about not being able to stay hidden forever. Sooner or later Brad would find them, and she had to be prepared to fight him. It wouldn't be easy, because he was Lexie's father. In the eyes of the law, Brad was an innocent man, a victim of a horrible crime. She could end up not only as a kidnapper, but also a murder suspect. Brad could paint a picture of sisterly rivalry. He could claim she came into the house and killed Kelly.

And how could she refute his accusations? She knew so little about her sister's life. She needed to know a lot more, and with Reid's help, she hoped, she'd find the ammunition she needed. Then she could go on the attack.

Reid stared at the computer screen. The image of Kelly Winters gazed back at him, and he felt as if he was looking at Lexie. Mother and daughter shared a striking resemblance, something Jenna should have considered when she'd run. She could have dyed Lexie's hair brown; that might have helped. Then he remembered Lexie proudly stating that she looked just like her mommy, and he suspected that Jenna hadn't been able to take that away from the little girl.

He'd gone through the online archives of every newspaper and media outlet that had covered the death of Kelly Winters, wife of police officer Bradley Winters, and he now had a few more facts. On Friday, April 12, at four o'clock in the afternoon, Brad Winters had come home from work to find his house ransacked and his wife dead on the kitchen floor. She'd been stabbed repeatedly. According to Brad, his daughter, Caroline, had gone to spend the weekend with a relative in Maine and, thankfully, had not been home at the time of the attack.

So Lexie was really Caroline. And Jenna was Juliette Harrison, a renowned pianist who had played with every major orchestra in the world. Her father, Damien Harrison, was a famous conductor. The two were supposedly residing in London at the time of the attack, although several papers alleged that Juliette was in rehab after a drug overdose had made her collapse onstage before a concert in Vienna.

That gave him pause. Jenna certainly hadn't mentioned a drug addiction, although she had glossed over some sort of mini-crisis. Still, drugs didn't ring true. There had to be another explanation.

Turning his attention away from Jenna, he focused on Brad Winters. He'd found several photos of Brad, including one taken about three weeks before the murder. Brad had been hailed as a hero by a local woman he'd saved from a carjacking while off duty. Although Brad's face was partially covered by the hand he'd put up to ward off photographers, Reid could see that Brad Winters was a big man with a strong, sturdy build, a square face, military haircut, and a serious expression. More important, he was a hero. No wonder Kelly didn't think anyone would believe he was beating his wife. But was that all that had been going on?

Reid had searched for biographical information on Brad Winters but came up with only limited facts. It didn't appear that anyone knew much about him before he'd joined the police force. The thing that puzzled him the most was why Brad hadn't raised the alarm that Lexie was missing. He knew she wasn't with relatives. If he was the killer, there was no other intruder. So why not report Lexie's absence? The only answer Reid could come up with was that Brad didn't want anyone to find Lexie.

Either Brad knew that Lexie was with Jenna, or he knew that Lexie had witnessed her mother's murder and he didn't want her to be interrogated. Or maybe it was both.

Reid picked up his phone and called Pete. It was risky, but he knew he could trust Pete. And he needed a middleman to get some information for him.

"McAvoy," Pete answered. "You better tell me you have the story done, Reid."

"Almost. I just finished an interview with our young filmmakers."

"Good. Finally some progress. Is that it?"

"No, I need a favor."

Pete gave a heavy sigh. "I already did you a favor. I got you a paying gig."

"I need information on a Massachusetts cop by the name of Bradley Winters and a murder investigation that took place at his home a little over two months ago. The wife, Kelly Winters, was killed during an alleged home burglary."

"What are you looking for?"

"Whatever you can get. I was thinking you might ask Stan," Reid said, referring to a PI he and Pete had both used over the years. "But you can't tell him it's for me."

"Murder, Reid? I think I liked it better when you were retired from hard news."

"You're the one who's been telling me to get back into the game," Reid reminded him.

"Why can't you call Stan yourself?"

"I don't want the inquiry traced to me."

"I'll see what I can do," Pete said. "But Stan's money is coming out of your paycheck. This doesn't involve a female, does it?"

"Two of them."

"Great. Double trouble. I should have known."

"I've got everything under control," Reid said.

"I've heard that before."

"Just get me the info. Oh, and I need it yesterday."

"Of course you do. I'll trade you the info for my angel article."

"You'll get your angels, don't worry." Reid hung up the phone, far more interested in a devil by the name of Brad Winters.

"This property is fantastic," Rachel said to Joe as she stepped out of the car.

"It's a burned down house," Joe said, unable to share her enthusiasm. He followed her along an overgrown path. He'd taken Rachel for a drive along the coast to show her the new developments going up, to whet her appetite for the Angel's Bay real estate market. He hadn't intended to show her the Ramsay property, but she'd seen the structure and insisted on seeing the house—what was left of it.

"Look at the view," Rachel said, with the most excitement he'd heard in her voice in years. "Imagine the possibilities. You know what else . . ." She turned to him with a light in her eyes. "This is a perfect film location. Mark would love this."

"Who's Mark?"

"He's a movie producer I know. He's looking for some coastal property to use in one of those slasher/horror films."

"Where did you meet this guy?" Joe asked.

She gave a breezy wave of her hand. "I sold him his house last year. He's friends with Aidan, my mixed doubles partner."

"I don't think I've met Aidan."

"Oh, right. He might have joined the club after you moved."

Joe noticed that Rachel didn't say "*we* moved." It was clear she still hadn't accepted the fact that her husband and her marriage were four hours north of Los Angeles. But they were getting along at the moment, and he didn't feel like rocking the boat.

"What happened to this place anyway?" she asked.

"Arson—about six months ago. The property is allegedly haunted. There was a dead body found in the basement about fourteen years ago. Since then, every time someone attempts to remodel the house or build an addition, something happens."

"That's quite a story," Rachel said. "I guess every small town has its haunted house. What else do you have to show me?"

"This was the last house for today. I have to go to work. You should come to the beach tonight."

"And sit by myself while you patrol?" she asked. "That doesn't sound like fun."

"You won't be alone. I'll introduce you around.

Everyone is very friendly and they're all dying to meet you."

"I can't imagine what I'd talk about with anyone up here."

He smiled at her baffled expression. "Rachel, this isn't Mars. The people here aren't that different from those four hours south. Although I must admit, sometimes L.A. does feel like another planet."

"Joe—why did you ask me to come this weekend if you were going to be working all night?"

"I'll be home by midnight. We'll have all day tomorrow. We can sleep in." He moved closer to her and slid his arms around her. "We can spend the day in bed. It's been a while. I've missed you."

"I've missed you, too," she admitted.

He was surprised by her words. "You did?"

"Joe, I love you. But you're turning into someone I don't know."

"Get to know me again."

"What about me? Are you willing to get to know me? Because I've changed, too, in case you hadn't noticed."

"Of course I've noticed."

"And you don't like what you see, do you?"

That was a loaded question. "I want you to be happy," he said carefully. "Your career makes you happy; I understand that. But you can do that job here. Maybe I'm being unreasonable, expecting you to uproot your life for me. But I've made compromises, too. I moved into the house your parents bought us, even though it went against the grain."

"It was a generous present, and you should have been grateful that my parents had the means to provide that for us."

"I was grateful. I'm sorry. I don't want to talk about that again." He kissed her on the lips, but she broke away. "What's wrong?"

Her eyes flickered with indecision. Then she said, "Don't you wonder if there's a reason we never got pregnant?"

"What are you talking about?" he asked warily.

"Maybe we weren't supposed to have kids or stay together."

A wave of fear swept through him. He didn't want her to cross the line they'd both been careful not to step over. He didn't want her to say something she couldn't take back, or something he wouldn't be able to fight.

"No, there is no reason. We're supposed to stay together," he said finally. "I've loved you since I was fifteen."

She gave him a sad smile. "But I'm not that fifteen-year-old girl, and you're not that fifteen-year-old boy. I'm really scared that we've outgrown each other."

"If you believed that, you wouldn't be here." He hoped that was true.

"I'm here because I guess I'm not ready to give up."

Relief flooded through him. "Me, either." He

wanted to kiss her again, but he didn't want to taste the coldness on her lips so soon.

"Okay, then." She took a deep breath and let it out. "I guess I'll come to the festival and meet your friends. We'll be a couple again."

He wanted to believe that she was still with him. But despite her words, it felt very much like she was slipping away.

Sixteen

Charlotte could have been walking with a celebrity, for all the attention they were getting. She took Annie's hand in hers, sensing that the girl wanted to flee. In the few short blocks they'd walked, they'd drawn countless stares, and people weren't even pretending not to talk about them as they passed.

"It's better to just get it over with," Charlotte advised. "Once everyone sees that you're all right, they'll focus on someone else."

"I don't think they're gossiping about whether I'm all right. They want to know who my baby's father is."

It was the first time Annie had mentioned the father, and Charlotte took the opening. "Do you want to tell me about him?"

Annie shook her head. "I can't tell anyone who he is."

"I know you said that he didn't hurt you, that he didn't force you, but if he's holding something over you, he doesn't have any right to do that."

"He's a good person. He cared about me. At least I think he did," Annie said slowly. "I don't want to get him in trouble."

"He knows you're pregnant, doesn't he?"

Annie stopped abruptly. "I want to go back to your mother's house."

"Annie, you have to tell him. This man is responsible for that baby, too. You shouldn't have to shoulder the entire burden. He should at least give you financial support. If he's a good person, maybe you're selling him short. Maybe he'd want to help you." Even as Charlotte said the words, she felt like a traitor. She'd been in Annie's position once, and she hadn't done any of the things she'd just suggested. "I'm sorry," she said immediately. "I shouldn't be telling you what to do. You're an adult. It's your baby and your life. I just want to help."

"I appreciate your help. I just can't tell you about him."

"All right. I'll walk back to the house with you. I just thought you could use a break from my mother."

"I like your mother, but she's very sad, isn't she? She was crying in her room earlier."

Charlotte had never seen her mother cry, although she'd heard some sobs in the deep quiet of the night. Her mother didn't like to show emotion in front of her children, or even her friends. "She loved my father very much."

Annie nodded. "She told me how they met at the ice skating rink. She said she pretended not to know how to skate, so he'd have to hold her hand." Annie smiled. "But then she found out that he didn't know how to skate, either, and they fell down together, all tangled up on the ice. When she looked into his eyes, she knew at that moment that she would marry him. And she never ever told him that she knew how to skate, not in all the years that they were together."

Charlotte stared at Annie in amazement. Her mother had never told her the ice skating story—had she? Or had she just not been paying attention? She'd learned how to tune out her mother's criticism; maybe she'd missed other things along the way.

"You don't have to come with me," Annie said. "I know the way back. You go to the bonfire. I'll be fine."

As Annie turned around, Charlotte hesitated, wondering if *she* had it in her to go to the bonfire. But Annie was already halfway down the block. She might as well check out the bonfire. As she started down the path toward the beach, the last of the sun disappeared over the horizon. The air had chilled, and she drew her jacket more closely around her. When she reached the beach, she slipped off her shoes, and walked barefoot across the sand toward the group gathered by the fire that was just beginning to catch flame.

The first few sparks took her back in time, to another place, another beach. There had been a fire that night, too . . .

Joey had snuck two bottles of vodka out of his father's liquor cabinet. Marcia had snatched a bottle of tequila, and Ronny had gotten his older brother to buy three six-

packs of beer. It was the end of the school year, the beginning of summer, and the small fire on the beach was surrounded by teenagers. They'd built the blaze on a secluded beach a few miles out of town, hoping that no one would see them.

"Charlie, take a shot," her friend Beth said, handing her a shot glass of tequila. "Come on, live a little. We're going to be seniors next year."

Charlotte glanced across the flames of the fire, seeing Andrew Schilling talking to Pamela Baines—Pamela with the big breasts and the long legs and the cocky smile. Charlotte hated her. But mostly she hated her because Andrew seemed to like her so much. Andrew was supposed to be her boyfriend. He was supposed to love her. They'd had sex the week before—her first time ever. But maybe she'd done something wrong, because now Andrew was avoiding her.

She took the shot glass from Beth and downed the tequila. It burned her throat, and she coughed. Beth laughed at her and poured another shot. She knew she should stop; her mother would be so disappointed in her. But what did it matter? Her parents would hate her more if they knew she'd had sex. She wasn't the good girl anymore, so she might as well go all the way bad.

One shot followed another, until she lost track. Propelled by anger and tequila, she decided to have it out with Andrew. She stumbled across the beach toward him, almost falling into the fire at one point. Someone pulled her back—Shane Murray. He gave her a scornful look then moved on. But she didn't care what he thought. She just needed to find out why Andrew didn't like her anymore.

Andrew had his arm around Pamela now. "Andrew," she said. "Can I talk to you?"

"What are you doing, Charlie? You're drunk."

"So what? Come with me. We have to talk."

"I'm busy. You should go home. Get Teri to take you. She's leaving soon, and she hasn't been drinking."

"I don't want to go home with Teri. I want to talk to you."

"He can't talk to you right now, because we're going skinny dipping," Pamela interrupted. She stepped away from Andrew and pulled off her shirt, revealing full breasts supported by a hot pink bra. Charlotte's jaw dropped. No wonder Andrew wanted Pamela. She was a woman.

Pamela grabbed Andrew's hand and they ran toward the water, stripping off their clothes along the way. The other kids followed suit, until there was nothing but clothes on the beach and naked teenagers in the water.

Tears burned Charlotte's eyes. She looked for Beth but couldn't find her. She must be in the water, too. Teri wasn't around, either. Charlotte was all alone, looking like a stupid idiot. She felt like crying, but she couldn't make herself look like a bigger fool. Her stomach churned. She thought she was going to throw up. She ran down the sand, through the trees, toward the parking lot. She saw some headlights go on. Maybe Teri hadn't left yet. Maybe she could get a ride home. And then a hand came out of nowhere . . .

"Charlotte," Andrew said, his voice shocking her back to the present.

She blinked in confusion.

"Are you all right?" he asked with concern in his eyes.

"I'm—fine," she said.

"You looked like you were a million miles away."

"Not quite that far."

His gaze settled on her face and she saw something that looked like regret.

"You were remembering that night on Refuge Beach, weren't you?" he murmured.

"The one where you and Pamela Baines stripped down and went into the water? Yes, I was."

"Not my proudest moment," he admitted.

"It was a long time ago." She shrugged, hoping he would leave it at that, but of course he didn't.

"You wouldn't talk to me after that night. I wanted to apologize for the way I'd acted, but you wouldn't take my calls."

"It was just one call, Andrew. You didn't try all that hard to reach me." She knew; she'd waited by the phone. She hadn't called him back after the first time because she'd wanted to make him sorry, assuming he'd call again. She'd assumed wrong.

"I was a stupid kid, Charlie. I made mistakes."

"So did I. I never should have slept with you. Or rather, had sex in the backseat of your car."

Andrew cast a quick look over his shoulder. "Let's not talk about that here."

"Don't want to ruin your reputation?"

"Or yours," he said pointedly. "You know, I didn't intend to get into all this tonight. I thought we'd say hello and talk about the festival."

That would have been a far better way to go. "You're right. This isn't the time or the place." She turned to leave, but he fell into step alongside her.

"I did love you, Charlotte," he said.

His words shocked her. She stopped abruptly. "How can you say that? Why the hell would you lie to me now?"

He looked taken aback by her reply. "I'm not lying. You scared me back then. I didn't know how to deal with what I was feeling. I didn't want to be in love. I was too young."

"I was young, too. Did you think I knew how to handle what I was feeling?"

"You wanted more than I could give."

"You didn't want to give anything," she returned. "And how could you know what I wanted, when I didn't even know myself?"

"I messed up," he said quietly. "I screwed things up with you when I hooked up with Pamela. I know you must have heard what happened between us, because you couldn't look at me after that night."

She couldn't look at him now. Not just because of what he and Pamela had done, but because of what she'd done. "Let's just forget it, Andrew."

"I'd like to start over, Charlie. We were friends once."

"You're probably a big believer in that whole 'turn the other cheek' thing, but I'm not so much. You hurt me, and even though it was a long time ago, I haven't forgotten."

"You can still forgive me."

She sighed. "Fine. It's forgiven and forgotten. Are you happy now, Reverend?"

He smiled at her tone. "You always hated being wrong."

"I'm not wrong."

"And you always hated being told what to do." He put up a hand as she opened her mouth to protest. "Let's change topics. I'm really sorry about your dad's passing. He was a good man. I won't come close to filling his shoes."

She gave him a thoughtful look. "Why did you become a minister, Andrew? I don't even remember you liking church. You snuck out with me a few times."

"I actually enjoyed the services, but I didn't think it was cool to admit that, especially to you." He paused. "When I left here to go to college, I let go of a lot of my values—went a little crazy, in fact. I finally woke up one day and wasn't proud of the life I was living. I started going to church and I got on track again, and realized that being a minister was what I really wanted to do with my life."

"And your path led you back here," Charlotte said.

"You came back, too," he reminded her. "Looks like we have a second chance, Charlie."

Her heart skipped a beat at the look in his eyes. Andrew couldn't possibly want her now, after all these years. But even if he did, did she want him? No other man had ever touched her in quite the same way. But still . . .

It was too much, too soon. "I have to go," she said abruptly. "I'm sure I'll see you around town."

"At least you didn't say no," he called after her.

She hadn't said yes, either, but she knew someday soon, she would have to come up with an answer. If not for him, then for herself.

The first person Joe saw on the beach was Charlotte—but then, she seemed to be the first person he saw anytime there was a crowd. She seemed to be having a heated conversation with the new minister. Joe knew that Andrew Schilling had grown up in Angel's Bay; he just hadn't known there was a relationship between Andrew and Charlotte. He frowned at the thought.

"Joe." Rachel tugged on his hand. "What are you looking at?"

"Nothing. Sorry." He smiled at her. He'd gotten her to the beach; now he had to make sure she had a good time while he was working. He perused the crowd, relieved when he saw Kara Lynch. Kara was in real estate and knew a ton of people. She was the perfect woman to help introduce his wife around town.

"This is *so* not my scene," Rachel said. "I'm used to Malibu and beach clubs, where people serve me champagne and don't kick up sand," she said as a group of kids ran by.

"We used to go to Manhattan Beach, where you watched me surf," he reminded her. "There was no champagne back then."

"In those days I just liked seeing you with no shirt on," she said, a small smile playing at the corner of her mouth.

"And I enjoyed seeing you in a bikini. Maybe we should come down here tomorrow and re-create the old days."

"We'll see. Too much sun can add years to the skin."

"Well, we don't want that. Come meet some of my friends. Kara," he said as they drew near. "I'd like you to meet my wife. Rachel, this is Kara Lynch."

"Rachel, it's so wonderful to meet you," Kara said with genuine warmth. "Joe has talked a lot about you."

"Hello," Rachel said, shaking Kara's hand.

"Kara is married to Colin Lynch, one of my officers," Joe added. "And we owe them a couple of barbecues."

"Well, you're the barbecue king," Rachel said.

"Joe tells me you're in real estate," Kara said. "I work at a local real estate office here in Angel's Bay. We could always use another salesperson."

"Really?" Rachel's eyes lit up. "What kind of property do you list? Joe showed me some of the new developments going up. Are those being handled by your office?"

"Some of them. There are two offices in town, and with the new developments, we're both getting a lot more business."

Joe let out a sigh of relief as Kara and Rachel discussed the real estate market. One problem solved.

He glanced around the crowd, wondering where Charlotte and her friend had gone. They were nowhere in sight. He didn't know if that was a good thing or a bad thing. The only thing he did know was that he really shouldn't care.

Turning his head the other direction, he saw Jenna Davies sitting on a blanket. Some distance away, Reid Tanner appeared to be watching Jenna. Joe's gaze narrowed. He knew a reporter of Reid Tanner's caliber was interested in more than angels. He also knew that Jenna Davies acted like a woman with something to hide. Put the two together, and it was all very interesting.

Maybe he needed to find out more about both of them.

SEVENTEEN

Reid hadn't felt so eager to see someone in ages. That sense of anticipation disturbed him, made him pause. He felt almost optimistic, and that wasn't a feeling he knew how to handle. For eleven months he'd wanted to check out of his life, but tonight he found himself looking forward instead of back. He wanted to think of Jenna as only a story, but he couldn't forget the way she tasted, the feel of her breasts in his hands, the softness of her body under his. He'd had to take a long, cold shower after she left his hotel room. He was involved with her, whether he liked it or not—whether *she* liked it or not. And he was worried that the real problem was that he liked it too much.

Jenna wore her long hair down tonight. It was dark and tangled from the ocean breeze, and he imagined himself running his fingers through it, cupping her face with his hands, staring into those big, beautiful, haunted blue eyes, sliding his mouth against hers, taking them both to another place. He wanted to chase the loneliness and fear out of her eyes, to see her smile, hear the catch of her breath when his lips touched hers. He wanted to unleash the passion she kept so rigidly under control while pretending to be an ordinary suburban mom.

Jenna had gotten into his head, under his skin. She'd woken him up, and there was no going back. So he walked across the sand and took a seat next to her on the blanket.

Jenna gave him a wary smile. "Took you long enough. You've been watching me for a while. Second thoughts?"

"A few," he admitted.

"Lexie and I are not your problem. You can still walk away if you want to."

Her offer only reminded him of how generous she was. Terrified, in danger, and completely on her own, she was still offering him a way out. "I don't want to. I'm in."

Jenna brought her knees up to her chest and wrapped her arms around them. She wore faded blue jeans, a knit shirt that clung to her curves, and a soft sweater. Her feet were bare, and Reid smiled at the red polish on her toenails. He had a feeling he was catching another glimpse of the real Jenna. She must have caught him looking, because she quickly dug her toes into the nearby sand.

"Don't worry. The red polish won't give you away—Juliette." He deliberately used her real name.

"Shh," she said quickly, looking around to be sure no one was eavesdropping.

"Relax. No one can hear us." Lexie was playing tag several yards away with her friends. "You seem more like a Jenna to me," he mused.

"I'm starting to feel like a Jenna. Juliette fit the old me—classical, romantic, a little removed from mundane reality. But that's certainly not my life anymore. How did you find out my name?"

"The Internet. It wasn't difficult once you gave me Brad and Kelly's names." He spoke quietly. They were separated from the crowd, but he didn't want his words to carry. "The facts you have correlate with the police reports. It still surprises me that Brad has managed to keep Lexie's whereabouts a secret. He must be concerned about keeping up the pretense indefinitely. He has friends, neighbors, people who will begin to question where his daughter is."

"He put his house up for sale," Jenna said. "My contact keeps me up to date on his movements."

"That would certainly eliminate questions from the neighbors."

"Maybe that's the reason he did it, but it bothers me. He's putting some plan into motion, and we would be safer if I knew what it was."

Reid didn't tell her not to worry. Her brother-in-law was a dangerous man, and Jenna needed to feel the danger. She couldn't relax and let down her guard. She had too much on the line.

"I have some things to tell you," he said briskly.

Her mouth curved down as she sighed. "Am I going to like them?"

"No."

"You're always so honest. Don't you know there is nothing wrong with a little sugar-coating?"

"There is when your life is at stake."

She turned to face him. "Okay. Go ahead."

Reid pulled out the email Pete had sent him. Dusk was turning to night, but there was enough light left for Jenna to see the photo. "Do you recognize this guy?"

Jenna stared at the picture for a long minute. "I don't think so. Should I?"

"His name is Brad Winters."

"That's not the man my sister was married to."

"I know. But he has the same Social Security number, went to the same school, and worked at the same places that Brad claimed on his application to the police academy."

"I don't understand, Reid."

"Your Brad stole this guy's identity," he said bluntly.

Her eyes widened in disbelief. "That can't be true. Brad Winters is a common name. This has to be a mistake."

"It's not. I asked a PI friend of mine to do a rush background check on your brother-in-law." He took out the other image he'd printed, the one of her brother-in-law and the carjacking story. In the photo, Brad had put a hand up over his face. Now Reid knew why: he'd been trying to avoid getting his picture in the newspaper. "This photo was taken about three weeks before Kelly died. Your brother-in-law was a local hero."

"Kelly never told me about this," she said, taking the paper from his hand.

"But your sister *did* tell you that someone had recently come to her with information about Brad."

"I don't see the connection."

"The timing fits with when this article appeared. There is a possibility that this newspaper photo tipped someone off. They recognized your brother-in-law, and knew he wasn't Brad Winters."

"So who is he?"

"I don't know yet."

"This just gets worse and worse." Jenna's gaze moved toward Lexie, who was making a sand castle with her friend. "He's her father, Reid. What am I ever going to tell her? How will I make this right for her?"

He heard the anguish in her voice and knew that there was no way to make it right. "You'll help her deal with the truth when it's time."

"I can't allow Lexie to go back to him, Reid. I have to find a way to prove that Brad murdered Kelly." Her chin came up.

Jenna was a fighter. Her determination was probably what had gotten her to the top of the classical music world. Even though she'd collapsed under that pressure, it just made her more human, more likeable. Because while she'd fallen, she'd also gotten up again—and maybe that was all that mattered. Maybe that's what he was supposed to do. Get back up and fight, instead of letting the weight of his guilt keep him down.

"Lexie will never be able to handle the fact that

her father killed her mother," Jenna continued. "She'll always be scarred."

"What have you told her so far?"

"That her father is sick and needs to get help, and he has to be by himself to do that. Kelly must have prepared Lexie for an escape, because she knew that she was going to be called Lexie and that her mom was going to be Jenna." She blinked away the moisture in her eyes. "Kelly was supposed to be Jenna, not me. I don't know why she picked the name. But using it makes me feel close to her, like it's a bridge between us. It's as if both of us died, and we became one person—Jenna. Does that sound crazy?"

"No, it doesn't. I think your sister would be very proud of you."

"I hope so. Is there any way that Brad will find out your detective is checking up on him, and that he'll be able to trace your inquiry back here?"

"I used a middleman. I covered my tracks, Jenna."

She nodded, relieved. "So if Brad isn't really Brad, then who is he?"

Reid shrugged. "Someone who wanted to escape from his past."

"What about the real Brad Winters? If Kelly's Brad was using someone else's Social Security number, then wouldn't the other guy have found out at some point in the last eight to ten years?"

"I'm hoping to get more information, but there's a good chance that he's not alive."

Her face paled. "You think that Brad didn't just steal this man's life—he took it?"

"I could be wrong."

"Or you're not. Kelly must have found out. That's why she started making an escape plan."

"It's possible that the other Brad isn't dead, that he was the one who showed up and told Kelly what was going on. Or it could be someone else entirely," he said. "It could be someone who knows who Brad really is. We have no idea what kind of past your brother-in-law was running from. If someone saw his photo in the newspaper and had something on him, they might have considered going to Kelly and not to Brad. We'll be able to figure it out when we get more pieces of the puzzle."

She stared at him for a long moment. "Is that it?"

"I have a few more questions for you."

"Of course you do," she said with a sigh.

"Where does your father think you are? Rehab?"

A gleam of disappointment flashed in her eyes. "My father knows I don't do drugs. He thinks I'm resting at a resort in the Caribbean. A friend of mine has a house on Antigua."

Her answer reminded him that they came from very different worlds. "A male friend?"

She raised an eyebrow. "Is that important?"

"Just wondering why you didn't call anyone to help you. A beautiful, celebrated pianist, and you don't have a boyfriend?"

"I never had time for serious relationships. The piano came first." She ran her hand through the sand, letting the grains fall through her fingers. "Music was my sole purpose and reason for being, from the time I was three years old until two months ago."

"You said you had a career crisis. What happened?"

"I collapsed on the stage. I don't know why. Exhaustion, depression, anxiety, panic . . . Pick one or all of the above. I wasn't sleeping well or eating right. I was on a grueling tour, different cities across Europe every other week. The pressure had been building for years; the endless quest for perfection, the constant falling short. I was never as good as I was supposed to be. The performances took a lot out of me. I felt tremendous anxiety every time I went onstage. Finally I snapped. I took the coward's way out. I collapsed so I wouldn't have to tell my father I was done."

He was impressed with her self-analysis, but also reminded of how much she expected of herself. "Is that the only reason you didn't walk away—fear of how your father would react?"

"No. There was also the music. I love it. It sweeps me away, transports me to another place. It's a release, a joy. It's who I am. Unfortunately, the flip side of the music is the business: the pressures of performance, and the criticism of the critics, the conductors, the audience, and my father. I needed a rest, but there was never time to take one. My father insisted that I had to keep going while I was popular, that I couldn't let people forget me, that if I didn't tour, if I didn't stay up with the best, I'd be done. I didn't want to disappoint him. I was an extension of his success. He made me."

"No, he didn't," Reid argued. "You made yourself."

"He was my teacher."

"You were the one who played the notes. That was *your* accomplishment."

"In my head I know that, but it's far more complicated where my heart is concerned," she said, gazing into his eyes. "After my mother died, my father was the only parent I had. He saw my mother in me, and I felt her presence when I played. Her voice ran through me. If I didn't play, I thought I'd lose that connection with her. Then I'd lose him. I'd be alone." She turned to stare at the bonfire, the light of the flames dancing off her face. "The really sad thing is that I was never afraid I'd lose Kelly. I took her presence for granted, assuming she'd always be there. I was so wrong. So wrong about a lot of things."

Reid had to fight the urge to put his arms around her. He knew what it felt like to be alone, really alone. He'd spent years trying to be part of families that didn't want him. In the end, it had been easier to stay separate, to stop risking disappointment. But Jenna had known love, and she still had two important people in her life. "You'll see your father again. He might be angry, but I'm betting he'll be back in your life. And you have Lexie, too."

"You're right. You're also too easy to talk to," she said with a regretful smile. "For the last two months, I've kept everyone at arm's length. Then you show up, and I spill my guts."

He smiled back at her. "I'm a good listener. Your father had to have heard that your sister was murdered. Did he go to the funeral? Did he get in touch with you? Even if the press thought you were in rehab, he knew that wasn't the case."

"I called my father from a pay phone the day after Kelly was killed. He'd already heard the news, but couldn't get out of his commitments to attend the funeral. He wanted me to go to the service and represent the family, and to keep him advised of any developments in the search for her killer. At first I wasn't going to call him, but I worried that if I dropped completely out of sight, he might start looking for me, so I left him a few messages, calling at times I knew he wouldn't be available. I used pay phones so no one could trace the calls."

Reid shook his head in disgust. "Your father sounds like a complete ass. His daughter was murdered. How could he not fly home and get justice for her? How could he not be concerned about his granddaughter?"

Jenna frowned. "My father let Kelly go a long time ago. She had no musical talent, so she was left behind with nannies or housekeepers while he took me around the world. He didn't even go to Kelly's wedding. He's seen Lexie maybe twice in her life."

"He really *is* an ass."

"He's a sophisticated, intelligent, accomplished man, but you're right: he's also an ass. Where Kelly was concerned, I wasn't much better. I let her go, too. It sounds crazy, because I had so much more than she did, but I was jealous of her. She was free of my father. She didn't have his expectations hanging over her head. She didn't have to constantly try to please him; she could do whatever she wanted. I'm sure Kelly saw it differently. She must have felt abandoned by both of us."

Jenna looked at him with guilt in her eyes. "You don't know how much I regret the distance between my sister and me. If I had been paying attention to Kelly, I might have seen that she was in trouble. Maybe she would have come to me earlier, when I could have done something to help her. Maybe, maybe, maybe," she said, her voice rising with each frustrated word. "I wish I could go back in time to change things."

Reid knew that feeling all too well. "You're doing something now. You're protecting Lexie. You've given up your life to do that."

"It's not enough."

"It's a hell of a lot. You're that little girl's salvation."

"I hope so. I want to give Lexie the life that Kelly wanted her to have, but I know I'll be a poor replacement. I'm not her mother. And I know what it feels like to lose a mother. I wasn't much older than Lexie when my mom died."

"How did she die?" Reid asked.

"A car accident. She was supposed to play at our church on Christmas Eve—she was a pianist, too. On the way, her car hit an icy patch and flipped over. She was killed instantly." She drew in a shaky breath.

"I've lost two people in a second. Twice I didn't say good-bye. I don't want to take anyone else for granted."

Reid stared at the bonfire. He knew exactly what she meant. But what the hell were good-byes worth, anyway? What mattered was what came before the end. He didn't regret not saying good-bye to Allison. He regretted involving her in his life.

"Do you mind if we change the subject?" Jenna asked.

"Definitely not," he said, relieved.

"How is your article coming? Have you started to believe in angels yet?"

"I have not been converted, no."

"You're a tough nut to crack."

"I'm a realist. You're not going to tell me you believe there are angels flying around the cliffs, are you?"

"It's an intriguing thought."

He shook his head. "The angel video could have been easily constructed with special effects available on any personal computer. The markings on the cliff could be the result of the tides, the winds, natural erosion."

She tilted her head, a quizzical look in her eyes. "Is that what you're going to write in your article?"

He smiled. "Hell, no. Erosion doesn't sell magazines. I'm going to relate all the wonderful tales I've heard about miracle experiences, and let people think what they want."

"Even though you don't believe?"

He shrugged. "I'm reporting what people tell me. I'm not their judge and jury."

"My mother used to say that you can't find hope if you're not looking up. Maybe that's why everyone's gaze is on the sky." Jenna stretched out to rest on her elbows, her head tilted upward. "It's a beautiful night. Try it, Reid."

"I've seen the sky before."

"Not this night's sky, not with me. Come on. What do you have to lose?"

He hesitated one more second, and then followed suit, stretching out on the blanket. He'd lost hope and faith and all that other shit a long time ago. It was true that he'd spent most of the past eleven months looking down, but he didn't think gazing at the sky would change his attitude. He had to admit he was surprised by the multitude of stars, though, more than he could ever remember seeing.

He'd grown up in a big city where skyscrapers and city lights drowned out the stars. He liked the energy, the rush, the adrenaline of the busy streets. But there were downsides to that, too. In Angel's Bay people knew one another. They cared about their neighbors. They had hope, he realized. And just as Jenna had predicted, he was starting to feel that hope seep into his bones.

"Kelly used to know the constellations," Jenna said. "I can never remember what they are. That group of stars looks like a lion, don't you think?"

"I think you see whatever you need to see," Reid replied, surprising himself with the same words that had once come out of Henry's mouth. If he didn't get out of Angel's Bay soon, he had a feeling he'd lose all sense of reason.

"I need to see Kelly's face," Jenna continued, the sad note back in her voice. "I need to know I'm doing what she wanted."

His hand slid across the blanket, covering hers. "You are, Jenna, and you already know that. You don't need an angel to tell you. You don't need me to tell you."

"Thanks anyway," she said quietly.

"You're welcome." With his fingers intertwined with hers, he felt connected again—to the world, to his life, and most importantly, to her. The connection scared the hell out of him.

He pulled his hand away from hers and sat up just as Lexie and her friend came racing over to them. Lexie's face was lit up like a Christmas tree. She had sand clinging to her cheeks and probably in her hair, but there was a simple joy in her eyes. Jenna had given Lexie this moment, this feeling of being safe and protected. Reid hoped she could see that.

"We're going to make s'mores," Lexie said excitedly.

"What's that?" Jenna asked.

"You don't know?" the little girl with Lexie asked, clearly astonished. "You take two graham crackers and put a piece of chocolate in the middle and then a melted marshmallow. It's *really* good."

"Do you want one?" Lexie asked.

"I don't think—" Jenna began.

"She'd love one," Reid said. "And so would I. Come on, Jenna." He pulled her to her feet.

"I really don't think I want one," she said to him. "It sounds disgusting."

"Trust me: you do, and it's not." He led her over to the picnic table where the s'mores were under construction. Lexie and her friend were already busy making their own.

"It looks messy," Jenna said, with a wrinkle of her nose.

"Messy can be good." He picked up two graham crackers and handed them to her. Then he grabbed a piece of chocolate and slid a half-melted marshmallow off a stick. "You put the chocolate down, then the marshmallow over that," he instructed. "Now bite."

She gave him a doubtful look but took a bite. He watched the look of delight come over her face, and felt more proud and pleased than he had in a long time. "Well?"

"Excellent," she said with surprise, her mouth full of marshmallow. "This is fantastic!"

"Told you."

"I can't believe I never had one of these. And I can't imagine how many calories are in this."

"Don't imagine. Just enjoy." He leaned over and took a bite.

"Hey, get your own," she complained.

"You wouldn't have even tried this if I hadn't dragged you over here. Now you don't want to share?"

"No, but thank you for bringing me over here. Now get your own," she told him with a laugh. She popped the rest of the cracker into her mouth.

"I've got a better idea." He grabbed her finger and licked off the remaining chocolate. Her eyes darkened with desire, and his heart thumped against his rib cage.

Jenna jerked her hand away, grabbed a napkin off the table, and wiped off her hands. Whatever she'd been feeling for the brief second that had passed between them, she'd shut it down.

He followed her across the beach. "You shouldn't have done that," she told him as she sat down with an angry flounce. "Anyone could have seen you."

"So what?" he asked, sitting next to her.

"So I don't need the attention."

"No one was watching."

"You don't know that," she said, her gaze sweeping the beach. "I always feel like someone is watching."

"That's your fear talking. But even if someone saw us, what's the crime? You're living as a widow. I'm a single guy. We can share a kiss. We can share whatever we want."

"No, we can't. You're leaving in a day or two, and I'm on the run with a small child. I'm not in a position to get involved with anyone, even if you wanted that, which I'm sure you don't. This isn't the time to start anything, even anything casual."

"Who says it would be casual?" he challenged, not sure why he threw the words out. But they were on the table, and he couldn't take them back.

"Because you're not a serious relationship kind of guy, and I'm not a one-night-stand kind of woman."

He would have liked to argue that she had him wrong, but unfortunately she was on the money where his relationships were concerned. For the past year he had steered clear of anything longer than one night. If he were honest, he would admit that had been the case for most of his life. He didn't know how to stay. His years in foster care had taught him to leave before someone left him. He'd never been able to trust that a relationship would work any other way. So he didn't put himself in that position. He didn't put his heart on the line.

"I'm right, aren't I?" Jenna prodded.

"I've spent most of my life pursuing my career."

"Your career as a freelance tabloid reporter?" she asked with a disbelieving raise of her eyebrow.

"I've worked a few other places."

"Like . . ."

He sighed. "*The New York Times*, the *San Francisco Chronicle*, and most recently *The Washington D.C. Journal*."

"Very impressive. So why the fall?"

"Who said it was a fall? Maybe I just wanted a change."

"And maybe I'm not a fool. Come on, Reid. I know there's something going on with you. Your intensity, your personality, your drive—it doesn't add up to your current job." She looked long and hard at him. "I get the feeling that you're running away from something, too."

"I'm just here doing my job."

"No. I may have been a little self-involved in the past, too caught up in my own problems to consider what other people were going through, but that changed when I grabbed Lexie and ran. I can't afford not to notice what's going on with other people now. So talk to me, Reid. Tell me your story."

He didn't know how to answer that question. He certainly didn't feel like confessing his sins to Jenna. Fortunately he was saved by Lexie's reappearance. The kid had chocolate smeared across her mouth, but she was holding something out in her hand. It looked like a pebble, but then he saw blood. He tensed, until he heard Lexie say, "My tooth came out! Look."

"Wow," Jenna said. "I guess it got stuck in the s'mores." She took the tooth out of Lexie's palm. "Why don't I hang on to this for you?"

"Do you think the tooth fairy will be able to find me?" Lexie asked, worry in her eyes. "What if she can't?"

"The tooth fairy can find anyone." Jenna pulled a tissue out of her purse and wrapped up the tooth, then applied another tissue to Lexie's face. "Trust me, she'll come when you're fast asleep in dreamland."

"Do you think so, too?" Lexie asked Reid.

"Absolutely," he said.

Lexie gave him a thoughtful look, as if she were judging the truthfulness of his answer. "Okay. I'm going to watch the fireworks with Kimmy's family, all right? They have a better spot." Lexie pointed across the beach. Kimmy's mother gave a wave in return.

"Fine, but stay right there. I mean it, Lexie—no running off to look for angels," Jenna warned.

"I won't. I promise." Lexie took off at a dead run.

"She's a bundle of energy," Jenna said to Reid. "Kelly was like that, too. Thank God that tooth came out. I was terribly afraid I would have to pull it, and while there are some parts of motherhood I'm able to handle, yanking out loose baby teeth is not my idea of fun." She paused, giving a shake of her head. "But we were talking about how you went from the *Journal* to *Spotlight Magazine*."

"It doesn't matter how, because I'm here now. And I'm not looking back; I'm not looking forward. I'm just concentrating on the present."

Jenna started as a testing sky rocket lit up the night. She turned her head and the moonlight caught the stark beauty of her face. Reid drew in a quick breath. Her dark hair flowed loosely about her shoulders, and he was tempted to pull her hair to one side and kiss the curve of her neck.

"I guess the fireworks are starting," Jenna said as the crowd began to murmur with excitement.

"I think they already started—for me, anyway," he murmured.

She turned her head and met his gaze. "Reid. Don't."

Fireworks rattled the sky, a shower of red, gold, blue sparkles lighting the air, shimmering to the ground. They were nowhere near as spectacular as the fireworks going off in his head.

"I can't resist." He leaned over and stole a kiss.

Her mouth was soft, her breath warm. He wanted more.

She put a hand against his chest, but she didn't push him away. Instead her fingers curled in the material of his shirt. "Someone will see."

"No one is looking at us."

"Lexie—"

"Is fine," he said, lowering his head again. "Relax. Live for the moment. It's allowed."

"Maybe one moment," she murmured. "But that's all."

Eighteen

Jenna went back for a lot more than one kiss before she finally pushed Reid away. Her pulse was pounding, her lips tingling, and her body was more than ready to take things a lot further. Judging by the look in Reid's eyes, he was, too.

"Jenna . . ." he began.

"Don't say anything," she whispered as the fireworks exploded in a climactic frenzy. The crowd cheered as the last colors rained out of the sky. She got to her feet, drawing in several deep breaths of air as she did so. Her eyes sought out Lexie, who was with the Coopers, thank goodness.

Reid moved in behind her, his breath warm on her neck. It wouldn't take much for her to lean back against his chest, for him to slide his hands around her waist, for her to turn her head ever so slightly . . .

"Kissing me isn't a crime," Reid said.

"This isn't me. I'm breaking all the rules."

"What rules?"

"No public displays of emotion or affection. No scandals. No wrong notes. No bad hair days. No breakdowns. No forgetting what I'm supposed to do, who I'm supposed to be."

"Those sound like your father's rules. You can choose your own, Jenna." Reid put his hand on her waist. "Stop worrying so much," he whispered by her ear. "You didn't do anything wrong."

She put her hand over his, and the warmth of his fingers seeped into her soul. Why this man? Why now, when she had so many other things to deal with?

As usual, the universe wasn't including her in its plans. She was just going along for a very wild ride.

As the fireworks ended, the crowd began to break up. Jenna stepped away from Reid as Kara and Colin walked over to them. She was grateful for their interruption.

Kara's face was glowing, and Colin had his arm around his wife as if he never intended to let her go. If the word *happiness* had a picture next to it in the dictionary, it would be an image of Kara and Colin.

"Hey there, Jenna," Kara said with a smile. "Weren't the fireworks spectacular?"

"They were amazing," Jenna replied.

"Spectacular," Reid agreed.

Jenna heard the smile in his voice and knew he wasn't thinking about the fireworks. She felt a blush warm her cheeks and hoped no one noticed.

"I don't think we've met." Kara gave Reid a curious look. "I'm Kara Lynch, and this is my husband, Colin."

"Reid Tanner." He stepped forward to shake Kara's hand. Reid offered his hand to Colin next, but Colin simply scowled at him.

Kara glanced up at her husband. "What's wrong with you? You're being rude."

"We've already met," Colin told his wife. "He was one of the men in the bar fight last night."

"I thought one of the Harlan brothers punched you." Kara frowned at Reid. "You're not the one who put that bruise on my husband's face, are you?"

"No," Reid replied. "I am sorry about the fight. The Harlan brothers misunderstood my desire to get across the room as being impolite. They assumed that I had shoved one of them, which wasn't the case. Unfortunately, when someone takes a swing at me, I swing back."

Colin's scowl lifted as he gave a nod. "Roger and Bill have hot tempers; always have. I got into my share of misunderstandings with them when we were kids. I'd suggest you steer clear of them when they're drinking. Otherwise, they're not bad guys." He stuck out his hand. "I guess I should officially welcome you to Angel's Bay. What's your business here? Or are you just vacationing?"

"I'm covering the angels for a magazine."

Colin tipped his head in acknowledgment. "I'm a big fan of our local legends, but I wouldn't mind if the angels disappeared for a while. We've had more vandalism this weekend than we've had in a long time. A few break-ins, too. So make sure you lock your doors at night. We're stepping up patrols, but there are a lot of strangers in town and I'll be happy when they go home. Speaking of which . . ." Colin glanced down at his wife. "We should go. The baby needs to sleep."

"Does that mean we'll be going right to sleep?" Kara asked with a mischievous twinkle in her eye.

"We'll have to see how tired you are," Colin said with a laugh, as he brushed a strand of hair from her face in a tender gesture.

"Bye, Jenna," Kara said as her husband led her away.

"They're a nice couple," Jenna commented. "Very much in love."

Reid didn't answer. He seemed lost in thought.

"Reid?" she prodded. "What are you thinking?"

"I was just considering what Colin said about vandalism. It makes me wonder if there's a link between the break-ins, the video, the angel fanatics, and the symbols on the cliff. I don't know how anyone could get to that cliff face now; there are too many eyes on it. But even though the angels haven't appeared in at least a week, no one seems to be going home."

"I guess faith doesn't have a time limit. And here I thought I was your favorite story," she added lightly.

He smiled at her. "I can multitask." His expression grew serious. "About your story, Jenna. What about confiding in Colin?"

"Absolutely not. He might be a good guy, but he's also a cop. It's too big a risk."

"One you may have to take."

He might be right, but she wasn't ready to make that decision. "I'll think about it. Right now, I need to get Lexie home." She picked up the blanket and shook out the sand.

"I'll walk back with you," Reid said as volunteers began breaking down the tables next to the bonfire.

"I don't think that's a good idea."

"Don't worry. I'll say good night at the door."

She didn't believe him for a second. "You are too good at talking me into things I don't want to do."

He grinned. "Oh, I think you want to do them; you just need a little encouragement."

"You're very cocky, did you know that?"

"I've been told," he said.

Jenna sighed. Reid was pretty irresistible. The more she knew about him, the better she liked him, cockiness and all.

A moment later Lexie came running over, talking a mile a minute about the fireworks show. When she finally slowed down to take a breath, Jenna said, "I'm glad you had fun, but it's way past your bedtime. We need to go home."

"Kimmy said I could come over to her house tomorrow if I want," Lexie volunteered. "She has swings in her backyard. I really like to swing."

Jenna blew out a breath. There seemed to be no end to the many things Lexie wanted to do that would take her away from Jenna's protective care, which was normal, and somehow she'd have to find a way to deal. "Let's talk about that in the morning."

As they headed up the stairs from the beach, Jenna saw Lexie grab Reid's hand as she talked about her favorite fireworks. Reid was good with Lexie. He talked *to* her, not down to her, and Lexie blossomed under his smile. She probably missed the presence of a father figure in her life, but it worried Jenna that Lexie might get attached to Reid. He was only temporary; she'd have to make sure that Lexie understood that.

About two blocks from the beach, Lexie's energy gave out. She stopped walking abruptly and raised her arms in the air.

"I'm tired. Could you give me a piggyback ride?" Lexie asked Reid.

"Sure." Reid squatted down. "Climb on, kid."

Lexie threw her arms around Reid's neck and wrapped her legs around his waist as he stood up. She let out a squeal as Reid took off on a jog.

Jenna smiled to herself. The man was showing off—no doubt about it. She just hoped he knew there was a hill coming.

Annie stared at the phone in the Adamses' study for a long moment. It was almost ten o'clock at night, and she thought both Charlotte and her mother had gone to bed. They were in their bedrooms, and she hadn't heard any sounds in a long time. Mrs. Adams had had two lady visitors for most of the night, and they'd spent the evening in the kitchen. Charlotte had been in her room, talking on the phone to her sister, Doreen, for at least a half hour, and it was clear they were arguing about something.

Charlotte didn't seem to get along very well with either her mother or her sister, but Annie couldn't figure out why. Charlotte was the nicest person she'd ever met. Mrs. Adams was nice, too. She was strict, though. Mrs. Adams liked things a certain way, and Annie hoped she wouldn't screw up. She really didn't know where else she could go. Maybe she could help cheer Mrs. Adams up, and then she'd be allowed to stay.

Annie understood sadness. She'd felt it throughout most of her life, but she'd especially grieved for her mother. She hadn't just lost a parent; she'd lost her best friend. She couldn't imagine living the rest of her life without her mom. She couldn't imagine giving birth to her own child without her mother being there to help her. But she was gone. And that was that.

Her gaze moved from the phone and swept the rest of the room. This was the room that Reverend Adams had used as his office. There was a family photo on the desk right next to a Bible. She wondered if Charlotte's father had made her memorize the Bible, the way her father had done.

Seeing the Bible reminded her of the shame she'd brought to her father. He hated her now. She was dead to him. She shouldn't care. He hadn't loved her in a long time. In truth, he might never have loved her—or at least not since she was a small child and the war changed him.

She didn't miss living in the latest shack he called home. She didn't miss worrying that he'd accidentally shoot her if she got up to go to the bathroom in the middle of the night. She didn't miss the harsh slap of his hand upon her face or hearing him call her a whore. But . . .

She missed having a home, a family. She put a hand to her stomach. There was a baby growing inside. The thought terrified her, yet she felt secretly happy that she'd finally have someone to love, someone who would love her back. But the baby wasn't just hers. Maybe . . .

Maybe she should just call.

She picked up the phone and punched in the number before she could change her mind.

It rang three times and then his voice came over the line. Her heart melted at the strong masculine tone. She remembered how it had felt to hear her name on his lips as he'd made love to her. He'd told her she was beautiful, and she'd believed him. A tear slid down her cheek.

"Hello," he said impatiently. "Who is this?"

She heard another voice in the background and knew what she had to do. She hung up the phone. She and the baby were on their own. She had to accept that.

It was nice not to come home alone, Jenna thought as they approached her house. She didn't like the nights, the dark silence, the tall shadows from the trees surrounding her property. But while she was grateful for Reid's presence, she'd need to send him home before she did something stupid—like kiss him again. She liked him a little too much.

Most of the men she'd dated had come from her world; they'd been smooth, sophisticated, polished, educated in culture, the arts, music. They had season tickets to the opera and to the ballet. Reid had lots of rough edges. He obviously knew how to fight. He was blunt, honest, and she doubted he was ever politically correct. But he was also intelligent, charming, sexy, and he seemed to understand her almost better than she understood herself. He'd been kind to her, offering his shoulder to cry on, and listening to all of her concerns and insecurities. She wasn't too naïve to see that there was something in it for a him, a potential story to break, but she knew it wasn't all about that. He had a good heart. He cared even when he didn't want to.

"I'm coming inside," Reid said as they stepped onto the porch.

She unlocked the door, not bothering to argue. She always dreaded the first few moments when they entered the dark, empty house. She began turning on lights and moving through the rooms. Lexie ran down the hall to her bedroom to get into her pajamas. Jenna quickly checked the rest of the house, acutely aware that Reid was watching her every moment.

"Everything okay?" He followed her into the kitchen, tipping his head toward the basement door. "Where does that go?"

"The basement," she said. "There's no access to it from outside the house."

"Why don't we check it anyway?"

"All right." She opened the door and flipped the light at the top of the stairs.

Reid went down first. "What is this stuff?" he asked, looking around.

"It belongs to the woman who owned this house before she died. And you're not going to believe this, but she seems to have a tie to my family."

An immediate gleam of curiosity flashed in his eyes. "Don't stop there."

"In that trunk, I found some old clothes and a journal. It seems that Rose Littleton, the woman who lived here for most of her life, gave up a baby when she was very young. That baby had a birthmark on her heel in the shape of an angel's wing, much like the angel's wing featured on the centerpiece square of the Angel's Bay quilt. I don't know if you've heard any of the history of the town, but the baby was washed ashore without its parents and the town took care of her, named her Gabriella. According to the journal I found, every first daughter descended from Gabriella carries the birthmark."

"I heard something about the baby," Reid said, as he glanced around the basement. "How does it connect to you? I thought you came here by chance, that the underground network placed you here."

"That's what I thought, too. Until I read the journal. It seems that Rose gave up a baby for adoption, a baby who bore a birthmark in the shape of an angel's wing. My mother and Rose's baby had the same birthdate."

"And your mother was adopted?"

"I didn't know that she was. No one ever said, but since she died I've had no contact with her family. They lived in another state, and my father didn't encourage any kind of relationship."

"So all you have is a common birthdate?"

"No. Kelly had the same birthmark on her heel, and so does Lexie. I'm not sure about my mother, but I think there's a good chance she had it, too. I believe Kelly figured out the connection to Rose, and that's why she came here. That's why we're renting this house—the house of the person who was probably our biological grandmother." She could see by the doubt in Reid's expression that he wasn't buying it. "You don't believe me."

"What about you? Do you have a birthmark?"

"I'm not the firstborn daughter, and according to Rose's journal, the mark only goes to the first daughter. You want proof? I'll show you."

She led Reid out of the basement and down the hall to Lexie's room. Lexie had changed into her pajamas and was sitting in the middle of her bed, with a hairbrush in her hand. She was trying to get the tangles out of her hair to no avail.

Jenna took the brush out of Lexie's hand and sat down behind her on the bed. "I'll do that, honey. Why don't you show Mr. Tanner the angel's kiss on your foot? He wants to see it."

Lexie immediately stuck out her foot. Reid sat down on the bed and examined her foot.

"That's cool," he said, tracing the lines with his finger.

"Only very special people have one. It's the kiss of an angel," Lexie said. "My mommy had one. I mean . . ." She licked her lips and gave Jenna a quick look.

"It's okay, honey. Mr. Tanner knows that I'm your aunt. But he's the only one, so we have to keep it that way. You understand, right?"

Lexie nodded solemnly and then turned back to Reid. "My name used to be Caroline, but I like Lexie better. Mommy told me that I could pick any name I wanted. We used to read a story about a girl named Lexie, and she had a lot of fun. She climbed trees, and surfed in the ocean, and looked for buried treasure. I'm going to learn to surf when I'm older."

Reid smiled. "I always wanted to surf, too."

"Maybe we can do it together."

"Maybe," Reid said lightly, but Jenna could see that he was uncomfortable.

"I like the name Lexie," Reid continued. "I always wanted to change my name."

"To what?" Lexie asked.

"Dragon," Reid said very seriously.

Lexie laughed. "No one is called Dragon. That's silly."

"I didn't think so. If someone told me something I didn't want to hear, or forced me to do something I didn't want to do, I'd breathe fire and scare them away. I thought it was the perfect name."

Reid's childhood must have been rough, Jenna thought. He'd mentioned growing up in foster care, and she felt a rush of emotion for his loss. No wonder he kept himself closed off. He'd already suffered through a great deal of pain. Perhaps it was his past that made him connect with Lexie. He knew what it was like to lose parents.

"Will you read me a story, Mr. Tanner?" Lexie asked. "I don't have any about dragons, but I do have one about mermaids."

"Uh, I think Jenna wants me to leave," Reid said.

"You have time for a story, if you want," Jenna replied with a smile.

Lexie handed Reid the book she'd borrowed from the library. It was about mermaids living in an enchanted sea until the pirates came along to steal their gold. Jenna brushed Lexie's hair while Reid read the story. She was impressed with the way he got into it, changing his voice for the different characters. Reid was certainly not a man to do anything halfway.

After she finished brushing out the tangles, Lexie slid down on the bed, her eyes drifting closed as Reid read the climactic scene where the mermaids outwit the pirates and retrieve their gold. Jenna liked the story because the mermaids saved themselves, not a hero in sight, which was unusual for a fairy tale.

"And they all lived happily ever after," Reid said, shutting the book.

"Night, Reid," Lexie whispered, then she rolled onto her side and tucked her hand under her chin. She was asleep in a second.

Jenna covered Lexie up, turned on a nightlight and a monitor, and then ushered Reid out of the room. She closed the door behind them and followed Reid down the hall and into the living room. "You were great with Lexie."

He shrugged. "She's a good kid. It was the least I could do. I wish I could do more."

"You said you were raised in foster care. What happened to your parents, Reid? Did they die?"

"No, they disappeared." Reid dug his hands into the pockets of his jeans, rocking back on his heels. "My father took off before I was born. I never met him."

"And your mother?"

"She bailed on me a few years later. She took me to a church one day." He gave a bitter smile. "And I thought it was a good sign. We knelt down at a pew in the back. She bowed her head, said some prayers I guess. Then she told me to stay there and she'd be right back. Five hours later I was still waiting when the priest came to lock up the church."

She caught her breath at the look of bitter betrayal in his eyes and her heart tore for the little boy who'd been abandoned without a word. "I'm so sorry, Reid." No wonder he'd wanted to be a dragon. He'd had a lot of anger and nowhere to put it. "Did you ever see her again?"

"About a year later. She came to find me because she wanted to get her child welfare money back. Unfortunately, the judge didn't think she was a fit mother and left me where I was. I was furious at the time. I wanted to be with her. I believed in her even after everything she'd done. I was a fool."

"You were a child."

"After that, I saw her a few times over the years. She'd try to get clean, but she always fell back into the drugs."

"So who raised you?"

"No one, really. I lived in a half dozen homes. I wasn't a very popular kid; I kept trying to run away to find my mother."

"When was the last time you saw her?"

"Ten, twelve years ago . . . she could be dead for all I know."

"Don't you want to know? You're a journalist. I'm sure you could find out."

"I'm done looking for her. Sometimes you have to cut your losses."

She nodded, understanding him a little more. "Do you want to sit down for a few minutes?"

He hesitated. "Why?"

She smiled. "Because there's more to say." She walked over to the couch and sat down, patting the cushion beside her.

He came over, but sat in the armchair across from her. "Okay, here's the deal—you get two more questions; that's it."

"That deal really didn't stop you," she reminded him. "You've asked about a hundred questions since then."

He smiled back at her. "All I have to say is, choose your words carefully."

"Fine. How did you get from foster homes and

poverty to reporting for major newspapers? That's an amazing feat."

"I knew that I would have to get whatever I was going to have in life myself. I wanted to be in the newspaper business for a long time. I wanted to be someone that people had to listen to, that they couldn't ignore. I wanted the power of the press. And I got it."

"Why did you give it up?"

"A lot of reasons."

"Be specific."

He stared down at the floor, then raised his gaze to hers. "I was doing a story on counterfeit drugs. It's a booming business, and a dangerous one. People are dying because they're getting placebos or watered-down medication. One of my best friends, Allison, was a nurse at a hospital suspected of using fake drugs. I asked her to help me get the inside story. She dug up some information for me over a period of weeks. Then one day when she was leaving work, she was run down by a car. No one saw the driver. She died a few hours later. It was made to look like an accident, but it was murder."

She was shocked. What had happened was horrifying.

"Allison was killed because I involved her in my story—my all-important story that I had to break before anyone else," Reid continued. "She was a nurse, not an undercover spy, and I shouldn't have used her that way."

Jenna wanted to tell him that it wasn't his fault,

but she knew he wouldn't hear her. Instead she got up and knelt in front of him, putting her hands over his. She could feel the tension in his body, and was sorry she'd made him talk about something so painful.

His fingers closed around hers. "When I asked Allison for help, she jumped at the chance. She told me that I always kept her at a distance, that I never let her into my life. And now she's dead." His gaze bored into hers. "Maybe you should be pushing me away, Jenna. I might be as dangerous to you as Brad."

"I don't believe that."

"I told you to trust me. The last person who did that is dead."

"So Allison's death is the reason why you're punishing yourself—working for a tabloid, pretending not to care anymore what you write."

"I'm not pretending," he said flatly. "I don't care."

"Yes, you do," she said, holding his gaze. "Maybe you didn't before. Maybe you managed to get through most of the year believing that you were done with your old life. But then you came here—and I made you care." She saw the truth in his eyes. "You met me, and you sensed a story. I made you want to do real news again. I made you want to help someone."

"You give yourself a lot of credit."

"I'm right, aren't I?"

He stared back at her, the air between them thick with tension. "You had to jump off that damn pier. I couldn't believe anyone would do that to save a stranger. But you did. Even with everything you were trying to protect, you still couldn't walk away. Just like you couldn't walk away when your sister asked for help, when Lexie was hiding in the park, when you threw away your entire life to protect your niece. You amaze me, Jenna."

"You amaze me, too. You've had a difficult life, but you've accomplished a lot. And you did it all on your own."

"I just survived, that's all. Don't make it more than it is."

She shook her head. "You really don't see how great you are."

"Jenna—"

"No. Don't try to talk me out of my opinion. I can be stubborn when I have to be."

He smiled. "I've noticed."

"I *do* trust you, Reid. Nothing you've said has changed that. I'm sorry about what happened to your friend. But from what you've told me about her, I suspect she wanted to help not just because you asked her, but because of the people she wanted to protect. She was a nurse. She knew how dangerous counterfeit drugs could be. I'm sure you saved a lot of lives with that article, with her investigation. It wasn't all for nothing."

"I only snagged the small fish, and stopped one outlet. It wasn't nearly enough. I thought when I became a reporter that I could change the world, but the only world I changed was that of my best friends. And I destroyed it. I quit the day after she died."

It saddened Jenna to see the pain in his eyes, the guilt weighing him down. He'd loved only a handful of people in his life, and Allison had obviously been one of them. "I understand why you quit, even though I might not agree. You had to regroup. And now you're ready again. You're going to help me. We're going to be partners."

At her words, a mix of emotions ran through his eyes. He was fighting her and himself as hard as he could. He'd been alone a long time and had built an impenetrable wall around his heart. He didn't know how to believe in people. He didn't know how to believe in himself. But she saw what he couldn't see—a strong, intelligent, articulate, determined man who could make a difference in a lot of people's lives, including hers.

As the silence lengthened, the tension between them built. The anger and grief were replaced by something else, something that was far more dangerous.

"I don't want to *just* be your partner," Reid said.

His words stole the breath from her chest. There it was—on the table, front and center. Her stomach clenched at the new spark in his eyes, at the silent question in his gaze. He was giving her a choice, asking her if she really wanted to cross that line. She told herself that she didn't. She told herself that the best thing to do was tell him to go—but the words wouldn't come. She was tired of lying, tired of pretending. Maybe she needed to be honest for this one moment.

But Reid wasn't giving her the moment. He was on his feet, heading for the door.

Damn him! He could never wait two seconds for an answer. Just like the night before, he was running out on her. Was he quitting on her? Was this the end of their alliance, or just the end of this night? He always had to have the last word, and she was sick of it.

She raced over to the open door. Reid was halfway down the walk. "That's the second time you've left in the middle of a conversation," she called after him. "I don't like it."

He paused and glanced back at her.

"You don't want me to finish the conversation," he returned.

"Don't tell me what I want. I know what I want."

He hesitated for a long second, and then walked slowly back to the house, stopping a few inches away from her. "What's that?"

She drew in a deep breath, feeling as if she were about to leap off a cliff. "You."

His eyes glittered in the moonlight. "Jenna . . ."

"Have I scared you?" she asked, feeling more reckless with each passing second.

"Hell, yes," he murmured huskily. "Are you sure?"

"Yes. Stay." She held out her hand and for a very long moment, she worried that he wouldn't take it, but then his fingers curled around hers. She led him back into the house. He shut the door, threw the deadbolt, and then hauled her into his arms.

There was no slow buildup to his kiss, no tentative touch or hesitant caress. Reid took her mouth as if he owned it. His kiss was hot, demanding, intense. She felt his fire burning into her as his tongue tangled with hers. His hands were in her hair, holding her head where he wanted it. His lips moved from her mouth, roaming across her face, her cheek, her jaw. He nipped at the curve of her neck, a delicious sting of passion.

Then his hands dropped to her waist, his fingers bringing heat to her bare midriff. He helped her out of her sweater, their hands colliding as they both reached for the hem of her T-shirt, pulling it over her head.

He smiled as he saw her hot red bra. "So this is what you've been hiding. Sexy underwear. I like it." His eyes darkened as he gazed into hers. "I like you."

"I like you, too," she said.

He ran his lips along her collarbone, then his mouth slid lower. He opened her bra, flicking aside the cup, and feasted on her breast, sucking her nipple into his mouth. A rush of desire shot straight through her body. She ran her hands through his hair, pulling him closer. He moved from one breast to the other, teasing, tantalizing her with the promise of more.

Her legs weakening, she slid her hands under his T-shirt, running her fingers across the strong, supple muscles of his back. He lifted his head to remove his T-shirt. She pulled off her bra and moved into his embrace, loving the feel of the fine hairs of his chest brushing across her breasts.

He kissed her again, his finger reaching for the snap on her jeans. She returned the favor, wanting him completely naked, skin to skin, mouth to mouth, no barriers between them.

Stumbling out of their jeans, they made it to the living room couch. Jenna fell back against the soft cushions as Reid came down on top of her, his hand palming her breast, his lips running across her jawline, his leg separating her thighs. She ran her hand along his bicep, cupping the back of his head as she pulled his mouth back to hers.

"We've got to slow down," Reid muttered.

"Not this time," she said.

Desire flared in his eyes, and he ripped open the condom he snagged from his jeans. She helped him slide it on, and then he was moving on top of her, inside of her—everywhere she wanted him to be.

Nineteen

Reid stared at the shadows that danced off the living room wall, the moonlight coming through a slit in the curtains. His heart had yet to go back to an even beat, but that might have something to do with Jenna's sweet, naked body in his arms. He pulled the afghan off the back of the couch, covering them both. Jenna's cheek rested against his chest. She could probably hear the pounding of his heart. She had one leg thrown over his and one arm around his waist, as if she didn't intend to let him up any time soon.

He'd imagined making love to Jenna since he'd first met her, but the real thing had been better than any dream. Her understated appearance hid a passionate nature, a generous lover, a caring heart. He never should have let her get this close. She made him want things he couldn't have. She made him want to believe in possibilities, in a future, but there was no future for the two of them. Was there?

She stirred and he tightened his arm around her. He wasn't ready to let her go yet, either.

Jenna lifted her head and gave him a thoughtful smile. "I can hear you thinking. And the answer is no, it wasn't a mistake."

"That wasn't what I was thinking."

"Yes, it was." She pressed a kiss to his chest.

He smiled. "Okay, maybe."

"I'm not expecting anything."

"That's good, because I don't have anything to offer."

"You sell yourself short," she murmured, her eyes filling with tender concern.

Her words echoed what Allison had said to him so many times. But Allison had been wrong, and so was Jenna. He'd once believed that things could work out. Every time he'd gone to a new foster home, he'd thought that it would be the one, that he'd have a family again. But it had never happened. He wasn't destined to belong to anyone.

"It was just sex." He wanted to make it abundantly clear where they stood. He knew the statement would annoy her; with any luck she'd get pissed enough to throw him out.

His words only seemed to amuse her. "Nice try. I've had 'just sex.' That wasn't it."

He shrugged. "So I'm good. It doesn't mean anything."

She made a little face at him. "Okay, so you don't sell yourself short in *every* area—just where affection is concerned."

"I don't believe you ever had 'just sex.' You're not the type."

"He was another musician, a violinist. Let's just say he was better with an actual instrument."

Reid grinned and ran a hand through her hair. He didn't want to like her so much, but he couldn't seem to stop himself. Her unpretentiousness was very likable. "What about other guys?"

"There have been a few, but I don't have a long scorecard. I never had time for relationships. What about you? Any serious romances in your life?"

"You know, this is my least favorite part of the after-sex moments," he said.

She laughed. "You gotta take the bad with the good."

"You already reached your limit on questions."

"Fine—I know the answer anyway. You don't do serious. And for the most part I don't do casual sex, but this doesn't feel casual. Don't get all freaked out on me," she hastily warned. "I went into this with my eyes open. I have no regrets."

He frowned. No matter what she said, he suspected she would still want more than he could give her. But he didn't want to talk about it anymore, so he cupped the back of her neck and pulled her in for another kiss.

A shrill scream rent the air. Jenna jumped, taking the blanket with her as she stumbled to her feet. Lexie screamed again, a sound of pure terror.

"Wait!" Reid said as Jenna ran, but she didn't pay him any attention. He grabbed his jeans, hopping into them as he ran, wishing Jenna had waited two seconds. There could be someone in Lexie's room.

When he got to the door he saw Lexie thrashing in bed, fighting with the covers as if she were battling an impossibly strong assailant. She alternated between screaming and sobbing, her face dark red, sweat matting her hair against her head.

Jenna grabbed Lexie in her arms and held on tight. Pressing Lexie's head against her breast, Jenna said, "It's okay, honey. You're safe. I'm here. No one can hurt you."

Lexie's fear was so at odds with her usual personality that Reid had almost forgotten what she'd been through. Now he could see the trauma written all over her terrified face. During the day she could distract herself with friends and fun, but in the dark her nightmares caught up to her. Lexie's father had damaged her for life, and he needed to pay for what he'd done, how he'd destroyed his family.

Jenna held on to Lexie, murmuring soothing words over and over as the two of them rocked in the middle of the bed. There was love on Jenna's face, and a determination that made his gut clench. Jenna was something else—warrior mom, loyal sister, incredible friend—maybe she was the one who sold herself short.

She deserved better than him.

The thought rocketed through his head.

Turning, he went back down the hall and finished dressing. He gathered Jenna's clothes together and took them into her bedroom. She appeared in the doorway a moment later, the afghan still wrapped around her.

"You're leaving," she said, disappointment in her dark blue eyes.

"I'm sure you don't want me here when Lexie wakes up in the morning." He had to clench his fists to stop himself from reaching out for her.

"Lexie won't be up before eight, maybe later," Jenna said softly. "You really don't have to leave now."

"Does that happen a lot—the nightmares?" he asked, changing the subject.

Jenna nodded, drawing the blanket more tightly around her. "They're better now, usually no more than once a night. In the beginning she slept with me constantly, but eventually I got her into her own room, thinking that we needed to live a more normal life so she wouldn't feel so afraid. Maybe it was a mistake."

"You have good instincts, Jenna. Don't second-guess them. Lexie loves you. She trusts you completely."

"I love her, too, as if she were my own." Her blue eyes held his gaze. "Reid, do you really want to go?"

Want to go? Hell, no. Have to, absolutely. "I think I should—unless you're afraid to be here alone?" For a moment he hoped she would say she was, giving him a legitimate reason to spend the rest of the night with her.

Her look didn't waver. "I've been alone the past two months. I didn't ask you to stay tonight because I wanted a bodyguard. I wanted you."

Her words made his gut clench. "I wanted you, too. I just don't do the overnight thing. It's less complicated."

"And you're a man who likes things simple. Then you should leave. I'll lock the door after you."

Now that she'd told him go, perversely, he wanted to stay. "I told you I can't give you what you want."

"No, you're afraid to take what you want. This isn't about me. It's about you."

It terrified him that she could read him so easily.

"You've put your heart on the line before and got it stomped on. I get that," Jenna said. "You have to leave first because you can't get left again." She tucked her hair behind her ear, her eyes filled with understanding. "And while I'd like to say that I'd never walk out on you, I'm not in a position to make that promise. I don't know what direction my life will go. I have to put Lexie first, whatever that entails. So you're right, simpler is better. Good night, Reid." She kissed him on the mouth, a sweet, tender kiss that felt more like good-bye than good night.

Reid's stomach churned. There were a lot of things he wanted to say to her, but he couldn't get one single word out. She followed him to the front door, and as he stepped onto the porch, she shut the door and turned the deadbolt. Exactly as he'd wanted.

You're a complete idiot, Reid. Allison's voice rang through his head.

"I know," he muttered as he walked down the path. "I know."

* * *

Jenna's telephone rang early Sunday morning. She grabbed for it, disoriented. She'd gotten very little sleep after Reid left, reliving everything that had passed between them. "Hello?"

"Jenna, it's Kara Lynch. I'm sorry if I woke you, but I have a problem."

Jenna sat up in bed, rubbing the sleep out of her eyes. She glanced at the clock. It was a little before eight. "What's up?"

"Our piano player at the church is ill. The new minister is giving the service at ten a.m. and we don't want him to have to do it without music."

Jenna's stomach clenched. She didn't want to play in public. Giving lessons was one thing; playing for a congregation was another. "I doubt I would know the music," she prevaricated.

"Everyone says you're a fabulous teacher. I'm sure these songs would be easy for you to play. Or you could play what you know. It's just this one time," Kara pleaded.

Jenna had a feeling she was fighting a losing battle, but she made another attempt to beg off. "I have Lexie."

"Bring her along. She'll like it. There's a lunch afterwards to welcome the new minister. He's actually a guy I went to school with—Andrew Schilling. I can hardly believe he's a minister, but that's another story. Just get here by nine forty-five, so they can show you what to do. We all really, really appreciate this."

Jenna opened her mouth to protest, but Kara had already hung up. If she called Kara back and refused to play, she would draw more interest than if she just went and played.

She could do it. She could play a couple of easy songs. No one would suspect that she was more than a simple piano teacher.

Lexie came into the bedroom and jumped on the bed with a big grin, her nightmare long forgotten. In her hand was a dollar bill, the one Jenna had slipped under her pillow the night before. She'd almost forgotten, but after Reid had left she'd gone back into Lexie's room to check on her and remembered the tooth.

"Look what I got," Lexie said with delight as she waved the dollar bill. "The tooth fairy came after all!"

Jenna smiled. "I told you."

"Maybe the tooth fairy is Mr. Tanner. He was in my room last night. I like him," Lexie declared. "He's nice. And he reads stories really good."

"I like him, too," Jenna said with a small sigh.

"Who was on the phone?"

"Mrs. Lynch. They want me to play the piano at church today."

"We're going to church?" Lexie asked, sounding excited. "You said we couldn't go to church."

Because she'd wanted to avoid getting more involved with the town, but that seemed to be impossible. "Well, we'll make an exception." She'd made a lot of exceptions in the past few days. She hoped this one wouldn't land her in any more trouble.

Reid stared out at the ocean, watching the waves crash along the rocky shoreline. It was a beautiful sunny day, the blue sky filled with promise. He would have preferred dark and stormy to suit his mood. He'd been an absolute idiot last night, afraid to spend the night with a woman he actually cared about, one with whom he could have shared a lot more incredible sex.

He'd never met a woman who was so clear about her intentions, her expectations, her own actions. It should have made things easier to have everything out on the table, but he wasn't used to such honesty. He also wasn't comfortable being with someone who was a giver. Most people were users, out to get whatever they could. In his experience, children had been an expendable commodity. But Jenna had given up her life for Lexie, a child who wasn't her own. She'd jumped into the bay to save a stranger. She was far too good for him.

He grabbed a beer bottle and thrust it into one of two large trash bags he was carrying along the beach, one for recyclables and the other for garbage. Roger and Bill Harlan were also sweeping the beach per their ordered community service. Roger had two of his boys with him, nine-year-old twins who took turns throwing a stick into the water so their dog could chase it.

In the light of day, stone cold sober, the Harlan brothers were family men and not the assholes Reid imagined. Bill had even apologized for shoving him. Reid had offered an apology in return. He knew he'd taken some of his anger and frustration out on them. Bill might have thrown the first punch, but he'd been eager to hit back.

Reid looked up at the sound of a whistle. Joe Silveira was ambling across the beach with a golden retriever. Joe had on jeans and a T-shirt. He gave Reid a nod as he threw a tennis ball to his dog. The golden retriever took off after the ball, but got sidetracked by the Harlans' dog, and the two of them wound up chasing each other into the sea.

"Looks like you're about done here," Joe said as he joined Reid.

"It wasn't bad."

"The locals take care of the beach. There's a lot of town pride around here."

"I've noticed. Nice dog," he added as the golden retriever came charging back, shaking seawater all over both of them.

"Rufus has turned out to be quite a pal. He was my uncle's dog. He came with the house I inherited."

Reid had always wanted a dog, but he'd never lived anywhere a dog would be happy. His apartment in D.C. was on the twelfth floor. He couldn't see taking a dog up and down in an elevator. His lifestyle didn't suit pets, women, or children, he thought with a sigh.

"You and the Harlan brothers getting along?" Joe asked.

"They're fine."

"Yeah." Joe leaned over to grab the tennis ball. He threw it down the beach and the dog took off at a sprint. "So how long you think you'll be in town?"

"Don't know yet."

"Nothing much happening out on the cliff these days. No new markings since three days ago. Too many people around, I suspect."

"You think there's someone actually getting to that rock face and carving lines into it?" Reid asked.

"I don't know how, but I don't believe in angels. So there has to be some other, more human explanation."

"I'd sure love to hear it."

"So would I." Joe tilted his head as he gave Reid a thoughtful look. "You and Jenna Davies are getting to be good friends."

Reid stiffened at Joe's comment, which he knew was anything but casual. Joe had something on his mind.

"No one knows much about her," Joe continued. "She has the gossips wondering, that's for sure. I did a little checking, and I couldn't find any information about her anywhere. It seemed a little odd."

"I doubt she's committed any crime, Chief. Why would you check up on her?"

Joe stared out at the ocean for a minute, and then said, "I don't use my resources to play Big Brother, but Jenna Davies is scared of something, and that worries me." He glanced back at Reid. "I think you know what I'm talking about."

Reid should have realized that the chief could see that Jenna was terrified. Both he and Silveira were used to dealing with people who had something to hide.

"I'd like to know if trouble is heading this way," Joe added, his gaze searching Reid's face.

"As far as I know, it's not," Reid said evenly. "But it's not my story to tell."

"No? I figured you were working something up with her. Or maybe it's not a story you're working on. She's a beautiful woman."

"Yes, she is," Reid agreed. He debated telling the chief more. Deep down he believed that Jenna needed the help of the police, but he'd made her a promise, and he couldn't break it.

"We've had reports of break-ins the last two days," Joe said. "It's probably petty thievery, but we're planning to patrol the residential areas more closely. If you think there's anything else I should know about, I'd appreciate a heads-up."

Joe's dog brought back the tennis ball, then barked. Joe picked up the ball and tossed it down the beach again. His dog kicked up sand as he ran after it, but got sidetracked by a bunch of seagulls landing on the beach. The birds scattered with a flutter of wings and cries.

"I can think of a few reasons why a woman wouldn't come to the police if she was in trouble," Joe continued. "One is that she's done something illegal, another is that she's protecting someone, and a third is that she doesn't think she can trust law enforcement." His gaze held Reid's. "If it's the third, she'd be dead wrong. I don't cover for anyone."

"That's good to know."

"Pass it on."

Reid nodded and moved down toward the water's edge, spotting something that looked like a bottle in a pile of seaweed. As he drew closer, he realized it wasn't a bottle but some metal object. He knelt down next to it. Tossing the seaweed to one side, he dug out the object, finally uncovering what appeared to be a very old and rusted bell that was almost a foot in diameter. He put his hand on the metal, his fingers tracing the letters of the word—*Gabriella, 1850.* His pulse quickened as he realized what he'd found.

The ship's bell—he'd just uncovered the bell from a ship that had sunk a hundred and fifty years ago.

Adrenaline shot through him. Henry had told him that there hadn't been one item to wash ashore since the morning after the ship went down. Reid laid his palm over the inscription, and as he did so, his skin began to sting. He felt light-headed, almost dizzy. He closed his eyes.

He could smell the fear on the ship, from the sailors battling the ocean's fury to the passengers huddled together in the main salon. No one was talking. The music had stopped playing. It was late at night but people were afraid to sleep, terrified they would never wake up. The storm was the worst they had encountered since they'd left San Francisco.

As he moved through the ship, his real concern was for her, the woman he had met earlier that day. He'd interviewed her as he'd done many of the others. He planned to publish his stories when he returned to New York, and her tale was fascinating. He had to speak to her again. He hadn't been able to stop thinking about her.

His pace quickened as he heard a woman scream. Instinctively, he knew it was her, but he had taken only one step forward when his feet went out from under him and the ship shattered around him. They must have hit some rocks in the storm.

Water poured through the portholes, the doors. He couldn't gain his footing. He was swept along to the outside deck, finally grabbing a piece of pipe, stopping his spiraling descent into the churning sea. People were running for lifeboats. Women, children, men, sailors.

He struggled to get up, but the ship was tilting at a dangerous angle. And then he saw her, the fear in her eyes, the blood on her dress . . .

"What have you got there?"

Reid's eyes flew open in shock, and he stared up at Joe in confusion. It took him a minute to realize where he was. The chief gave him an odd look, then knelt down next to him to see what he'd discovered.

Reid took his hand off the bell, his fingers still tingling, his heart racing from the images that had flashed through his head. He couldn't believe what he'd seen, what he'd felt, as if he'd been on that ship, been one of those people about to die. *Had* he died? But that was crazy. He didn't know any of the people onboard. He knew little to nothing about the wreck. So why did he feel like he'd just trespassed on someone else's life, someone else's memory?

"Shit!" Joe swore. "Is this what I think it is?"

"It's the bell from that ship that went down," Reid said slowly, still trying to get his wits about him.

"This is unbelievable. Do you know what this means?"

"That you'll have a hell of a lot more people coming to town?"

Joe gave him a sharp look. "What's wrong with you? You look like you saw a ghost."

"I got an odd feeling when I touched the bell." He had barely finished speaking when the Harlan brothers, the two kids, and the two dogs joined them to see what they were looking at.

"Oh, my God," Roger Harlan said in shock. "It's the bell from the *Gabriella*! The angels must have brought it up. That's what they've been doing—flying around, stirring up the waters so the bell would come up, so people would believe again. They want that ship to be found."

"This bell could have easily washed ashore because of the tides," Joe said.

Reid's pulse began to pound as he looked out at the water. A wisp of cloud passed in front of the sun. Or was it an angel? He blinked the image out of his head. He had *not* just seen an angel. He had to get hold of himself.

"I'm taking this into police custody," Joe said.

"Hey, wait a second," Reid said. "I found it."

Joe frowned. "You're not going to tell me you think you get to keep this?"

"Not keep it, but I would like to take some photographs of it and include it in my story," Reid said, his mind racing ahead.

"You can come down to the station and shoot your pictures. Until I can sort out just what this is and where it needs to go, it stays with me." Joe sighed as the Harlan brothers took off down the beach to share news of the discovery. "Those two will have this discovery spread all over town before I can get to the station. It's just an old bell from an old ship. Why do people have to make so much of things?"

"You don't feel anything when you're touching it?" Reid asked, the words coming out before he could stop them.

"No." Joe got to his feet. "You don't think the angels brought this bell up from the deep, do you?"

Reid was shocked to realize that he couldn't dismiss that scenario out of hand—but the images of what he'd seen and felt still raced around in his head. Where the hell had they come from?

He realized that the chief was still waiting for an answer. "Of course not. I don't believe in angels."

"That's what I thought," Joe said. "So why do I have the feeling you're not as sure as you used to be?"

Twenty

Kara saw uncertainty in Andrew's eyes, and suspected the new minister was having a bad case of nerves. She'd been watching him fiddle with the microphone at the podium, his movements clumsy and awkward. Andrew was probably worried that the town still saw him as a kid. She could understand that. It was difficult to shake hometown labels. Most of her parents' friends still saw her as one of the Murray children and not an adult woman in her own right, with a marriage and a career. In her line of work, it didn't matter all that much what people thought of her. She provided a service. It was different for Andrew; he was supposed to be the new spiritual leader of the town. That was a heavy burden to carry. He looked up and caught her staring. She smiled.

He gave her a sheepish grin in return and walked down the steps to join her.

He was handsome in his robe, his blond hair

neatly styled, his face clean shaven. The women in Angel's Bay were going to go crazy over him.

"How stupid did I look up there?" he asked.

"You looked nervous—not stupid."

"I grew up in this church. It doesn't feel quite right to be giving the sermon where I spent so many years listening to Reverend Adams. He was a good speaker. He made me listen even when I didn't think I wanted to."

Kara suspected Andrew would have the same effect on people. He had a natural charisma, a smile that drew a person in. "You'll do great, Andrew. And it's nice to have a different voice in the pulpit. Not that I didn't care for Reverend Adams, but you'll speak to a new generation. Your mother and father must be so proud."

"They're beside themselves. I think my mother has decided that my taking on this position has suddenly made her first lady of the town, even above the mayor's wife."

"Your mother may have competition when all the single women start lining up to see who will become the new reverend's wife," Kara teased.

"I don't think it will be a long line."

"Oh, come on, Andrew. You were one of the most popular boys in school. Half of the women you grew up with are still single and still live here. And then there are the new ones. The casseroles and baked goods will be arriving shortly, and you'll have more volunteers for the ladies' auxiliary than you know what to do with."

As she finished speaking, Kara realized Andrew wasn't listening to her. His attention was at the other end of the church. She saw Charlotte in the vestibule, talking to her mother. "Or maybe someone already has the lead in that race," she added.

"What?" Andrew asked, his gaze still on Charlotte.

"Never mind. I see Jenna, our replacement piano player. I'll go get her."

Kara met up with Jenna at the back of the church. Jenna looked more nervous than Andrew, her face pale, her eyes worried. Kara had noticed that Jenna often appeared wary. She wondered what was in Jenna's past to make her so cautious, but they weren't good enough friends for her to broach that subject. Maybe someday they would be.

"Thanks again for doing this," she said to Jenna. "The music is at the piano. I think it's self-explanatory, but Mrs. Adams said she'd run through it with you. She's Reverend Adams's widow," Kara explained at Jenna's blank look. "She knows everything there is to know about how the church is run and how the service goes. Now, take a deep breath and relax."

"I don't think I'll relax until the service is over."

"You will be great," Kara said, wondering how many more people she'd have to pump up today.

"I'll take a look at the music," Jenna said, heading toward the piano.

"I'll see if I can find Mrs. Adams," Kara replied. She walked down the center aisle, saying hello to some of the early arrivals. When she reached the vestibule, she said, "Good morning, Charlotte, Mrs. Adams. The piano player is awaiting your instructions."

"Excellent. I'll talk to you later, Charlotte," Monica said, then headed into the church.

"Are you and your mother fighting?" Kara asked Charlotte when they were alone. "She sounded a little ticked-off."

"Always," Charlotte replied in a weary voice.

"It must be difficult since your dad died."

"It was hard before that, almost impossible now."

"Sorry. Maybe you can pray she'll change."

Charlotte smiled. "God has already heard that prayer from me a million times. So far he's not answering."

"I thought you might bring Annie with you today."

Charlotte shook her head. "I wanted to, but it's too soon for her to face being the center of attention."

"Well, I can understand that. Although I would love to meet her sometime." While Charlotte appeared to be listening, her gaze seemed to be focused on Andrew. So that's how the wind blew. "Okay, what's going on?" Kara asked.

"Excuse me?"

"First Andrew, then you. You're both checking each other out when the other one isn't looking."

Charlotte flushed. "Don't be silly. It's just strange to see him in his robe, looking so spiritual."

"You two had a thing in high school. I bet *that* wasn't spiritual," she said with a laugh.

"Kara, we're in church. Please."

"Oh, please yourself. Andrew was hot back then and he's hot now. What's not to like?"

"It was a long time ago. Ancient history, not to be repeated."

"Why not? He's handsome and single, innately good, probably has the inside track on heaven. And you're beautiful and single. If I add that up—"

"Don't," Charlotte said quickly. "I am not going down that road again."

"Your mother would love it. Imagine—you could be the next minister's wife." She laughed at Charlotte's pained expression. "Is that the real obstacle between you and Andrew?"

"Well, being a minister's wife would not be my first choice."

"You could do worse."

"I am fine the way I am," Charlotte said. "Why do all married women want to set up their single friends?"

"We want you to be as happy as we are." Kara grinned.

"Who's happy?" Colin asked, coming up behind her. He kissed her on the cheek and put his arm around her. "Hi, Charlotte."

"Colin, tell your wife not to match-make."

"Who are we matchmaking, honey?"

"Don't even say it," Charlotte warned Kara. "You'll start a rumor before you know it," she added as families began to fill the church. "Let's sit down."

Kara followed Colin and Charlotte down the aisle. They took a seat in the third pew from the front as Jenna began to play. The music flowed from her fingers with a beauty that made Kara pause. She'd heard the same song played every Sunday, but for some reason it sounded different today.

"She's good," Colin whispered in her ear.

"Very good," Kara agreed, wondering why a woman who played so well would be so nervous.

The song ended, and Andrew took his place at the podium. He gazed out at the crowd and smiled. "Friends," he said. "It's good to be back."

More than a dozen people stopped Jenna on her way out of the church to tell her how much they had enjoyed her music. Playing for someone besides herself had made her feel a little more connected to her old life, her old self. As the number of compliments grew, she realized that she'd probably gone overboard, judging by some of the reviews of "amazing," "fabulous," and "the best we've ever heard." She had meant to play like an average pianist, but once her fingers had hit the keys, she hadn't been able to stop herself. She didn't miss the pressure of her old life, but she did miss the music.

Outside the church, she stopped under a tree. Lexie was in the playground with Kimmy, twirling on the merry-go-round. The ladies' auxiliary had set up a buffet picnic with sandwiches, pastas, salads, desserts, even a Sno-Cone machine. At another table they were serving lemonade and punch. Angel's Bay certainly celebrated every moment of life.

If anyone had told her that she could trade London, Paris, Vienna, and Rome for a small seaside community on the California coast and be happy, she wouldn't have believed them. But aside from the constant worries about Brad, she was starting to fit in quite well here. She was getting to know people, making friends. She'd never really had girlfriends and she found the idea immensely appealing. She also saw Lexie blossoming with friends who already loved her. The two of them could bloom here.

"Jenna."

The sound of Reid's voice brought her head around. She'd been so caught up in her thoughts she hadn't seen him approach. Her heart skipped a beat at the sight of his face, still bruised from his fight but incredibly handsome. Her gaze dropped to the sexy mouth that had driven her crazy the night before. When she lifted her head, she saw a smoldering look of desire in his eyes and she knew that he was remembering, too. They might not agree on everything, but neither of them could deny they had chemistry.

"Hey," she said lightly. "I didn't figure you for a church-going guy."

He dug his hands into the pockets of his dark jeans. He had on a dark blue sweater today, the sleeves pushed up to his elbows. "I'm not, but as I was walking down the street, I heard a bunch of people talking about the best piano player Angel's Bay has ever had. They said it was almost as if an angel had come to play music in the church." He smiled. "I knew it was you."

"I'm no angel."

"You told me that the first day we met." He pulled a leaf out of her hair that must have fallen from the tree above. "I'm not so convinced anymore."

"I wasn't sure I'd see you again, after the way things ended last night."

"We're still partners."

"Business allies," she said. "I know it's simpler that way."

"I thought you didn't have regrets."

"I don't. I just . . ." Her voice trailed away as she realized she didn't know how to finish the sentence. Her emotions were all over the map where Reid was concerned. "I just want to change the subject. Would that be all right?"

"I'd be eternally grateful."

She couldn't help but smile at the relief on his face. "You are such a guy."

He smiled back at her. "Since we're on to a new topic, I have some interesting news. I was down on the beach this morning, doing my community clean-up for my bar fight, and I found something interesting in the sand."

"What's that?"

"The ship's bell from the *Gabriella*."

"Are you serious?"

"Yes, I am, and apparently nothing from that ship has washed ashore for the last hundred and fifty years—until today."

"Wow. And you were the one to find it. That's amazing. Almost a miracle!" She laughed at his expression of chagrin. "Sorry, I couldn't resist."

"There's nothing magical or miraculous about an old bell that came from a ship that sank offshore."

"I don't know about that. It feels a little magical to me, especially with the timing. This weekend is the anniversary of the wreck, the founding of the town, the reappearance of angels that haven't been seen in a long time. You don't find it all coincidental?"

He shrugged. "Coincidental perhaps, magical, no, but I might be the only one who sees it that way. The Harlan brothers also witnessed the discovery, and they're convinced that the angel flurries stirred up the waves and the ocean floor, and sent that bell to the surface. Roger claims the angels want the wreck to be found and that's why they've been flying around the cliffs."

"That's quite a theory. Sounds like you have a new twist for your article. So where is the bell now?"

"The chief took it into custody for the time being. I'm going down there later today to photograph it."

She was surprised at his level of interest, and the odd shadow that flitted through his eyes made her more curious. "What aren't you telling me?"

He shrugged. "I got a strange feeling when I put my hand on the bell. I felt as if I was on the ship when it shattered against the rocks. I could see the scene, the people scrambling to hang on as the ship tilted precariously, the water rushing over the side . . . It's crazy. It was so vivid in my mind."

"You're really caught up in this."

He inclined his head. "I do find it intriguing that

the wreck has never been found. The ship was allegedly carrying a great deal of gold, which has certainly lured many treasure hunters into looking for it, yet, its whereabouts remain a mystery. The ocean has hidden it away somewhere."

"Or the angels," she said. "Despite your cynical edge, you've tapped into the spiritual energy around here."

"The angels and the wreck are two separate things."

"Not according to the people who live here."

He gave her a thoughtful look. "You're starting to feel connected to this town, aren't you?"

"How can I not? If Rose Littleton really was my grandmother, and if Lexie's birthmark is the same as the one on Baby Gabriella, then both she and I are connected to that child, to that wreck." She paused. "If I ever get free of Brad, I'd like to spend some time researching it all. But first things first. Did you receive any more information from your private investigator?"

"Not yet, but I did have a disturbing conversation with Joe."

Hcr ncrvcs tightened at the mention of the chief. She didn't care for the turn in conversation or the way Reid called the chief "Joe," as if they were becoming friends.

"He's suspicious of you," Reid continued.

Her heart skipped a beat. "What do you mean?"

"He senses that you're scared and hiding something. He's already checked up on you."

"He told you that?" A wave of panic ran through her, and her breath came short and fast. "I have to go. I have to pack. I have to leave." She turned her head, searching for Lexie. "Where is she? Where's Lexie?" She started to move forward, but Reid grabbed her by the arm.

"Whoa, Jenna, calm down."

"Are you kidding me? If the chief is looking into my background, he'll find out I'm not Lexie's mother—if he hasn't already."

"He hasn't," Reid cut in.

"Are you sure?"

"Yes. Whatever cover story was set up for you has held true."

"But for how long? I can't stay here and wait for him to find out who I am. I can't take the chance that he won't discover the truth, won't call Brad, won't turn Lexie over to her father." She tried to pull away from Reid, but he held on tight.

"Chief Silveira has a great deal of integrity."

"And you would know this how—from a five-minute conversation on the beach?"

"Jenna—you're going to need to trust someone besides me."

She didn't care for the fact that Reid suddenly seemed to be on the chief's side instead of hers. "You can trust him if you want. I don't have to do the same."

"You need protection."

"Brad is a cop. The chief will not protect me. He'll protect his fellow officer."

"Brad is an imposter, Jenna, and I have enough information to prove that, if you'll let me."

He had a point, but what if the chief looked the other way? "He still might not believe us. He might want to give Brad the benefit of the doubt; call him up, talk to him."

"I think if we explain exactly what happened, the chief will be willing to work with us."

Since Reid had discovered the information about Brad's Social Security number and identity, there was a chance the police *would* listen to her—but that might not stop them from removing Lexie from her care. "Even if we can get the chief on my side, he could take Lexie away from me. Maybe he wouldn't give her to Brad, but she'd go into foster care. And you know what that's like."

Reid's mouth set in a grim line. "I do know, and I admit it's a possibility. But losing Lexie to foster care on a short-term basis is nowhere near as bad as losing her forever."

"I couldn't protect her if I wasn't with her," she said with a definitive shake of her head. "Kelly wanted me to stay with her. I promised, Reid. It was the last thing I said to my sister. I can't go back on my word."

Reid raked a hand through his hair, his expression one of frustration and reluctant understanding. "I hear you, Jenna, but Kelly tried to escape without help, and she lost her life. Some things you can't do alone. And while I'll do anything I can to protect the two of you, I'm afraid it won't be enough."

"I'm not asking you to protect me. The best thing for me to do is leave. I'm getting too close to people here. I'm sure the chief isn't the only one who has noticed my secrecy. The longer I stay in Angel's Bay, the more questions I'll have to answer."

"All of that is true, but then there's Lexie," Reid said, looking to where Lexie was playing happily on the merry-go-round. "She's thriving here. She has friends, a sense of security. You don't want to take that away from her. And if you're honest, you'll admit that you're happy here, too."

They *were* happy here, and this carefree existence was the kind of life Lexie deserved. But danger lurked in the shadows; a danger that could strike at any moment. Was Reid right? Was it time to take the risk of involving the cops in order to gain true freedom, to vanquish Brad forever? "I'll think about it," she said slowly.

Reid's gaze turned speculative. "Jenna, will you make me one promise?"

"What's that?"

"That you won't run without telling me first?"

She stared back at him for a long minute. "I'll think about that, too."

Joe was surprised to find a strange car parked in his driveway. He got out of his truck and took Rufus through the back gate. The sandy dog was in no condition to spend time with Rachel.

As he walked into the side yard, he heard voices

on the back deck. Rachel was talking to a man. She laughed at something the man said, and Joe stopped in his tracks, realizing it was the first time in forever that he'd heard her laugh so freely. It bothered him to realize that he wasn't the one who had made her sound so happy.

He moved out of the yard and up the back stairs. Sitting on the loveseat was a man who appeared to be in his mid thirties. He had the look of Beverly Hills about him: polo shirt, black slacks, slicked-down blond hair. Rachel looked up and saw him. Was there was a flicker of guilt in her eyes, or was he imagining it?

"Joe," she said quickly, jumping to her feet. "I was wondering where you'd gotten to. That was a long run on the beach."

"I had to go by the station for a while."

"This is Mark Devlin," she said. "Mark, my husband, Joe."

Devlin stood up to shake his hand. He had an easy smile on his face. "It's about time I got to meet you. Rachel has told me a lot about you."

"Really? She's told me nothing about you." He gave Devlin's hand a brief shake and then moved back to lean against the railing.

"Of course I have," Rachel interjected. "Mark is a film producer. I sold him his house in Beverly Hills last year. He's scouting locations for a new movie, so I called him this morning and told him about the haunted house on the bluff, and he drove up here to see it."

"That's quite a drive for an impulse," Joe said.

"Rachel is very convincing. She told me I needed to see this property right away," Mark returned.

"I doubt the house is going anywhere anytime soon," Joe said.

"Actually, when I spoke to Kara Lynch last night, she told me that they've had an offer on the house," Rachel interjected. "Kara is supposed to be here at two. She's bringing me some information on the property lines, and also said she'd show us some other locations that might work for the movie. Isn't that great?"

He supposed it was great that Rachel had found something of interest in Angel's Bay. He just didn't like that part of that interest seemed to be tied to Devlin, a man who had dropped everything to drive four hours north to check out an abandoned house.

"Oh, and I invited Mark to dinner," Rachel said. "Do you think you could barbecue some steaks?"

"So you're spending the night?" Joe asked.

"I thought I might check out the rest of town tomorrow," Mark replied. "I booked a room at the Seagull Inn. Nice place, a lot of atmosphere. I love small towns."

"Angel's Bay has nothing but atmosphere," Rachel said as the doorbell rang. "That's Kara. We should go." She waved Mark through the living room door, then poked her head back out to give Joe a smile. "Isn't this great? You get what you want and I get what I want. We're both happy."

She gave him an airy wave and walked into the house. He heard her introduce Mark to Kara, and then the door shut behind them. It was quiet again—too quiet, with the sound of their laughter still lingering in his mind. He couldn't help wondering if what Rachel wanted wasn't just a real estate deal, but also Mark Devlin.

TWENTY-ONE

"According to the phone records Stan was able to procure," Pete told Reid, "Kelly Winters called a man by the name of Rodney Harris three weeks before she was killed."

"Who is Rodney Harris?" Reid switched his cell phone to his other ear so he could jot down some notes.

"Who *was* Rodney Harris is a better question. He was robbed outside of his apartment and killed, a day after she called him."

Reid's pulse began to pick up. "You should have started with that."

"I like to save the best for last. Harris was a small-town insurance agent in North Carolina. His adult sister died about a decade ago, drowned in the backyard swimming pool. Harris thought her husband did it, but the man had an airtight alibi, and she had a high blood alcohol level. Her death was ruled an accidental drowning."

"What's the connection to Kelly Winters?"

"The husband's name was Steve Dunsmore. He vanished about a year after his wife's death, and I do mean vanished: no use of credit cards, no employment history, no bank accounts, nothing. But we did manage to locate an old photograph. And guess what?"

"Steve Dunsmore is Brad Winters," Reid said, putting the pieces together. "So he did this before. He killed his first wife and his second wife." His pulse began to race at the implications.

"I'm guessing that Rodney Harris told Kelly Winters that her husband wasn't who she thought he was."

"And Brad figured she was on to him, so he got rid of her. But the police who investigated Kelly's death must have known about Mr. Harris. The fact that Harris died after meeting with Kelly Winters should have alerted them to investigate further." Unless someone had stonewalled the investigation, or buried the connection between Harris and Kelly.

"I'm emailing you the photo of Steve Dunsmore now. If you want to catch this guy, you might have to move fast. His house is for sale, and this morning Stan did a drive-by and saw him loading up some boxes. He's going to run."

Judging by past history, Brad knew how to start fresh with a new identity. But in the past, he hadn't had a daughter. Would he want to disappear with Lexie? Or would he be more interested in saving himself? Brad had to know that with Lexie out there somewhere, and Jenna unaccounted for, they both posed a threat to him. The real question was, how far would Brad go to get rid of that threat?

"So, where's my angel story?" Pete asked.

"You'll have it by tonight. I'm just waiting on a photo. My story has a new twist."

"What's that?"

"You'll find out when you read it," Reid said, as he ended the call. He got up from the chair, grabbed his camera and jacket, and headed to Jenna's house.

Jenna ran her fingers over the piano keys, feeling a desperate need to play through her emotions. Since she'd left Reid at the church, she'd been going over and over her options. Running seemed the best idea, but the how and when eluded her. Lexie and Kimmy were happily ensconced in a game of dress-up in Lexie's bedroom, and their easy, happy laughter tormented her.

How could she rip Lexie's life apart again by taking her away from her new best friend, from a place she'd begun to think of as home? Yet how could she stay and take the risk that Brad would find her, or that the local cops would arrest her and send Lexie back to her father? Running seemed like the best plan. But while that might take her away from the local scrutiny, being alone on the road didn't mean she'd be safe from Brad.

She had to think. She had to be smart.

The panic inside of her was clouding her judgment. She had to release the tension, so she hit one note and then another. The melody took over. Her fingers knew what to do. She just went along for the ride, hoping that by the end of the song everything would be clear.

At first she didn't hear the doorbell. The ring blurred with the music, but her critical ear soon discerned the jarring sound from the beauty of her piece. She lifted her hands and went to answer it. Glancing through the peephole, she saw Reid on the step and her heart jumped in spite of herself. She'd told herself that getting more involved with him was out of the question, but her body hadn't quite caught up with her brain.

She opened the door and Reid strode in, purposeful and decisive.

"I have more information," he said.

"One second." She walked over and closed the door to the hall, not wanting the girls to hear their conversation. Then she took a seat on the couch. "Okay. Go ahead." As Reid related the facts he'd uncovered about Brad's true identity, Jenna's bewilderment grew. "I don't understand how your detective could figure all this out, but the cops investigating Kelly's murder couldn't," she said after he finished.

"They never considered Brad a suspect. Or someone covered up the facts. Brad was their friend, their partner; he actually had an exemplary record as a police officer."

"But he was a murderous husband of two innocent women. And God knows who else he killed along the way." She lifted her gaze to Reid's. "I'm ready to talk to the chief. I just hope we have enough evidence to make our case."

"We do, and I'm glad you've come to that decision," Reid said with an approving nod. "Joe is meeting me at the station in thirty minutes so I can photograph the bell. Why don't you come with me?"

"Thirty minutes? That seems so soon." It was one thing to make the decision; another to act on it.

"The only way to truly be free of Brad is to make sure someone catches him before he catches you. This is the first step."

"I'm just scared. I don't want to mess this up."

"You won't. What about Lexie? Are we taking her with us?"

"I'll call Kimmy's mother and see if she can watch Lexie for an hour. We can drop the girls off on the way."

Reid put a hand on her arm as she stood up. "I heard you playing when I came up to the house. I'm glad you're finding your way back into the music."

"It helps calm me down."

"Hearing you play has the opposite effect on me. I can see your hands on the keys, and I can see your hands on me."

She sucked in a breath at the look in his eyes. "I thought we were keeping things all business."

"Yeah, me, too. But I still want to kiss you."

"It won't make it easier to say good-bye."

"We're not saying good-bye."

"Not yet," she whispered. Despite her words, she

was the one who leaned forward and pressed her lips against his. She needed him as much as he needed her. Whatever else would be decided later—much later.

Joe Silveira stared down at the information Reid Tanner had compiled on Brad Winters aka Steve Dunsmore. Jenna's story was much worse than he'd suspected. He'd believed that she was a battered wife, possibly on the run from an abusive husband who wasn't as dead as she'd claimed, but things were far more complicated than that.

He set the papers down and lifted his gaze to meet Jenna's. Her face was pale, her eyes resolute. Her expression reminded him of when he'd seen her on the docks after she'd jumped into the bay to save Annie Dupont. This was a woman who did what she had to do, even at great personal risk. She was terrified but also determined. He found himself liking her, wanting to help her. He was glad she'd finally decided to trust him. He suspected that he had Reid Tanner to thank for that. It was obvious the reporter had more than a business interest in Jenna. He stood behind Jenna's chair with one hand on her shoulder, his stance clearly protective.

Joe turned his focus to Jenna, whose nervousness was palpable, but from what he'd read she had a lot of good reasons to be wary of him. "I can understand your hesitation to involve the police, but I'm glad you came in. I want to help you and Lexie."

"My main concern is Lexie's safety and that she and I stay together," Jenna said quickly. "Lexie has been through a terrible trauma, and if she were to be taken from me now, I don't know how she could cope. There's no way she can go back to her father. I hope you're not considering that as an option."

Joe suspected that if he gave Jenna the wrong answer, she'd take Lexie and bolt before he had time to get social services on the phone. "I understand your concern. Let's take this one step at a time."

"The police department where Brad works could have discovered this information if they'd only looked," Jenna said. "Or perhaps they did look and chose to cover it up because he's their fellow police officer."

"That's a serious charge."

"And not one I'm making lightly," she said forcefully. "If you call Brad's department, someone will tell him where I am, where his daughter is. He'll come after us. I'm sure of that." She hesitated, giving Reid a quick look before she continued. "There's a good possibility that Lexie saw her father murder her mother. I think that's the reason why Brad didn't tell anyone that Lexie was in the house, why no one is looking for her. He doesn't want her to identify him as her mother's murderer."

Joe had already checked the missing persons' database to ensure that Lexie/Caroline Winters wasn't on it. There had been no report filed indicating that Lexie was missing or in jeopardy. So far Jenna seemed to be telling the truth, which gave him a little breathing room. The fact that Brad Winters had not reported his daughter missing was an unusual choice for a man whose wife had been murdered. It was certainly one that warranted investigation.

"Brad told the detectives that Lexie was with a relative," Jenna added. "So, technically that's true. She's with me. And the fact that I have her isn't a crime, right? If Brad wanted her back, he'd have told people to look for her."

Jenna was skating on thin ice, but for the moment he would go along with it, at least until he had more information. "I will handle this with the utmost discretion," he assured her.

"But you can't make me any promises."

"The issue of custody is not one I can decide."

"Lexie's father is a murderer."

"That hasn't been proven."

"So you would send Lexie back to him in the meantime?" she asked in horror.

"I didn't say that."

She jerked to her feet. "Look, I promised my sister that I would protect Lexie. She can't go back to Brad, not for a second. And aside from my father, I'm Lexie's closest blood relative. She loves me, and I love her. We belong together. I would give up my life for her."

He saw the desperation in her eyes, and he wanted to reassure her, if for no other reason than to prevent her from taking immediate flight. "I'll do everything I can to make sure Lexie is protected and that she stays with you until I'm legally obligated to place her somewhere else."

"I don't like the sound of that. This was a mistake."

"Jenna—" Reid cut in, grabbing her by the arm as she turned toward the door.

She shook him off. "You heard him. Lexie might have to go back to Brad."

"That's not what he said, and we won't let that happen," Reid said. "Will we, Chief?"

Joe stood up, meeting Reid's gaze. "Certainly not without a thorough investigation." He turned to Jenna. "Give me a chance to sort through this information, and then we'll see where we're at. I have no intention of placing Lexie into any situation that could be harmful to her, and that includes her father's custody. You have my word on that. In the meantime, I'm going to have my officers keep an eye on your house."

"Do you really believe us?" Jenna asked. "You're not just playing along, are you?"

"No. I don't think you would have come to me if you were guilty of anything. And I have no tolerance for a police officer who uses his position and his power to get away with any crime, much less murder. I have no allegiance to this man or to anyone who might be helping him cover up a crime. I don't care if they're wearing a uniform or not."

She gave him a long searching look, then let out a sigh. "I guess I have to trust you. I hope I'm not wrong."

"You're not. What I would like to do is meet tomorrow, first thing in the morning."

"Lexie has summer school. I can come in after I drop her off at nine."

"Perfect."

"I suppose that officer who's going to be watching my house is probably also going to be watching me, isn't he?" she asked.

"Don't think about leaving town," Joe said. "It's not the answer. You need help, and right now I'm your best chance."

She nodded with reluctant acceptance. "I'm not sure I could leave Angel's Bay even if I tried. This town seems to have a grip on us."

He smiled. "I know what you mean. I've only been here a few weeks longer than you, but it feels like I've been here forever. There's something about Angel's Bay that gets under your skin."

"Speaking of Angel's Bay," Reid interjected. "I still need to get a few photos of that bell before we take off."

"Right. I'd almost forgotten." Joe opened the locked cabinet behind his desk and placed the bell on his desk. Reid and Jenna both leaned in for a closer look.

"Wow, this is amazing," Jenna said, as her fingers traced the engraved letters. "I can't believe it's been lost all these years and then it's suddenly found."

"Unless someone put it on the beach to be discovered," Joe said, unable to keep the cynicism out of his voice.

"Someone wanting to drum up more tourist business?" Reid asked as he snapped photos.

"Could be," Joe replied. "I find the timing interesting, with the sudden influx of angel sightings."

"Maybe the angels really did bring it to the surface," Jenna suggested.

"You believe in the angels?" he asked her.

"Well, right now I really need to believe in something hopeful—so why not angels?"

"I'm sure there are a lot of people who will feel the same way you do," he replied. "Unfortunately, I think this bell will bring more than angel fanatics to town. I'm betting we'll soon see fortune hunters and who knows who else."

"Who knows," Jenna muttered, exchanging a quick look with Reid as she took his hand.

Their joined hands reminded Joe that he had a woman waiting at home for him, too. Unfortunately, she was with another man.

After their trip to the police station, Reid saw Jenna home and then returned to the hotel to finish his angel article. It was difficult to concentrate—his mind kept replaying their meeting with the chief. He believed that Joe would help them end Jenna's nightmare, but he didn't know what the cost would be. It was possible that Jenna might still lose Lexie to foster care, and he couldn't imagine either one of them being able to handle such a split. But as Joe had said, first things first...

He uploaded the photographs of the ship's bell to his computer, and attached them to the file he was about to send. He knew Pete would love this twist, tying the angels into an old shipwreck and a missing fortune. No doubt he'd want a follow-up story, but Reid wouldn't be the one to write it. Once he sent in the article, his assignment in Angel's Bay would be officially over. He would have no reason to stay in town except for Jenna.

He'd told her he would stay until Brad was captured, until she and Lexie were safe. He couldn't possibly walk away from her while she was in danger. Walking away afterward—that was another story.

He had to go. He knew he had to go.

But Jenna wasn't an easy woman to leave. She was more than just a good time, more than a casual lover. She was his friend. She understood him in a way that no one ever had, which scared the shit out of him. He'd never done love, but Lord, he was tempted. Jenna was beautiful, sexy, wonderful, kind—and she also had some very heavy baggage in the form of one energetic seven-year-old. Jenna and Lexie needed a man who could be a husband, a father, and he didn't know how to do either. He'd let them down. He knew he would.

Shaking his head, he hit the send button on his email. Then he shut down his computer and walked over to the window. The moon had risen high in the sky. Another day had come and gone. Tomorrow would do the same. He could continue counting off the days, the way he'd been doing since Allison's death, or he could start making the days count.

But he didn't know how to do that.

Didn't he? A voice in his head countered. All he had to do was call her, or better yet, go over to her house and see her, care about her, love her.

His stomach clenched.

Then his cell phone rang. He'd given Jenna his number earlier. He knew it was her before he opened the phone.

"What's wrong?" he asked, not bothering to say hello.

"Nothing. Everything's fine," Jenna said. "Well, as close to fine as it can be, under the circumstances. It's been a crazy day."

"Yeah, I know. You did the right thing."

"I hope so." She paused. "This probably sounds strange since we were together most of the day, but I—I miss you, Reid. I know we're not talking forever, but do you want to come over tonight? Lexie's gone to bed. We could have coffee, whatever."

Her sweet invitation, filled with so much promise, made his heart turn over. "I can't," he said, making an abrupt decision. "I'm sorry." His hand tightened around the phone. He knew he should offer an explanation, but he suspected she'd only see through it, and the last thing he wanted to do was lie to her.

"I'm sorry, too," she said.

"I'll call you tomorrow, or you call me back if there's any problem. Okay? I'm here for you."

"If there's a problem," Jenna repeated, making it clear that she understood the boundaries. "Good night, Reid."

The phone clicked in his ear. He hung up, feeling

like the biggest coward in the world. What the fuck was wrong with him?

He needed a drink.

But even as the thought crossed his mind, he knew that wasn't what he needed. He needed Jenna. And he'd just told her to back the hell away. He might be the stupidest man on the planet.

TWENTY-TWO

Jenna tossed and turned in bed, feeling hot, unsettled, worried, and angry. She'd known all along Reid was just looking for a casual fling. She shouldn't have been surprised that he'd backed off. She just hadn't expected it quite so soon.

The man was crazy. They were good together. They connected. Why couldn't he see that?

Maybe he did, but he just didn't want to accept it. They came from different worlds, and after this was over they'd go back to those different worlds—maybe. She actually liked Angel's Bay, and Lexie was happy here. They could stay. They could share their true ties to the town. They could make friends; bloom where they'd been planted.

But this wasn't Reid's life. He didn't want a wife, a child, a small cottage in a small town with a small newspaper. Did he?

Maybe what he really wanted was just that—the family he'd missed his entire life. Not that he'd ever admit it. He wouldn't take that risk. He'd probably stay closed off and guilt-ridden and eager to live a life on the road, where he never had to confront the idea of permanence.

She sighed and turned over again, squeezing her lids shut, trying to drive Reid out of her head. She needed to sleep. She had to get up early to make breakfast for Lexie and take her to summer school.

She brought up some of her favorite going-to-sleep images: the sun setting over the ocean, the moon rising in the twilight. A puffy cloud of white floated in front of her eyes. She saw a face—Kelly's face. She wasn't smiling; she was worried. Why was she worried? Because of Brad.

Deep in the recesses of her brain, she could hear Brad's voice . . .

"Hey, baby, did you miss me?"

"Daddy?" Lexie asked sleepily. "Is that you?"

"That's right, baby. It's me. I finally found you. And now we're going to be together forever."

"Are we going home? What about Mommy?"

"Your mommy left you, baby. I'm all you've got, and I'm never going to let you go again. You still love me, don't you?"

"Yes, but—but you—you hurt Mommy," she stuttered.

"That was an accident. Now let's go. Put on your shoes."

"No, I want Mommy."

"I'll take you to see her."

"But . . . Mommy is in heaven."

"No, she's not, baby. I'll take you to her. You just have to come with me."

Jenna awoke with a start, her heart pounding. Had she just heard Brad's voice? Or had she been dreaming? She turned toward the monitor. Everything was quiet, but his voice had seemed so real, so near.

She got out of bed and walked down the hall. Lexie's door was closed. Jenna put her hand on the frame, listening. Then she slowly turned the knob and opened the door.

Her heart stopped. Brad had Lexie in his arms. She had on tennis shoes and a jacket over her pajamas. Her arms were around her father's neck. She looked both guilty and scared.

"Daddy is going to take me to see Mommy," Lexie said, her voice uncertain.

Jenna drew in a shaky breath, knowing she had to tread carefully. "Put her down, Brad."

"Did you really think you could keep my daughter away from me?" Brad asked.

"I won't let you take her."

"But I want to see Mommy," Lexie said. "Daddy is taking me to see her. He said so. He promised."

The desperate agony on Lexie's face showed how badly she wanted to believe that her mother was alive. Jenna knew she had to kill that impossible dream, but it tore her apart to say the words. "Your mommy is dead. You know that. You can't see her. You have to stay here with me. That's what your mommy wanted."

"She's lying," Brad said in a quiet voice. "Your mommy is waiting for you. She can't wait to see you. We're going to make hot fudge sundaes the way we used to, remember, baby?"

Jenna could see the indecision on Lexie's face. The lies Brad was willing to tell weren't just wrong; they were cruel. "Don't do this, Brad. Let her go. She's safe with me, and no one ever has to know where we are. You can go on with your life. We won't say anything."

"I can't take that chance."

"You're hurting her," Jenna pleaded, seeing the tears streaming down Lexie's face.

"Daddy, I don't want to go anymore," Lexie said. "I want to stay here."

"I need you, baby. You're my little girl. We have to be together, or I'll be lonely—and you don't want that, do you?"

Jenna's heart broke at the pain on Lexie's face. She wanted to believe her father, but somewhere down in the recesses of her mind she knew that her father had done something horrible.

Brad moved toward the open window. Jenna had nailed the window shut, but Brad had somehow gotten it open.

She started forward, intent on stopping him, but he pulled out a gun and pointed it at her head. There was no mistaking the determination in his eyes.

"Don't move," he said. "My daughter is going with me."

"I'm scared," Lexie cried. "Daddy, I don't want to go anymore!"

"You're going," he repeated as Lexie began to squirm in his arms. "Goddammit, stop moving. If you try to get away, I'll kill your aunt."

Lexie froze, her terrified eyes meeting Jenna's.

Jenna had never felt so scared or so helpless in her life.

Reid had decided to take a walk to burn off his restless energy. He was only a few blocks from his hotel when he saw a female figure walking along the sidewalk in front of him. As she passed under a streetlight, he caught a glimpse of her red hair. It was the woman he'd seen in the bar a few nights earlier. He was sure of it. It couldn't possibly be Allison—but he needed proof, so he could leave town and never look back, never wonder if he'd seen a ghost or an angel.

She turned the corner, walking down a narrow path between buildings, and Reid took off after her. He could see her shadow as she turned another corner; she seemed to be moving more quickly. He picked up the pace, his heart racing as he tried to keep up with the elusive figure. He told himself over and over again that he was chasing a real person, but his instincts told him that no woman could move so fast, so quietly, so quickly into the night.

The salty ocean air blew wisps of fog against his face, turning the shadowy buildings into eerie shapes. He blinked the moisture out of his eyes, and it wasn't until he turned the next corner that he realized he was on Jenna's street. His steps slowed, faltered. His gaze swept the neighborhood. There was no sign of the woman he'd been following, but there was a police car parked at the end of the street, a few houses away from Jenna's house. The front door on the driver's side was open, and there was a figure lying on the ground.

Reid moved into a dead run. When he reached the car, he dropped to his knees next to the officer on the ground. The man was on his back, blood coming from a wound in his head. It was Colin Lynch. He was unconscious.

Reid put a hand on his neck. There was a faint pulse, a whisper of breath coming from his parted lips. Reid leaned into the car and grabbed the radio, reporting an officer down at 910 Elmwood Lane. He could hear the dispatcher shouting questions at him, but he couldn't take the time to answer. Every instinct he had told him that Jenna was in trouble.

He took off his jacket and laid it over Colin. Hearing the sound of a siren in the distance, he knew that help was on its way. He ran down the street to Jenna's house. The front door was locked. He jerked at the handle, but it wouldn't budge. He vaulted over the porch railing, grabbed a heavy vase filled with flowers, and hurled it at the window. As the glass shattered, he heard a woman scream.

And he knew that Jenna's worst fear had come true. Brad Winters had found her.

A window shattered somewhere in the house, then Reid shouted her name. Jenna was torn between wanting him to come to her rescue, and terror that Brad would hurt him. "It's too late," she said to Brad. "Just leave your daughter and go."

"She's mine! I'm not going anywhere without her." Brad forced Lexie through the open window. It was at least a four-foot drop to the ground below. Lexie struggled in his arms, but he was too big and too strong. She screamed as she tumbled to the ground.

"Run, Lexie, run," Jenna yelled.

Brad raised his gun and fired at Jenna. She ducked, but a burning pain seared through her shoulder as she fell to her knees in shock.

Reid burst through the bedroom door behind her, his wild gaze taking in the scene in one swift second. Brad fired again, forcing Reid to jump to one side as Brad climbed out the window, dropping to the ground below.

Police sirens roared through the night. Would they be in time to save Lexie?

Jenna stumbled to her feet, dizzy and terrified. Reid grabbed her hands. "You're hurt. You're bleeding."

"I'm okay. Find Lexie!" she said. "Save her, Reid! Please, you have to save her."

"I will. Don't die on me, Jenna. Don't you die on me." He grabbed her face, kissed her hard on the lips, then ran to the window. He climbed out, and Jenna prayed he would find Lexie before Brad did.

Reid ran through the side yard, cursing the fact that Jenna's house was surrounded by woods. He heard dogs barking, and then he saw a flash of pink through the trees. It had to be Lexie's sweater. She was headed toward the bluffs. He ran through the woods, seeing a dark figure in front of him also pursuing Lexie. He couldn't let Lexie go with that monster. He had to get to her first.

It was difficult to see in the thick crush of trees. He stumbled over rocks and branches, battling through them for almost a quarter mile, before he finally burst into an open area. Brad and Lexie were struggling on the edge of the cliff.

He ran toward them, trying to stay out of Brad's sightline. Lexie punched her small fists against Brad's chest as he tried to get her into his arms. She was a small tornado of fury, and their struggle was taking them closer and closer to the edge. One wild jerk, one hard kick to Brad's groin area, and suddenly Brad lost his grip on his daughter. Lexie waved her arms in wide windmill circles as her feet slipped out from under her on the loose dirt. She was going over the side!

Reid sprinted toward them. He wasn't going to get there in time.

Brad grabbed Lexie by the foot, but her momentum took them both over the edge.

Reid's heart jumped into his throat. For one terrified moment he thought Lexie was gone forever, but when he got to the edge of the cliff he saw that Brad and Lexie had landed about ten yards down the hillside, right before it turned into a sheer wall of rock. Brad was hanging on to a boulder with one arm, his other hand gripping Lexie's leg. Her hands were dug into the dirt, but there was only a foot of hillside left in front of her. Brad was struggling to pull her up next to him without losing his grip on the boulder, which was the only thing stopping them from tumbling into the dark sea.

Lexie was sobbing hysterically, her terrified movements making it more difficult for Brad to hang on to her.

Reid picked his way down the hill as fast as he could, his feet sliding on the loose dirt. Tiny pebbles scattered with each step. He stayed low, keeping his upper body against the hillside, slowing his descent by sliding his hands through the dirt and shrubs. Even if he got down to Lexie, he had no idea how he would make it back up. But somehow he would do it, because he wasn't going to lose her. He wasn't going to let her die.

Brad watched him with an intense gaze that made Reid wonder if he'd let go of Lexie and shoot him before he took another step. But he had to take the risk.

"Lexie? It's me, Reid. I'm going to take you home now." He was only a foot away from Lexie's free leg. She turned her head to look at him, her face streaked with tears, terror in her eyes. Her movement sent another scatter of pebbles over the sheer rock wall. He took a small sliding step, grabbing her free ankle. He felt better knowing he had a hold of her, but now she was stretched like a wishbone between him and her father, and Brad wasn't going to just give her up.

"Let her go," Reid yelled over the sound of the ocean. "The police will be here any second. They're already at the house. You're not getting away. It's over."

"She's my daughter. *Mine.*"

"And you can save her life. You can let me take her to safety. I know you don't want her to die."

Brad looked at his daughter, who now turned to him. "Daddy?" she asked in a voice that made Reid's heart break. She was scared of her father, yet some part of her still wanted him to be her dad, to love her, to save her.

"I know who you really are," Reid continued as Brad hesitated. "I know about your past, your first wife, your real name. We went to the local police today and told the chief everything. No one will protect you this time. You're going to jail." Brad didn't answer. "But you can do the right thing now. You can let your daughter live."

Brad's gaze moved to Lexie. "Baby, I love you. Do you hear me? I love you," he shouted.

Lexie began to cry.

"You were the only good thing that ever happened to me," Brad continued. "I'm sorry about your mother. It was an accident. You have to believe me."

"I believe you, Daddy," Lexie said with gulping sobs. "I love you. But I'm scared, and I want to go home."

"You will, baby. You'll go home, and you'll grow up, and you won't be anything like me. I only wanted the best for you. You have to remember that. Promise me."

"I promise, Daddy."

Brad looked over at Reid. "Don't let her fall." Then he slowly released Lexie's leg.

Reid carefully pulled Lexie toward him, her stomach scraping on the ground as he inched back up the hill. He wanted to catch hold of her arm, turn her around so she wasn't facing downward, but it was all he could do to keep his balance and continue moving upward. The fog had thickened around them, and the mist blew thick into his face. Or *was* it a mist?

He blinked as the image of a woman took shape before him. Her hair was blond, her eyes sad.

He suddenly felt a hand on his, adding strength to his grip. Lexie's weight lightened, and with a final surge of energy, he pulled himself and Lexie over the top of the hill. Taking her in his arms, he gasped for breath as he tried to assimilate what had just happened.

Lexie stared past him at the shape that had guided them to safety.

"Mommy, you're here," she whispered.

The words *I'll love you forever* floated across the air. *Be happy always.* The angel smiled and blew them a kiss. Then she was gone.

Reid wiped his wet eyes, sure he was hallucinating.

Lexie was smiling at him now, her cheeks streaked with tears and dirt. "Mommy's okay. She's in heaven. She still loves me."

Lexie threw her arms around Reid's neck and squeezed tight. He hugged her back, not sure he could ever let her go.

He heard shouts from afar and saw two policemen emerging through the trees—the chief and another officer. He stood up with Lexie in his arms, her face now buried in his chest. The fog seemed to have lifted again. He looked over the side of the cliff. Brad still clung to the boulder. Reid was surprised he hadn't tried to climb back up, but there was no escape for him now. Jenna and Lexie would have their justice.

"You two all right?" Joe asked.

Reid nodded. "He's down there."

When Brad saw the officers, he turned his gaze on the sea below.

Suddenly Reid knew why Brad hadn't scrambled up the hill. He didn't intend to be taken alive. "I'm getting Lexie out of here," he said to Joe.

He moved quickly, but they were still only a few feet away when he heard a loud cry that was quickly swallowed up by the sound of the waves crashing on the rocks below. Brad Winters was not going to hurt anyone ever again.

As Reid approached Jenna's house, an ambulance sped away. A fire engine and two other police cars were still parked in front. Jenna sat on the top step, a paramedic treating her shoulder. A bunch of neighbors had gathered nearby, and someone had laid a quilt over Jenna's knees.

Jenna let out a sob when she saw him and Lexie. He sat next to her on the step as the paramedic moved away, and Lexie took her head out of his chest long enough to see if her aunt was okay. Her mouth trembled when she saw the blood.

"I'm all right," Jenna told her with a tearful sniff. "I have to get some stitches, that's all. I'm fine."

"Why are you crying?" Lexie asked.

"Because I'm so happy you're okay," Jenna said. "I'm sorry, honey. I'm so sorry."

"I saw Mommy," Lexie told her. "She saved me, didn't she, Mr. Tanner?"

Reid didn't want to admit that he'd seen an angel, but he couldn't deny what had happened. He slowly nodded. "She did. She helped pull us up."

"Pull you up from where?" Jenna asked, searching his face with worried eyes.

"The cliff."

"Oh my God, Reid—"

"It's over, Jenna. She's safe."

"Mommy smiled at me," Lexie continued. "She said, 'I'll love you forever. Be happy.' She's going to heaven now. She just wanted to say good-bye."

Jenna's mouth trembled, and Reid felt tears gather in his own eyes. The little girl had lost both her parents, but she still believed in heaven. Maybe that was the *true* miracle.

Lexie's arms tightened around Reid's neck and then she buried her face in his chest.

"Brad?" Jenna whispered.

"It's over. You're safe now."

She nodded, relief in her eyes. "They want me to go to the hospital to get some stitches."

"We're coming with you."

"Thank you. I want you to be with me, and I don't think Lexie intends to let you go."

"I'm not letting her go, either." Reid looked up as Joe approached them. The chief's face was grim.

"Did you tell her what happened?" the chief asked, obviously not wanting to discuss Brad's death in front of Lexie.

"I will," Reid answered.

"I need to talk to both of you, but right now I have to get to the hospital," Joe said. "I'd prefer it if you spent the night elsewhere. I'd like to keep the crime scene intact. I understand your brother-in-law broke into your house."

"Yes, through the window in Lexie's bedroom." Jenna paused. "I'm so sorry that Brad shot Colin. I feel terrible. I brought this monster to the town, and it's my fault."

"No, it isn't. Officer Lynch was doing his duty," Joe said heavily. "One he chose gladly and willingly."

"I pray that he'll be all right," Jenna said.

"So do I," Joe returned. "So do I."

Twenty-Three

Kara Lynch woke up abruptly, and glanced at Colin's side of the bed. It was empty; he was on the night shift. Everything was fine, she thought—but a shiver ran down her body. The curtains rustled as if by a breeze, but the windows were shut.

Then the doorbell rang.

She knew she'd been waiting for it, though she didn't understand why.

Now she was afraid to answer it.

The bell pealed again, followed by a determined knock. Kara got up, put on her bathrobe, and walked slowly to the front door. Looking through the peephole, she saw Joe on the step, his face pale and grim under the porch light.

Her hand trembled as she opened the door.

"What happened to Colin?" she asked, her stomach turning over.

"He was shot, Kara. He's on his way to the hospital. I'll take you there now."

"He's going to be all right," she said. Because there was no alternative.

"Yes, of course he will," Joe said, but she saw the fear in his eyes.

"We're having a baby. Colin has to be okay. I need him. I can't do this alone. I *can't*."

"You'd better get dressed, Kara."

Terror swept through her like a wildfire, but she couldn't break down. She had to get to her husband. She had to believe in Colin. He was going to live. He was going to make it. He simply had to.

Colin had been airlifted to a hospital thirty miles away from Angel's Bay, a facility that handled serious trauma cases. Kara was barely aware of the drive along the foggy coast in Joe's squad car. The siren blazed through the night, the strobe lights flashing off the water. During the trip she prayed to God, to the angels that Colin believed in, to all of her family members who had passed on, and to the universe in general. She offered up bribes and bargains, things she would do if only Colin would live.

How could she go on without him? He was her husband, her lover, her best friend—the man she wanted to spend the rest of her life with. He was the father of her child. She put a hand to her abdomen, feeling the flutter of a tiny foot or hand against her rib cage. Her baby needed Colin. So did she. They'd been together forever. He was her first love—her last love. It could not end now—not like this, not without warning. She wasn't ready. She would never be ready.

Tears streamed down her face, and she was vaguely aware of Joe pressing a tissue into her hand. She wiped her eyes, knowing she had to be strong. She could hear Colin's voice in her head, telling her not to worry, that everything would be all right. She had to keep the faith.

When they arrived at the hospital, Joe took her upstairs to a waiting room. Two of Colin's fellow officers were already there, both in their street clothes. They hadn't been on duty, but they'd come as soon as they'd heard. They each gave her a hug, but she couldn't feel anything but mind-numbing pain. Someone helped her into a chair. Someone told her that Colin was in surgery and the doctor would be out as soon as it was over.

Over? If Colin didn't survive . . . She couldn't even finish the thought; it was too terrifying. So she stared at the clock on the wall, watching the minutes go by.

Whenever she woke in the night after a bad dream, Colin took her in his arms, smoothed her hair, kissed her on the lips, and told her that everything would be fine in the morning, that she wouldn't even remember the nightmare.

She wanted the sun to come up now. She wanted the nightmare to end. She couldn't wait until the morning.

* * *

After getting her stitches, Jenna found Reid and Lexie in the waiting room of the Redwood Medical Center emergency room. She knew that Colin Lynch had been taken to a trauma center down the coast, and she wanted to go there as soon as possible, but it was the middle of the night, and Lexie was exhausted. In fact, she was stretched out on a couch fast asleep. Reid stood up as soon as he saw Jenna and quickly moved to her side, concern in his eyes.

"Are you all right?" he asked, his gaze dropping to the sling supporting her arm and shoulder.

"I don't feel a thing now," she said with a tired smile. "They gave me something for the pain. But it was just a surface wound. I should have ducked more quickly."

"You shouldn't have had to duck at all. I should have been there with you."

She heard the self-recrimination in his voice and it bothered her. "You *were* there with me," she reminded him.

"Too late. If I'd come over earlier—"

She cut him off, putting her free hand against his mouth. "Shut up, Reid. I won't let you take on any more guilt. We were never your responsibility. And the truth is, you were there when it counted. You saved Lexie's life! I can't ever thank you enough." She lifted her hand. "Why *did* you come to my house? I thought we weren't going to see each other tonight."

An odd look entered his eyes. "I went out to take a walk, and I saw that woman again—the one with the red hair, the one who reminded me of Allison. At least I thought it was her. I followed the vision, and the next thing I knew I was on your street, and she'd disappeared. I saw Colin on the ground next to his squad car, and I knew Brad was in your house. It seemed to take forever for me to get to you." He put his hands on her waist, pulling her close. "When I walked into that room and saw Brad with a gun, and you on the ground—" He shook his head. "If I'd been a second later, he might have killed you."

"But you weren't a second later. And I'm all right."

He lifted one hand to her hair, tucking a strand behind her ear. "I might have to stare at you for the next couple of days just to make sure."

She gave him a soft smile. "That's okay with me." She pulled him farther away from Lexie, then drew in a breath. "I have to ask, Reid: What happened out on the bluff? How did Brad die? And are you sure he's dead?"

"When I found Brad, he was struggling with Lexie. She was fighting him like a little tiger cat, but they got too close to the edge, and she slipped. Brad reached for her and they both went over the side. The hillside goes down about ten yards and then hits a sheer wall of rock. Brad managed to grab on to Lexie's leg and a boulder before they reached the point of no return." Reid swallowed hard. "I went down to get her. I told him it was over, that we knew everything about him. For a minute I didn't think he'd let her go. But then she looked at him, and she said *Daddy* in that sweet little voice of hers, so full of hope that he'd do the right thing. She must have gotten through to him. He told her that he loved her, that she was best thing that ever happened to him, and that he was sorry for her mother's death." Reid paused. "Brad let me save her, Jenna. He could have taken her with him over the side, but some small piece of his soul wouldn't let him kill his child."

"Thank God for that. I can't believe he's really gone, though. I wish I could have seen it for myself." It would take a while to really feel safe.

"He's gone," Reid replied. "It was a hundred-foot drop to the sea with jagged boulders anywhere he would have landed. He couldn't have survived. But I'm sure the police will look for his body in the morning."

"What about the angel Lexie mentioned? Was it just her imagination?"

A small smile crossed Reid's lips. "I did see what appeared to be an angel—an angel that looked a lot like Lexie. There was a moment when I thought I wasn't going to be able to pull both of us up the cliff. The dirt was loose, I couldn't get my footing, and Lexie was in an awkward position. And then I felt new strength, as if someone had given me a hand. Want to tell me I'm crazy?"

"How could I? I'd like to believe that Kelly is all right, that she's in a better place. And the fact that Brad saved Lexie is something that she can cling to as she grows up, as she tries to make sense of it all. But I'm still afraid that she's going to be totally messed up."

"You'll straighten her out. It may not be easy, and it may take a long time and a lot of love—but Lexie is lucky to have you. You're an incredible woman, Jenna." His lips tightened. "When I heard you scream, I was so afraid that I'd lose you before—"

"Before what?" she asked.

"Before I had a chance to tell you that I loved you."

She sucked in a quick breath of air. "You don't do love, remember?"

"Yeah, I remember." Reid took her hand in his, his fingers curling around hers. "I didn't want to come over tonight because I was afraid to give in to what I was feeling. I wanted to be able to walk away without looking back—but I was lying to myself, Jenna. I'd already fallen for you; I just wasn't ready to admit it. Now I am. Because life is short, and I don't want to waste another second being stupid."

"Oh, Reid." She gave him a teary smile. "I'm crazy about you. I know it's fast, but it's also true. Maybe it's this place. I feel like this was meant to be—you and me and Lexie. She loves you, too. And just so you know, we can take things as slow as you want. We don't have to rush into anything. We don't even have to stay here," she said, wanting to make sure that he understood that. "If you want to go back to your paper or do something else, we can work it out. I'm finally free—not just of Brad, but also of my father and his expectations, and a life I didn't want anymore. I want you to be free, too. Free from your guilt over Allison, free from your difficult past. I want you to be happy. I want *us* to be happy."

Reid tilted up her face. "When I was a little kid, the only thing I ever really wanted was a family: people who I could love and who would love me back."

"You have that now."

"Then we'll figure out the rest as we go along," he said, with a tender kiss.

Jenna threw her arms around his neck and pulled his head down to hers, starting a kiss that would last for the rest of their lives.

It was just after seven o'clock on Monday morning when Charlotte found Joe standing alone at the end of the hospital corridor, down the hall from where Kara Lynch and her family and friends waited for a report on Colin's condition. She'd arrived at the hospital thirty minutes ago, wanting to check on Kara before she returned to the clinic and her schedule of patients.

"Hey," she said quietly.

Joe turned quickly. "Is there any news?"

She shook her head, wishing she didn't have to disappoint him. "No, not yet."

"He's hurt bad," Joe said.

"Yes, he is."

"I shouldn't have put him on patrol last night without more specific instructions. Jenna told me that her brother-in-law was after her, and I knew trouble was coming our way. I just didn't think it would get here so fast."

"I'm sure you prepared Colin."

"I didn't say enough. I didn't *do* enough." His eyes were pained and angry.

She put a hand on his arm. "You did your job, Joe, and so did Colin. I grew up with Colin, and he was always the first guy to jump into battle to save someone. When the bullies on the playground would come out, Colin would take them on, even when he was a scrawny, underweight, geeky kid. He loved the role of protector."

"He might die, Charlotte." Joe shook his head in despair. "I don't know if I can forgive myself—or if Kara can forgive me. She's having a baby, dammit. Do you know how much Colin has been talking about that kid? He's been over the moon."

"I do know. He never misses one of Kara's appointments. But I'm not giving up hope, and neither should you."

"I'm trying not to, but I've seen a lot of bad things happen to good people. It's difficult to be optimistic."

"I know. Sometimes life isn't fair." She hesitated for a long second. "Joe, would it be all right if I hugged you?"

He opened his arms. She moved into his embrace, holding on for far too long, but she couldn't help it. He was hurting, and she was hurting for him. His wife should be here with him. Charlotte wondered where Rachel was, but it was none of her business.

She pulled away and smiled. "Take care of yourself, Joe."

"You, too, Charlotte."

"I will. I'll see you around."

The entire town seemed to be crowded into the fourth floor waiting room at St. Mary's Hospital late Monday morning. Jenna wasn't sure how Kara would take to seeing her, knowing that her husband might lose his life because of the situation Jenna had brought to Angel's Bay, but she'd come anyway because she wanted to support the woman who'd given her nothing but friendship.

The Murrays were out in full force, as well as most of the police department, and Jenna recognized some other people from the town. Kara was sitting on a couch, a quilt over her shoulders. When she saw Jenna, she beckoned her over.

Reid gave her hand a squeeze of encouragement before she made her way across the room. She sat next to Kara, noting the extreme pallor of her face, the fear in her eyes, but also the hope.

"I'm so sorry, Kara," Jenna said. "So sorry this happened to you and to Colin. How is he?"

"They removed the bullet from his head," Kara said, "they don't know what's going to happen, or how bad the damage will be, but he's probably going to be asleep for a long while. Catching up on his rest, I guess," she said with a teary smile. "Colin could use a vacation. He always goes a mile a minute; tries to squeeze too many things into too little time." Her voice caught, and she drew in a shaky breath. "But I'm feeling hopeful, because . . . well, because I have to. And I don't want you to blame yourself."

"It's hard to blame anyone else."

"How about the monster who shot my husband? I heard that he's dead and I'm glad."

"Me, too," Jenna said. They'd found Brad's body just after dawn, ending the worst nightmare of her life.

"Joe told me a little about what you and Lexie went through," Kara continued. "I'm glad you're safe now. I knew you were afraid of something. I wanted to help, but I didn't want to be too pushy."

"You did help. You gave me your friendship. It meant a lot to me. It still does."

"So what now? Will you stay in Angel's Bay?" Kara asked.

"I'm not sure. I think we might, for a while anyway. I have a lot to tell you, but now isn't the time."

"I've got nothing but time," Kara said with a helpless shrug. "It's actually good to have a distraction."

"Well, to make it short, I think Lexie and I were sent here for a reason. I found Rose Littleton's journal, and I believe she was my grandmother. You see, Lexie has a birthmark on her heel, an angel's wing, just like Rose, just like the other descendants—"

"—Of Gabriella," Kara finished, her eyes filling with wonder. "Oh my God. That's incredible! I can't wait to tell Colin that he saved a child of Gabriella's. It's as if history came full circle. You know, it was right after you first came to town that the angels appeared. I wonder if they knew that Lexie would need them—that Gabriella's child had come home to be saved." She smiled. "I sound like Colin, don't I—believing in all that angel crap? I can hear his voice now saying, 'It's not crap, Kara; just believe.' And that's what I'm going to do. I'm going to keep believing until I can't anymore."

"That's a good plan."

Kara's gaze moved from Jenna to Reid, who was watching them closely, and she smiled. "So that's the way it goes. You didn't just find your history and a safe harbor at Angel's Bay. You found something else, too."

"Yes," Jenna said. "I found love."

Kara slipped her hand into hers. "That's what it's all about. Love. You won't let me forget that, will you? Because I have a feeling that in the days and weeks to come, I'm going to need a reminder."

"I won't let you forget," Jenna said, squeezing her hand. "And Colin won't, either."

"I'm going to fight for him. I'm going to fight for us," Kara declared.

"I know you will—and we're all going to fight with you." Jenna looked around the crowded room. "Because Angel's Bay takes care of its own."

Turn the page for a sneak peek at

On Shadow Beach

the next heart-tugging Angel's Bay romance
from bestselling author
Barbara Freethy

Coming from Pocket Books in April 2010

The marina was quiet. Most of the action occurred in the early morning or late afternoon when the sport and commercial fishermen took off for a day of work or pleasure. Lauren had spent a lot of time on these docks and in her father's boat, although she'd never been as big a fan of fishing or the sea as her sister. Abby and her father had loved trawling for fish, spending hours on the water just waiting for something to happen. She'd been far too impatient to enjoy idling the day away waiting for some poor fish to take the bait.

Her pulse quickened as the lights on her father's boat suddenly came on, followed by the sound of an engine. She could see his silhouette in the inside cabin. What on earth was he doing?

"Dad," she yelled, breaking into a run. She waved her arms and screamed his name again, but either he couldn't hear her or he was ignoring her. By the time she reached the slip, her father's boat was chugging toward the middle of the bay. She had to find a way to stop him. Her father had Alzheimer's. He couldn't be out on the open sea by himself. She needed to call the Coast Guard, find someone to go after him. "Hello, hello, anyone here?" she called.

A man emerged from a nearby boat. She hurried down the dock.

"What's going on?" he asked.

The familiar voice stopped her dead in her tracks, and as he hopped on to the dock, her heart skipped a beat.

Shane. Shane Murray.

He moved toward her with the same purposeful, determined step she remembered. She wasn't ready for this—ready for him.

She knew the split second that he recognized her. She saw his step falter, his shoulders stiffen, and his jaw set in a hard line. He didn't say her name. He just stared at her, waiting. Shane had never been one for words. He'd always believed actions spoke louder than explanations. But sometimes the truth needed to be spoken, not just implied or assumed.

"Shane." She breathed his name, wishing her voice didn't sound so husky, so filled with memories. She cleared her throat. "I—I need help. My father just took off in his boat." She waved her hand toward the *Leonora,* the lights of which were fading in the distance. "I need to stop him. Will you help me? There doesn't seem to be anyone else around." When he didn't answer right away, she added, "I guess I could call the Coast Guard."

For a moment she thought he might say no. They were not friends anymore. If anything, they were enemies, but finally Shane gave her a crisp nod. "Let's go." He didn't wait for her to reply, he just headed back to his boat.

The last thing she wanted to do was go with him, but she could hardly stand on the dock while her father sailed off to sea with probably no idea of who he was or where he was going. She walked quickly down the dock. Shane's boat was a newer thirty-foot sports fishing boat. There were rod holders in the gunwales, tackle drawers, and ice coolers built in to the hull. As she hopped onboard, Shane released the lines and pulled in the bumpers, then headed toward the center console. He started the engine and pulled out of the slip.

She stood a few feet away from him, feeling awkward and uncomfortable. She wondered how long it would take before he'd actually speak to her. And if he did speak, what would he say? There was a lot of history between them, a lot of pain. Part of her wanted him to break the silence—the other part was afraid of where any conversation would lead. So she waited, and while she waited, she let her gaze run down Shane's body.

Shane was the first man she'd ever loved. She'd fallen for him just after her seventeenth birthday. He'd been eighteen, only one year older in age, but a half dozen in experience. She'd been a shy good girl, and he'd been the town bad boy.

Shane definitely wasn't a teenager anymore. In his faded blue jeans, T-shirt, and black jacket, it was quite apparent that he was all man. He'd filled out his six-foot frame, with broad shoulders and long, lean legs. His black hair was wavy, and windblown, the ends brushing the collar of his jacket, and his skin bore the dark ruddy tan of a man who spent a lot of time outdoors.

The set of his jaw had always been his no-trespassing sign, and that hadn't changed a bit. Shane had never let people in easily. She'd had to fight to get past his barriers, but as close as they'd once been, she'd never managed to figure out the mysterious shadows in his dark eyes, or the sudden, sharp glimpses of pain that flashed briefly and then disappeared just as quickly. Shane had always kept a big part of himself under lock and key.

Her gaze dropped to his hands, noting the surety of his fingers on the wheel. His hands were strong, capable, and she couldn't help but remember the way they'd once felt on her breasts, rough and hungry, the same way his mouth had felt against hers, as if he couldn't wait to have her, couldn't ever get enough.

Damn. Her heart thumped against her chest and she forced herself to look away. She was not going back to that place. She couldn't. She'd barely survived the first time. He'd broken her heart. And it had taken her a very long time to recover.

"It took you long enough to come home," he said, glancing over at her, his expression unreadable.

She cleared her throat, hoping she could hide her emotions, but unlike him she'd never been good at pretending. "I just came back to get my dad."

"Get him?" Shane queried.

"He has Alzheimer's. I'm planning to take him back to San Francisco with me."

"Does he know that?"

"He will when you can catch him."

Doubt filled Shane's eyes. "Your father has lived in Angel's Bay his entire life. I can't see him moving anywhere else."

"It's the best solution."

"For you or for him?"

"For both of us." Her father might not like the idea of leaving Angel's Bay, but it was the most practical decision. If she moved him closer to her, she could take care of him. Her mother, who lived in the wine country, an hour north of San Francisco, might also drive down to see him once in a while. And there was David, who planned to live in the city after he finished with college. Her father's family was in San Francisco and that's where he should be.

Of course her dad hadn't really cared to be with his family for the past thirteen years, but she was trying to look beyond that fact. Since it also appeared that her father was rapidly losing touch with the world—would it really matter where he was?

Shane opened a nearby compartment and pulled out a jacket. "You might want to put this on. It will get colder outside the bay."

She accepted the coat with a grateful nod, relieved with both the change in subject and the warm jacket. She just wished they could go faster, but Shane couldn't increase his speed until they left the harbor. "This is a nice boat. Is it yours?"

"Yes, I picked it up last year when I came back," he said shortly.

"Came back from where?"

"Everywhere," he said with a vague wave of his hand. "Wherever there was water and fish and a boat to run."

"Sounds like you got the life you always wanted," she murmured.

He shot her a look that she couldn't begin to decipher. "Is that what it sounds like, Lauren?"

Her name rolled off his tongue like a silky caress. She'd always loved the way he'd said her name, as if she were the most important person in the world. But that wasn't the way he'd said her name now. Now there was anger in the word and God knew what else.

She sighed. "I don't know what to say to you, Shane. I guess I never did."

His gaze hardened. "You knew what to say, Lauren. You just wouldn't say it."

That was true. Thirteen years ago he'd wanted her to say that she believed in him, that she trusted him, that she knew in her heart that he didn't kill her sister.

All she'd been able to say was good-bye.

"I don't want to talk about the past." The words had barely left her lips when she found herself compelled to speak again. "You lied to me, Shane. I trusted you more than I'd ever trusted anyone, and you lied to me."

He gave a little nod, his eyes dark and unreadable. "Yeah, I did."

"And you're still not going to tell me why, are you?"

"I thought you didn't want to talk about the past."

She debated that for another second. There were so many things she still wanted Shane to explain, but what was the point? He'd refused before. He'd do the same now.

"You're right. I don't want to talk about that night. It wouldn't change anything. We made choices. We can't take them back. And in the end, Abby—Abby would still be gone." Despite the heavy coat, she felt a chill run through her. She glanced at the coastline. It was too dark now to see the Ramsay house where her sister had been found murdered, but she knew where it was; she could feel its presence even if she couldn't see it.

"Someone set fire to the house about nine months ago," Shane said, following her gaze. "One wing was completely destroyed."

"It's too bad the entire house didn't burn to the ground." She'd never understood how her father could stay in Angel's Bay, wake up every day and see the house where her sister had spent the last minutes of her life. But then there were a lot of things she couldn't understand about her father.

Lauren grabbed hold of the back of the captain's seat as Shane increased their speed. They'd finally made it past the breakwater. Waves slapped against the boat, and the wind increased, lifting her hair off the back of her neck. Her nerves began to tingle. She could handle being on the ocean when the day was sunny and bright, and she could see the shoreline, but she'd never liked going out at night or being hours away from land, where she'd be vulnerable to the mercy of an unpredictable sea.

"Where is my father?" She couldn't keep the rising note of panic out of her voice. "I don't see any lights. How are we going to find him out here? Maybe we should go back." She hated being a coward, especially in front of Shane, who had never met a fear he didn't want to look straight in the eye and take down.

"Your father didn't disappear. He's just around the point." Shane pointed to the GPS on his console.

"See that dot—that's him. We'll catch up in a couple of minutes."

"Okay, good." She gulped in a deep breath of air and wrapped her arms around her waist.

"Are you scared of me?" Shane asked.

She turned her head to look at him. "Don't be ridiculous."

"You seem nervous."

"I just want to get this over with."

A few minutes passed, then Shane said, "Your father loves this town. Do you really think you can drop in after all this time and sweep him away without an argument?"

"I don't know how much he'll fight me, but I have to do something. When I arrived at my father's house tonight, the lights were on, as well as the TV, and the stove. If I hadn't come home, the house could have burned down, and if I hadn't seen him take off in his boat, who knows what could have happened? I didn't realize his condition was this bad." She shook her head in confusion. Her father was only sixty-six years old. He was far too young to be losing his memory, losing his mind.

"Some days are worse than others," Shane commented.

She gave him a curious look. "You talk to my father?"

"All the time. He's on his boat almost every day. Mort took his key away from him a while ago. I don't know where he got another one."

"My father doesn't—" She broke off the sentence, realizing she was heading into dangerous territory.

"Blame me for Abby's death?" Shane finished, a hard note in his voice. "Some days he does, some days he doesn't. But he does blame me for you going away and never coming back."

"That wasn't because of you."

"Wasn't it?" He tilted his head, giving her a considering look. "What's making you so jumpy, Lauren? Don't try to tell me it's just the water. You don't like being alone with me."

"I got over you a long time ago." She waited for him to say that he'd done the same, but he remained silent. "It was a ridiculous crush, that's all. We were kids, caught up in the moment. It didn't mean anything. It's not like I'm still attracted to you. I don't think about you at all. I am way, way over you. I have moved on."

"Are you done?" he asked when she finally ran out of steam.

"Yes."

He eased up on the throttle so abruptly she stumbled right into his arms. Her lips had barely parted in protest when his mouth came down on hers, hot, insistent, demanding the truth. A mix of conflicting emotions raced through her. She should break it off, pull away, but she couldn't bring herself to move.

What the hell was she doing? She didn't want this. She didn't want him. But God, he tasted good. She felt seventeen again, hot, needy, passionate, reckless, on the verge of something incredible and exciting and . . .

She had to stop. Finally, she found the strength to push him away. She stared at him in shock, her heart pounding, her breathing ragged.

He gave her a long look in return. "Yeah, I'm over

you, too," he said as he put his hands back on the wheel.

Okay, so she was a liar. Her body still had a thing for him. That didn't mean her head or her heart intended to go along. Loving Shane had never gotten her anything but a heart full of pain.

"I'm glad we've settled that," she said sharply.

"Me, too."

A tense silence fell between them, and the air around them grew thicker, colder, damp. As minutes passed, her hair started to curl and a fine sheen of moisture covered her face. As they sailed around the point, a silvery mist surrounded them. Her father had spoken often of the angels that danced above the bay, the angels that watched over them, protected them. She'd believed him with the innocence of a child, but she'd lost her faith when Abby died. What kind of angel could let a fifteen-year-old girl be killed?

She felt a wave of panic as the mist enveloped them in a chilling hug. It had been clear only moments ago. Where had the fog come from? Why did she feel so cold? She had to fight a powerful desire to fling herself back into Shane's arms.

Why are you fighting? He's the man you've always wanted.

The voice wasn't in her head, it was on the wind. Lauren certainly hadn't said the words, because they weren't true. She didn't want Shane, not anymore.

A melodic laugh seemed to bounce off the waves, as if the ocean found her amusing. She shook her head, forcing the fanciful thought away. Her father had always talked to the sea, but that was her father, not her. She didn't believe in angels, or voices, or much of anything for that matter. Believing in someone or something always led to disappointment.

She let out a breath of relief as the mist lifted, and a beam of light danced off the waves ahead of them—her father's boat.

Shane's boat was moving at a faster pace now. They'd reach the *Leonora* within minutes. But then what? "How are we going to stop him?" she asked.

"We'll pull up next to him and see if we can get him to stop on his own and turn around. If not, one of us will have to jump onto his boat and take over."

"Excuse me. Did you say one of us is going to jump between the boats while they're moving?"

"It's not that difficult."

"Well, it's not going to be me," she declared.

"Then you can drive."

She didn't like that scenario, either. "I haven't driven a boat in a long time, Shane."

"You can do it. Take the wheel. Get comfortable with it. I'm going to see if I can get your dad on the radio."

She gripped the wheel with tight and nervous hands as Shane tried to roust her father on the radio. When they neared her father's boat, she could see him standing inside the cabin. He had the door closed and seemed oblivious to their presence. Shane switched frequencies and the sound of classical music blasted through. Her father had always loved opera, a strange passion for a simple fisherman, but he found some affinity between the music and the sea.

"I don't think he can hear us," Shane said. "Bring the boat as close as you can."

"Are you sure you don't want to do it?"

"Just hold her steady, Lauren. I'm going to jump onto your dad's boat."

"And then what?"

"I'll drive him back. You can follow us."

"You're going to leave me alone on this boat—on the ocean?" The idea terrified her more than just a little. It had been a long time since she'd allowed herself to get into a situation she couldn't control. And this one was way out of her comfort zone. "I don't think I can do this."

"You can."

His words echoed a conversation from a lifetime ago when he'd handed her a helmet and taught her how to drive his motorcycle. He'd always pushed her beyond her limits.

"You always could," he added, a slight knowing smile curving his lips as his gaze met hers.

"And you always knew how to get me to do things I didn't want to do."

"This isn't about me; it's about your father. You want him back or not?"

"Of course I do. All right." She lifted her chin and drew in a deep breath. "You jump. I'll drive."

"I won't let you out of my sight," Shane said. "It took me a long time to save enough cash to buy this boat. I don't intend to lose it."

"I'm touched by your sentiment." While she was getting dreamy-eyed about their past, he was thinking only about his boat.

"Just keep as close and as steady as you can. I don't feel like going for a swim, even though at the moment you look like you'd enjoy tossing me into the sea."

"The idea has some merit, but then I'd have to rescue you."

"Would you?"

"Don't miss, then neither of us will have to find out."

She bit down on her bottom lip as Shane moved toward the side of the boat. She wasn't worried about him. She was more concerned about her father, about this not working. Shane could take care of himself. Fearlessness and recklessness were part of his makeup. He wasn't a man to sit on the sidelines and wait for someone else to take charge.

Shane stepped over the rail, paused for one second, and then jumped. He landed in the middle of the fishing platform on her father's boat. He stumbled slightly and then straightened and yanked open the door to the cabin. Her father finally turned his head. He exchanged a few words with Shane, and then Shane took over at the wheel. A moment later his voice came over the radio. "Let's go home, Lauren."

His words brought with them a bittersweet rush of emotion. She was going back to shore, but Angel's Bay wasn't her home now, and it never would be again.

It took about twenty minutes to get back to the marina. Shane kept in constant contact on the radio and Lauren made sure that she stayed as close to her father's boat as possible. She breathed a sigh of relief when they made it back. She bumped the edges of Shane's boat as she pulled it into the slip, but she was so happy to be off the ocean that she couldn't worry about it. Shane came onboard to tie the lines down while she joined her father, who was waiting for her on the dock.

Her dad wore a pair of khaki pants and a windbreaker that hung loosely on his thin frame. He'd lost a lot of weight in the years since she'd last seen him, and he'd aged quite a bit. His dark hair was all gray, including the stubble on his cheeks, and he stood with his shoulders hunched, but he didn't seem upset or concerned about his jaunt out to sea. She didn't know if that was good or bad.

When he saw her, his eyes widened with surprise, followed by what appeared to be teary emotion. He shook his head, as if he couldn't believe she was there, and she felt a rush of guilt at all the years she'd let go by. This man was her father. He'd tucked her in at night, scared away the monsters under her bed, been there for her—well, at least some of the time.

Maybe they hadn't shared a lot of common interests, but they were connected by blood, by love. How could she have let him go? How could she have forgotten what they were to each other?

"Hi, Dad," she said softly.

"Abby," he murmured, holding out his arms. "My sweet, precious girl. You've come back to me at last."

Lauren's heart came to a crashing halt. "I'm Lauren, Dad. I'm not Abby. I'm Lauren," she repeated, seeing the disappointment and fear fill his eyes.

"What have you done with Abby?" he asked in confusion, his arms dropping to his side. "What have you done with your sister?"

Suddenly it was easy to remember why she'd left and why she'd stayed away so long.